TO CATCH A LORD

EMMA ORCHARD

Boldwood

First published in Great Britain in 2025 by Boldwood Books Ltd.

Copyright © Emma Orchard, 2025

Cover Design by Rachel Lawston

Cover Images: Rachel Lawston

The moral right of Emma Orchard to be identified as the author of this work has been asserted in accordance with the Copyright, Designs and Patents Act 1988.

Every effort has been made to obtain the necessary permissions with reference to copyright material, both illustrative and quoted. We apologise for any omissions in this respect and will be pleased to make the appropriate acknowledgements in any future edition.

A CIP catalogue record for this book is available from the British Library.

Paperback ISBN 978-1-83633-852-9

Large Print ISBN 978-1-83633-853-6

Hardback ISBN 978-1-83633-851-2

Ebook ISBN 978-1-83633-854-3

Kindle ISBN 978-1-83633-855-0

Audio CD ISBN 978-1-83633-846-8

MP3 CD ISBN 978-1-83633-847-5

Digital audio download ISBN 978-1-83633-848-2

This book is printed on certified sustainable paper. Boldwood Books is dedicated to putting sustainability at the heart of our business. For more information please visit https://www.boldwoodbooks.com/about-us/sustainability/

Boldwood Books Ltd, 23 Bowerdean Street, London, SW6 3TN

www.boldwoodbooks.com

To my wonderful agent, Diana Beaumont.

PROLOGUE
LONDON, SPRING 1813

The Season wasn't called 'the marriage market' for nothing. For every debutante who enjoyed the excitement of dancing, the glamorous balls, the fine clothes and the decorous flirting, there might be five who found the whole experience miserable, distressing, even degrading. Not everyone could attract the attention of a gentleman worth ten thousand pounds a year, or five, or three. Not everyone could be an acknowledged diamond.

It wasn't surprising, then, that young ladies might find other ways to entertain themselves. An indulgence in gossip, even in the spreading of scandal, might not be virtuous or kind or wise – but was surely understandable.

Even if it was bound to lead to trouble.

'He's quite handsome,' said one young lady wistfully. Her hand had not been solicited for this set, and her friends were in the same situation, which gave them leisure to observe those they considered more fortunate, and the gentlemen who had singled them out. 'And he is well-connected, even if he's not supposed to be terribly rich.'

The group of young women watched critically as Mr Peacock

– the son and heir of a peer, and a gentleman of decided fashion, with carefully arranged golden locks – partnered tall, dark Lady Amelia Wyverne through the steps of the cotillion. It was plain he was enthralled by her beauty; his gaze sought to catch and hold hers whenever the figure brought them together, and the observers could see that his hands, when they met hers, did not easily let them go. His attentions to her were most marked.

'But she doesn't seem to enjoy dancing with him,' Miss Lancaster said shrewdly. She was right; Lady Amelia's glance did not linger responsively on her partner's, and her gloved hands appeared to slip out of his with as much swiftness as she could manage. Though she had a vague social smile pinned on her face, nobody could imagine that it reflected genuine pleasure. She looked as though she might be counting the minutes till the music stopped and released her.

'She's spoilt,' sniffed Miss Archer. 'I dare say she thinks because she is the daughter of a marquess, and a great heiress, she is above Mr Peacock and too good for him. It quite gives one a disgust of her, to see her so proud and disdainful.'

'Especially when one considers the reputation of her family!' tittered Miss Muswell. 'My mama says that she might consider herself lucky that she is accepted in society at all. It is well known that her late father could not have created any more scandal if he tried – imagine a man of rank and title actually marrying an actress, a woman from the gutter! – and as for her brother, the new marquess, the rumours of his conduct with his stepmother are far too shocking even to repeat. Her sister-in-law, though, is French, so I suppose she does not care what manner of man she has married as long as he is wealthy.'

The first lady who had spoken protested faintly, disturbed by the venom she had provoked with her unguarded comment, but Miss Lancaster said bluntly, 'It must be a fine thing, to be an heiress, and sought-after, so that gentlemen are prepared to over-look such disadvantages. She has probably had a dozen offers, and rejected them all. It's not fair!'

This was so obviously true and so unanswerable that all the ladies subsided into discontented silence. There was no doubt that one or two of them would do Lady Amelia a mischief if they could; luckily for her, it was hard to see how their bad intentions might go beyond spiteful gossip. For now.

1

'Damn it!' the Honourable Mr Peacock cried, stumbling and losing his place in the dance. The music stopped and the set came to an end a moment later, and he pushed his way off the crowded dance floor, not even pausing to take leave of his abandoned partner. He was limping.

Lady Amelia sighed, returning to stand with her aunt and await with gloomy resignation the next gentleman on her dance card. She tried to tread softly, so that the tapping of her shoes was not too obvious to those around her. She had learned through painful experience never to wear fashionable but flimsy silk evening slippers as the other young ladies did. Her shoes didn't appear all that different from theirs, at a casual glance, but they were in reality more substantial in construction, always made of stout leather, and they had a slight heel. Most unusually – especially for dancing shoes – these heels had metal segs on them. No doubt they scratched the floors upon which she walked, but Amelia could not be expected to care much for that. It was a matter of self-protection.

These precautions meant that when some man she'd rather

not dance with, or be anywhere near, leered at her and attempted to grow over-familiar during the quadrille or the cotillion – pinching, squeezing – she could stamp down hard on the bridge of his foot, or his toes, smiling falsely all the while. Men, providentially, wore light dancing slippers too, and so their feet were vulnerable. The trick was partly in the angle of the heel and partly in the force applied. She'd grown quite good at it last Season and now this one. She'd had plenty of practice and could inflict a surprising amount of pain; anger gave her impetus, and the howls of surprise and indignation she caused gave her wicked pleasure. For more serious nuisances, she had concealed pins about her person, and longer, more vicious examples hidden in her abundant dark hair. The Dishonourable Mr Peacock, her most recent dance partner, had hobbled off the floor in acute discomfort just now, and would have a fine bruise to show tomorrow; she hadn't had to resort to her sharper weapons this time. It wasn't clear to her whether he, or indeed any of them, just thought she was a terribly clumsy dancer. But almost all of them came back after a while, undiscouraged, and made further attempts on her virtue. Either they were very stupid, or they had very short memories. Perhaps both. Or – this was a horrible thought – her obvious reluctance to be courted gave the chase spice in their eyes.

She knew that there were much worse situations one could be in than hers. There was a war on – in all her nineteen years, it seemed there always had been. Men were dying or being dreadfully injured every day, in Spain and Portugal, America and Canada, leaving their wives and families grief-stricken at best, destitute and starving at worst. Here in London and elsewhere in England, people, many of them children, toiled in backbreaking jobs to earn enough to eat, or begged in the street for a crust. Women and girls sold themselves, or stole, and risked the harshest of punishments: the gallows, transportation. She'd led a sheltered life, ignorant of such things, until her brother Rafe's marriage two years ago to a woman from a mysterious and complicated background had broadened her horizons and made her realise how privileged she was – in some respects, not in all.

With her eyes newly opened by Sophie's influence, she'd realised too that in her own sphere of life, the haut ton, many young women much like herself might indeed be spared from the sharpest bite of physical want, but still faced the awareness that their futures were bleak indeed if they could not induce some man of property – any man of property, no matter his age or personal attributes – to offer for them. Their entire families' futures might depend on such an eventuality.

Amelia faced no such problems, and must be grateful that she did not. She *was* grateful. The daughter of one ridiculously wealthy marquess (now deceased) and sister of another, she had no need to work. Nor would she ever face the bitter, secret struggles of genteel poverty. She would never be obliged to marry where her heart did not lead her: not to secure some sort of future for herself, and certainly not to increase her family's fortune, for they had that in abundance. And there was yet more. She had no harsh, controlling relatives, either male or female, who would think to force her into some splendid match that went against her heart's wishes. Her half-brother Rafe was the kindest and most loving of guardians, always considerate of her welfare and putting it above his own, which she knew to be rare, in her sphere of society or any other. Her full brother Charlie, though nobody would ever claim he had been over-favoured with brains, loved her dearly too.

And to add to the ways in which fortune had blessed her, her health was good, as was that of both her brothers and her sister-in-law, who had recently been delivered of a strong, thriving son and heir, a tiny viscount. She even had a grandmother living, her father's mother, at the preposterous age of almost 102.

It was true that Lady Amelia was an orphan, which might make any girl in any walk of life an object of pity, but in her peculiar circumstances, even that could be described as a blessing, if a mixed one. She greatly missed knowing the mother she had lost in early childhood, but she had not for as much as a second regretted the death of her father, two years ago. What was more, nobody – not even the highest sticklers of society, not even Queen Charlotte herself – could expect her to make any show of mourning him still, because her father, the late Marquess of Wyverne, had been a man of terrible reputation, every bit of it earned, one with a positive addiction to stirring up scandal and making enemies.

Lord Wyverne had left his three adult children with a wicked stepmother, as in the fairy tales, but Amelia wasn't obliged to live with her or suffer any cruelty from her. She'd never even met her, and for the sake of her own good name, must never do so if it could possibly be avoided. Rosanna Wyverne was an actress – not an actress in the mould of Mrs Siddons, admired widely for her artistry and admitted to be a respectable woman. No, she was the other sort of actress. The disreputable kind. She might be a dowager marchioness, but she had never been received into society and never would be. Amelia knew that, in collusion with her late husband, Rosanna had done all sorts of hugely scandalous things that nobody, not even Rafe or Sophie, would ever agree to tell her properly about, which was most provoking. But the world still whispered about them, just out of her hearing.

And here lay the source of the difficulties Lady Amelia Wyverne was experiencing. Her brother Rafe had confided in her recently that he'd spent most of his adult life imagining that when their father died, as he had most providentially done after a seizure in the spring of 1811, their family's reputation would somehow magically be restored. His concern, she knew, was not so much for himself, or even for his wife, who had married him with her eyes open and cared little for social acceptance, but mostly for Amelia and Charlie, and for their futures and their happiness.

But soon after the late Marquess's death, Rafe told her, he'd realised that such enormous scandal as he'd created over a long, notoriously dissolute life could never be forgotten. The name of the Wyvernes could *never* be wiped completely clean, no matter what they did. The burden fell on all of them, but not equally (since such things were always easier for men), and they'd just have to live with it.

And Amelia was living with it. She wasn't starving, or suffering, she was surrounded by people she loved and who loved her, but she wasn't comfortable in her skin. She was always alert for trouble from the so-called gentlemen of the ton, and sometimes lay awake at night, worrying about what would become of her.

She'd made something of a splash on her come-out last Season, and under the aegis of her highly respectable aunt on her mother's side, Lady Keswick, she'd curtsied to the Queen and been graciously received by the monarch who was supposed to be the ultimate arbiter of public morality. With the chaperonage of Aunt Keswick and of Sophie, Amelia was invited everywhere, though it was possible that much of the public acceptance came from sheer curiosity, since it had been a long time since anyone named Wyverne had attempted to move in polite society. And her debut was successful, in a way. Nobody cut her, nobody insulted her, not in plain words nor to her face, and to a casual observer, nothing might appear to be wrong, but it was wrong, all the same. Her metal-heeled shoes bore witness to it, as did the pins. And one only needed to understand the nature of the offers her brother had received for her hand to see exactly what the problem was.

Rafe had been punctilious in sharing the names of her formal suitors with her, and she'd been horrified to hear them, though not completely surprised, since they'd been making up to her in public in a variety of unpleasant ways since her debut. She could even now, if she'd cared for it, have been a countess, a viscountess or a baroness. Or she could have been, if she'd taken leave of her senses (and her brother had) and been content to marry someone whose reputation for depravity matched that of her father. It seemed that every raddled rake in London, young or old, had decided that she, and her fortune, could be his for the asking. It seemed too that it had never occurred to any one of them that Rafe, his own good name irrevocably tainted by the baseless rumours that his stepmother Rosanna had been his mistress, might think to refuse them; why should he? He could hardly be a moral stickler himself, surely?

The new Lord Wyverne hadn't told her what the men – there had apparently been a great number of them – had said to him in private conversation, and what he'd said in return, and she was grateful for that, but the set of his mouth and the sombre expression in his blue-grey eyes had been enough. He'd refused all of them in no uncertain terms, and sent them on their way wondering. 'Better men will come,' he'd said gently. 'When it is seen and understood that I will always reject offers from fortune-hunters, libertines, men of low character even if their rank is high; when your own good qualities are realised, Melia, better men will come. An honourable man who loves you for yourself, who you can love and be happy with, will come, I promise you, my dear. It is merely a matter of having a little patience.'

But no such man had come, just more who merited pins and bruised feet, and she was beginning to think that Rafe was deluding himself. She didn't *need* to marry anybody at all, and she'd never dream of marrying a rake in the pattern of her father. She wanted a decent, honourable man if she were to settle down one day, a man like her brothers (though perhaps rather cleverer than Charlie, if possible). But she certainly didn't want to marry some stuffy person either, who would behave as though he were doing her a favour by singling her out, and think it his duty to reform her. She didn't need to be reformed, she was reasonably sure, and would not suffer to be lectured. Such people might disapprove of her as much as they liked.

It seemed most unfair to Amelia that she should labour under all the disadvantages and discomfort of a stained reputation when she'd never actually done anything to deserve it. Not one tiny thing. It shouldn't be necessary to defend one's honour so very frequently; it grew tedious. She was aware – Lady Keswick had not failed to impress it on her with many awful, if frustratingly obscure warnings – that she was obliged to be more careful even than the other debutantes who surrounded her. There could be no indulgence for any rash youthful folly on her part; she could not afford even the tiniest slip. Something must be done, she thought, to set this right, and she must do it herself rather than relying on others; it was her future at stake, not theirs, no matter how much they cared for her.

If anyone had asked Amelia what her hopes for the future were, and she'd been able to answer honestly, she'd have said, *To take control of my life. To make things happen, rather than have them happen to me at the whim of others. To be responsible for my own fate.* Was that a ridiculous ambition for a young lady? She would not concede that for a second. So, she needed a plan. But what?

2

Amelia did not waste much time in imagining that any conspicuously holy action of her own could redeem her reputation and give her more freedom of choice. They had discussed this as a family. Lady Keswick, a woman of highly conventional morality, suggested that they frequent services at one of the fashionable churches. She would have had her niece soberly dressed in a pointedly ugly bonnet and drab colours that suggested half-mourning, carrying a large prayerbook and sighing with deep feeling when appropriate, and shaking her dark ringlets sadly when that should be called for. But Lord Wyverne, fondly viewing his younger sister's lively little face and large, mischievously sparkling dark eyes, had offered the strong opinion that – setting aside the matter of quite odious hypocrisy – nobody would believe any of it for more than five minutes. And if they did by some strange chance believe it, he went on to say, the end result would be offers of marriage from sober, religious young men, perhaps even ambitious fellows in holy orders who might like the idea of a wife of exalted birth and be prepared to overlook the Wyverne reputation for the sake of a substantial dowry. Did her aunt seriously imagine that this was a good idea? Could she picture Lady Amelia living in a country rectory, as helpmeet and support to a clergyman?

'Perhaps she will read Fordyce's *Sermons* aloud to her maid-servants, as they sit together hemming her husband's shirts,' he said, though it required an extraordinary effort of imagination to summon up such a vision.

Lady Keswick, looking at her niece and letting out a deep sigh of her own, had been compelled to admit that he made a good point. Amelia didn't precisely appear wicked, she agreed, but she didn't have a noticeably saintly aspect either. Every lineament in her face spoke chiefly of wilful mischief.

While Lady Keswick pondered what could be done, Amelia looked for other solutions. 'What do you think I should do, Sophie?' she asked her sister-in-law as they sat together in the Marchioness's private sitting room in the Brook Street house.

Lady Wyverne was nursing her infant, and said nothing for a moment, her brows creased in thought. She was an attractive Frenchwoman in her late twenties, of most unusual colouring, with red-blonde hair and bright, dark-brown eyes, but the baby, Louis, Lord Drake, had dark hair, like his father and his aunt Amelia, and, at present, their Wyverne blue-grey eyes. 'I do sympathise,' she said at length. 'It might appear a trivial predicament, yours, in a world that is so harsh and cruel to so many – I know you have told yourself this. But since women of your class – of ours – must be defined by whom they marry, and place themselves entirely in a man's power, life, liberty and fortune, really it is not trivial at all. You have as much right to happiness as the next person, and at present, little chance of gaining it. You cannot spend years stamping on people's feet in the hope that they get the message. Every feeling revolts at it.'

'Exactly,' Amelia replied eagerly. 'Rafe counsels patience, and perhaps he is right. I am not desperate to marry – do not think that. It is true that I am young, and can afford to wait a number of years. One thing that concerns me, though, is that I am obliged to behave entirely irreproachably while I do so, which you must acknowledge will be hard. I am not by nature a very good person indeed. And even if I do manage that dreary perfection, and maintain such an unnatural state for years, maybe, which is daunting, I cannot see matters ever changing. Why should they? It's not as though anybody is likely to forget what my father was, and all the shocking things he did, especially not while his wife is alive and present in London to remind them. And Sophie, I am... I am *damned* if I will wed someone who behaves as if he is doing me a great favour, condescending to take me despite my many disadvantages. I'd far rather stay unmarried.'

'Of course you would. I have myself received an offer in such circumstances – not from your brother, I hope it is unnecessary to say – and I agree, no woman of spirit could accept such an insult in the guise of a compliment. But any man should consider himself lucky to have you, *ma petite soeur*,' said the Marchioness seriously, not in the least shocked by her sister-in-law's ungenteel language. Amelia had in the past wondered what might shock Sophie, and had so far thought of nothing. It was something to aspire to, she thought, when she could leave off being so good at last.

'It's very sweet of you to say so. But you know it isn't true. You've seen the way they look at me, the young gentlemen and the older ones – there's a sort of predatory gleam in their eyes, many of them, as if to say, "That Wyverne blood, eh? I wonder..." And they're always trying to get me to go out on terraces with them alone, or into dark corners. They don't do it to anyone else, as far as I can see, or not half as much. I must say, it is excessively tedious, and it appears to me that I don't get any credit from society for always resisting. Not that I *want* to go anywhere with any of them, since most of them are quite repulsive, but you know what I mean.'

'While the respectable ones are scared of you, and avoid you,' Sophie agreed with more truth than tact, smiling down at her infant but still listening, since, as Amelia had observed before now, most women, especially mothers, were able to do more than one thing at a time.

'So what is to be done? I beg you, please tell me anything that comes into your head, no matter how outlandish.'

'Very well,' Sophie said. 'I think we must first establish – and it is fortunate that Rafe is not here just now, for he might consider me a bad influence, which perhaps I am – whether, or how much, you care for respectability. I am not saying that you should not, you understand; I am only asking. Because it makes a difference, as I am sure you can perceive for yourself, in what you choose to do. But I should say also that your grandmother told me once that times are changing and the world becoming stricter, in terms of a person's reputation, and I am sure she was right. Nobody cared much for respectability when she was young, and your situation would hardly have been a problem at all. But then, most marriages between persons of rank in those days were arranged, and often worked out badly, as did her own. I expect a marriage would have been devised for you, and you would have had little or no say in it, nor your prospective husband, for that matter, whatever your reputation might be. Or his!'

Amelia smiled at the mention of her grandmother, who was a quite outrageous person who had once been the acknowledged mistress of a King of France. 'It's true. And Grand-mère would tell me – has told me – just to carry things off in the grand manner, and remember that I am an aristocrat and descendant of royalty. But I don't really see that as practical advice, especially since one of the monarchs I am descended from is King Charles II, which hardly helps matters. I don't know if I do care all that much for respectability, Sophie, but I quite see that to be entirely without it might be excessively uncomfortable. And I can't change my mind later, can I? Once it has gone, it will never come back.'

'Generally speaking, that is true, unless one is extremely lucky,' Sophie said with an odd little smile, stroking Louis's soft cheek with one finger.

'So there is no point you suggesting I run off to be a pirate, or join my stepmother on the stage, or anything of that extreme nature, though I quite see that both those things could be exciting. There would be a certain relief, I imagine, to taking either of those paths in life – not having to worry what anybody thought of me any more, because I'd know they'd all had their worse suspicions confirmed. But I can also see that I'd still have disagreeable men trying to get me alone to paw at me, just as they do now.'

'Probably more so, I should think,' said Sophie seriously. 'I understand that that happens to actresses a great deal, and must be counted as a grave disadvantage. Though if you were a pirate, Melia, you would have a pistol, and could shoot them, which might be agreeable.'

'I'd like that. But I don't suppose Rafe would.'

'No,' the Marchioness agreed a little regretfully. 'He'd probably come round eventually, since he loves you, but one must be sensible and face facts, and for a new member of the House of Lords to have a sister who was a pirate and forever shooting people might be a little awkward, perhaps. Even if they deserved it. It is a pity, I think, but it is undoubtedly so.'

'Yes. Respectability, then,' Lady Amelia said gloomily.

'Perhaps you could be a widow?' her sister-in-law proposed, doing something complicated with muslin cloths that ended with the baby sucking busily at her other breast without any perceptible interruption. 'If you were a widow, you would have much more freedom, and would not need to be anywhere near so careful of your behaviour. Then later, you might marry someone you truly cared for. And you would look excessively well in black, I think, which is a great consideration.'

'But wouldn't I have to marry someone first? And he might not die. Then I'd be saddled with him forever.'

'We must ask Rafe to enquire if there are any gentlemen he is acquainted with who are actually on the point of death and might like to marry you.'

'Why would a man wish to, if he's dying?'

'That's true. I suppose it is too much to ask that someone might be in love with you already, and also dying.'

Her sister-in-law agreed that it probably was, since persons on their deathbeds were not, in the nature of things, usually encountered in society. They had strayed rather from the point at issue, she thought.

'What about a false engagement, then – one that is all for show?' asked Sophie.

'I can't see how that would help,' Amelia objected reasonably. 'Even if anyone would agree, and again, I don't see why they should, I'd be obliged to cry off eventually, and that would do my reputation no good at all. I'd be a sad jilt along with everything else. Why is it so hard, Sophie?'

'What if you pretended to be engaged to someone quite rakish? Then when you broke it off because of his wicked ways, your reputation might improve because it would be clear that you were *not* of such a disposition yourself. Maybe.'

'That's a better idea,' Amelia said. 'But if he was quite rakish, and agreed to such a scheme, wouldn't he want to... to take advantage of me? Which is just what I don't want, you know. Though of course I am grateful for all your kind suggestions.'

'We must think further on the matter,' Sophie replied. 'I refuse to believe that there is not a solution, if we put our minds to it. Perhaps...'

'Perhaps?' There was a light in Sophie's eyes that worried Amelia a little.

'What if you were to be wooed by someone excessively good?'

'What do you mean?' Amelia couldn't help but think that someone excessively good sounded as though they might also be excessively dull, but she was prepared to hear Sophie out. Soon she would have to dress for the evening, in silks and jewels, so that she could go to another ball with her aunt and listen to whispered comments about her – not quite to her face, but not quite out of earshot either – and whispered suggestions *to* her, which had at first shocked her but now only made her weary and downcast. If Sophie had an idea with the least spark of merit in it, she could only be grateful, and listen to what she proposed.

'If someone with a famously unsullied reputation offered for you, Amelia, would it not change people's opinions?'

'I've already said, though, that I don't want to be condescended to and treated as though I'm terribly wicked when I'm not, and you agreed with me, not five minutes ago.'

'Yes, because we were talking of conspicuously moral, holy people. Of course that would be a dreadful idea, it has already been decided. That's not what I intend at all, though – I have had an idea of genius. You should engage yourself to a hero!'

Amelia had a sneaking idea she had guessed what her sister-in-law meant, or rather whom. 'Sophie! You surely can't be suggesting—'

'Yes!' broke in Lady Wyverne with such energy that her son, who had been sucking himself to sleep, started and let out a kitten-like mew of protest. 'Hush, Louis, there is no need to be alarmed, *mon coeur*. It is merely that I have realised that all your aunt Amelia needs to do to make everything right is to engage herself to Lord Thornfalcon!'

3

Marcus sighed and set down the brightly coloured print that the Honourable Mr Gastrell had just handed him for inspection. 'I suppose you think it's amusing?' he said with a touch of weariness. It wasn't really a question – he could see that Jem did from the broad grin that had spread across his pleasantly ugly face.

'It's damned amusing, Thorn. They all are, and this is one of the best yet. I'm very sorry to hear that you're losing your sense of humour under all your current trials, dear old boy.'

Marcus – Thorn to his friends, Major Lord Thornfalcon to the polite world – hoped he wasn't becoming a dull, dreary sort of fellow as his oldest friend implied, but feared he might be, and really, was it any wonder?

With just a hint of asperity in his deep voice, he said, 'I wish we might see how long you would retain your famous sense of humour if *you* were constantly being made the subject of this sort of monstrously annoying thing, *dear old boy*!' With a large, well-shaped hand, he gestured at the paper he'd laid down on the table between the two armchairs he and his friend occupied. He could quite happily have torn it into a dozen pieces and made Jeremy eat them.

It was a satirical print, such as might be bought – or viewed with ease in one of the large new plate-glass windows by those who could not afford to buy – in any of a dozen shops a few minutes' walk away from White's club, where the two friends sat this morning. And there was no mistaking the subject of it. Thorn was a gift from heaven to the caricaturists, and one they had seized on avidly. He was far above the average height and magnificently built, with a profile that one lady, swooning at the mere thought, had compared to that of Antinous, and another to that of Michael Angelo's David. It was not necessary to choose the ancient personage he most resembled; the effect, in all events, was unmistakeably classical. His brow was noble, his nose straight, his lips beautifully sculpted and his jawline strong. His chestnut hair curled crisply in a manner any lady might envy and seek to emulate. All of this splendour could be seen in garish colour in the print that he so disliked. Though he was currently dressed with propriety and sober good taste in top-boots, buckskin breeches and blue superfine coat, just like his slighter companion, the print had him arrayed – as they always did – in the new and rather splendid British Hussar's uniform, skin-tight, flattering to every inch of the athletic manly figure, and liberally trimmed with gold braid.

The scene depicted was not a military one, however. Far from it. As in all the prints that had bedevilled his existence since his most reluctant appearance in society a few weeks ago, the Hero of Salamanca and Huebra (here described instead in an unscrolling ribbon of text as *the Hero of Berkeley Square)* was besieged, not by fierce cuirassiers in shining metal breastplates or by Marshal Marmont's brave dragoons in martial green, but by a great many nubile young ladies in bright, flimsy silks and snowy white muslins. His expression, drawn in a few swift but powerfully expressive lines, suggested that they were a far more formidable foe than any of Napoleon's army.

This time, he was pictured in an elegant drawing room, his sabre in his hand but plainly useless as a weapon (there was an obvious implication here, given the lewd nature of many of these prints, and Thorn didn't care for it at all) because of the tender nature of his pursuers. These ladies climbed frantically over each other's bodies in a tangle of near-naked limbs, and fought among themselves, pulling hair and scratching, the better to approach him more closely. They had rent their garments, or each other's, which had not been enormously substantial to begin with, the better to expose yet more of their essential nakedness. He, the sole masculine figure in the scene, stood at bay on a satin sofa, and it seemed as though at any moment he would meet his fate, swallowed up by these modern maenads.

It was, as Jeremy Gastrell had said, excessively well done as these things went, and even among his embarrassment and distaste, he might have admitted as much, had not the chief of his persecutors, the most carefully drawn and also the one who appeared most likely to lay her eager hands upon him first, so greatly and unmistakeably resembled that famous silver-haired beauty, his widowed sister-in-law, Lavinia.

This could hardly be an accident; the artist had known exactly what he was about, and he was grateful that Jem had not seen fit to point it out, as he would not have known what to say in response. He did not in general lack for humour, despite his friend's gibe, but he could find no amusement at all in this matter. Lavinia – who was by cruel irony Lady Thornfalcon though most definitely not his wife, but rather his brother's widow – was, of course, currently residing with her parents in Berkeley Square, as all the world knew, including the printmaker.

Ten years ago, Lavinia Hall, as she had been then, would not have needed to pursue him. He had been hers, body and soul. And she had been his. He still believed that she had, when they had both been sixteen and seventeen. But fate, in the shape of the late Lord Thornfalcon and his neighbour and crony Sir Lionel Hall, had intervened. Lavinia, the loveliest girl in Somerset, had been destined for Lord Thornfalcon's heir Ambrose, a most suitable bride, so that their substantial estates might one day be joined. Her ambitious father had not the least notion of allowing her to marry the Viscount's far less eligible second son, who was to go for a soldier.

Marcus might have defied his father and hers, and suggested an elopement to Gretna Green to his love, had he not realised, without ever puzzling out the full significance of the thought, that his delicate, fragile, heartbreakingly beautiful Lavinia was not particularly well-suited to the life of a very junior officer without a fortune to his name, even one in a fashionable cavalry regiment. He'd hoped with the optimism of extreme youth to make a great career and rise to a high position in the army, but he could not flatter himself it would happen quickly. And so he had told her that he could not ask such a sacrifice of her, and she had cried prettily, and agreed. 'I must obey my father; it is my clear duty,' she had said, looking up at him with those mesmerising, drenched-violet eyes, as if challenging him to contradict her, or to take her in his arms again this one last time and kiss away her tears. He had kissed her – had done much more than that – but he hadn't told her she was wrong.

So she'd married his brother Ambrose in the family chapel at Thornfalcon, but luckily – his father, though proud and rigid in his outlook, hadn't been entirely devoid of sense, and his long-suffering mother must have had a part to play too – Marcus hadn't been there to witness it. He'd gained his lieutenant's commission with extraordinary swiftness and been packed off post-haste to his regiment. He had resigned himself, he'd believed then, to seeing Lavinia only as a sister as the years passed; it would hurt at first, he knew, but he hoped the pain would lessen. He knew too that Ambrose loved her, in his quiet fashion. Everyone did; she was so perfect. That was some sort of mercy; he need not think of her being anything less than adored. She deserved that.

And as far as he knew – from what his mother had told him, carefully, in her letters – the pair had been happy enough together. Certainly, nobody had ever hinted to him that they weren't. In time, she'd borne Ambrose a daughter, Priscilla, and Marcus had sent sincere congratulations and a generous gift, for this child, no doubt as lovely as her mother, who might so easily have been his.

Marcus had fought through Spain and Portugal and Spain again with little more than a few scratches and a concussion, until recently. But while he had been fighting and growing to manhood, the third Lord Thornfalcon had died, which was to be expected, given his age and state of health, and then a few months later, the fourth, which was not. Ambrose had broken his neck one winter afternoon in a stupid, pointless riding accident. He had no son, which mean that Marcus was still his heir. And now Lavinia was a widow.

He hadn't rushed back for his father's funeral, nor for his brother's, though it was doubtful if he could have made it in time on either occasion. He could have come after, of course, and probably should have done, but last year had been a crucial one in the fight for the Peninsula, and he'd chosen to believe that he could not be spared, though of course he was far from being indispensable and knew it. But a Frenchman's bayonet-thrust deep into his shoulder had broken his run of luck at last, in the desperately bloody hand-to-hand fighting among the trees along the River Huebra, and so he'd been sent back to England at last, much against his will, to face Lavinia.

Jeremy said now, clearly realising from the storm clouds gathering in his friend's normally amiable face, that it was past time for a change of subject. 'Do you go to Mrs Singleton's ball tonight, old man?'

Marcus would have been glad of a diversion, but this was scarcely that. 'Need you ask? I shall be there, naturally, escorting my sister and my mother, if she is well enough.'

'I expect Miss Helena's Season is a great strain on Her Ladyship,' Jeremy said sympathetically.

Thorn could not blame his friend, though it seemed as though every topic of conversation that presented itself brought unwelcome thoughts with it, as was unavoidable, unless they were to talk of trivialities, such as some impending boxing mill or the latest thrilling *on dit*. As the subject of a great deal of gossip himself, Marcus had not the least desire to spread scandal about others. So he said, 'Yes, it must be, though she puts a brave face on it. She rests in the daytime as much as she is able, but being in London is tiring enough in itself for her, without mentioning the ridiculous number of events she is obliged to attend with Helena. At least if I am there too, I can make sure she does not exert herself more than she needs.'

'You hate it all, don't you?'

'Can you marvel at it? I would have to be the most unconscionable coxcomb ever born to enjoy the attention I am currently receiving – the extent of it, and the nature of it too.' He was vehement, but there were others sitting nearby chatting or reading, and so he kept his voice low. Jeremy grimaced in understanding.

Marcus had been promoted after the Allied victory at Salamanca rather than having to purchase his Majority – promoted into dead men's shoes, of course, as he was never likely to forget – and mentioned by name in dispatches then, and again after the disastrous retreat that was Huebra. So had many others, of course, and with much greater cause as far as he could tell. The true heroes of those days were most of them dead. But it was only when he'd returned wounded to England that he'd realised how much of a public figure he'd become in his absence.

For this, he came to understand once his wound was healed and he began to mix in company, he had in great part Lavinia to thank. She was still so lovely – she always would be – and in black, she must have been incomparable. No wonder she dazzled wherever she went. She had put off her full mourning now, more than a year after Ambrose's death, but the muted colours – chiefly silver, palest blue and unadorned white – that she always wore became her ethereal beauty astonishingly well. Her hair was such a pale blonde as almost to be silver itself, though her brows and lashes were dark, and those extraordinary violet-blue eyes were like deep, mysterious pools at midsummer dusk, in which a man might drown. Poets wrote verses in her praise – so beautiful and so sad, and always (on appropriate occasions) accompanied by her poor fatherless child, as strikingly lovely as she was. Ladies of a susceptible nature had been known to weep at the mere sight of them together.

Society was disposed to be interested in tragic Lavinia, of course, and once the full details of her truly heartbreaking story were widely known (though surely she had not spread it abroad herself, but only told a very few trusted friends who had shockingly not kept her confidence), she became the sensation of the Season. And so did he.

He could not help being faintly nauseated by it all. He made a mawkish figure, he thought, in the tale – his chaste young love for her and hers for him, his noble renunciation of her at their fathers' command, the way he had stepped aside to let his brother wed her, and the distorted, highly sanitised civilian's-eye view of his subsequent military career. It was to be understood that his bravery had stemmed from the fact that he no longer cared if he lived or died, like some warrior of legend, as the love of his life was forever lost to him. And now, of course, the gossip-mongers eagerly picked over the torment he must be undergoing – and Lavinia too, poor suffering soul – to see her widowed, free to marry again, and yet tantalisingly out of his reach.

Or, came the whispers – and this was by far the worst of it as far as Marcus was concerned – was she?

When he had come home and as soon as he was well enough, his mother had put before him, expressionlessly, the legal papers that made his position perfectly clear. He had read them with an attention almost more painful than the lingering throb of his shoulder. But he had known it all already. It was not illegal to marry one's deceased brother's wife. It could be done, and was done, no doubt, every day, in every rank of society. But – was ever a legal judgment more perverse? – the marriage was voidable; if challenged, ever, for as long as the parties lived, it could be set aside in an instant. Rendered invalid, as if it had never happened. Which meant, of course, that any children of such a union would be made illegitimate, with no remedy for it. Marcus's heir at present was a distant cousin he barely knew, a clever young lawyer who was not a wealthy man; who could doubt for a second that he would challenge and overturn such a match if Lord Thornfalcon were ever improvident enough to make it? Of course he would – he had so much to gain, and Marcus so much to lose.

It was unsurprising that his mother, and his sister Helena too now that she was old enough to understand, had the strongest possible objections to such a scandalous marriage. But he paid them the compliment of believing that they had only a fleeting concern for public notoriety and even for the future of the title, the estate and the name. No, their worry was for him, because they loved him; for what such a life of uncertainty would do to him, and particularly the bitter knowledge of what he would be inflicting on his innocent unborn children if he chose love over duty this time. The polite world found the whole situation highly romantic, as if his deepest feelings were some sort of play set out for public entertainment, but he had no taste for melodrama and his opinions were far, far otherwise. He was living a species of nightmare as he smiled and danced and rode in the park and kept his face impassive all the while, and if his mother and sister hadn't needed him, London would have been the last place in the world he'd choose to set foot in.

Lavinia, in one of their endless, tormenting conversations, just last night, had accused him of caring only for stuffy respectability and the future of his noble name. For base inheritance and worldly gain. She could not help but marvel at it, she told him often. She had thought she had known him, that their souls were as one, indivisible and eternal, but now she realised that she had been sadly mistaken. 'I would give up the world for you,' she said, those extraordinary eyes huge and tragic in her pale little face. Who but a heartless monster could make her suffer so? 'I would risk my reputation, everything, to have your love again, to stand beside you proudly and openly as your wife. I would defy everyone and everything, and if anyone dared to question our marriage and brand me a whore, I would accept it as long as I had you. But I understand now that you would not do the same for me. It is excessively odd,' she went on lightly, each word worse than a bayonet-thrust, her melodious voice tinkling like silver bells, 'that you are the hero of the hour and feted everywhere, and yet in this, I am braver than you. I can only suppose —' and here her voice broke at last '—that you never really loved me. Only desired me. And even that has left you. Has it not?'

She had a room kept ready for her in his town house – she had that right, as his brother's widow and mother of a Thornfalcon child – and sometimes, she came to sleep there. There could be no impropriety, no whisper of scandal, since his mother and his sister lived there too. They were all one family, or supposed to be. The Dowager, frail and unwell as she was, must welcome the chance of spending precious time with her only grandchild, and of course someone as impeccably behaved as her daughter-in-law would not dream of denying her that. Lavinia had been heard to say publicly and frequently that never, never, no matter that it caused her the acutest pain to pass over the threshold of the house that had once been hers, would she think of keeping grandmother and granddaughter apart. If angelic little Priscilla should be present when these trembling words were spoken, as she often was, the fairy-like child would clutch at her mother's hand and say, in her adorably high, piping tones, 'Oh, Mama, dearest, I am sorry if it hurts you to be here, but do not keep me from Grandmama, I pray! I do love her so! And brave Uncle Marcus too!' Ladies who witnessed this manner of affecting scene had often to be revived afterwards with sal volatile and hartshorn.

But on the occasions Lavinia chose to spend the night in Half-Moon Street at Thornfalcon House, it was a very different matter. The sensitive ladies would have been shocked to see it, and the printmakers delighted. It was all too easy to imagine what they would have made of what they witnessed. Once her child had been put to bed, once the mansion was quiet, Lavinia would slip silently along the corridor. Marcus could have locked his door; he should have. But then he would have to lie there in the darkness waiting to hear the handle turn, dreading it and wanting it at the same time. Because he knew that if the door was not barred to her, she would appear in his bedchamber in her nightgown and robe again, barefoot, beautiful as a dream, and do her very best to drive him out of his senses.

4

Sophie's suggestion took possession of Amelia's mind over the next few days, no matter how she tried to push it away. She didn't think it was as sensible a notion as the Marchioness seemed to believe, but it wasn't quite crazy either, Amelia thought; like all her sister-in-law's schemes, it had a sort of relentless logic to it that was hard to argue with. Sophie, though they rarely spoke of it, had lived for many years outside society, fending for herself and surviving in ways that had made her sharp and ruthless and pitilessly clear-sighted. Public chatter said she had been a governess, but Amelia knew that, whatever she had been doing, it wasn't that. She had a sort of veneer she assumed now when she chose to. She was charmingly idiosyncratic, a little absent-minded and prone to amusing mistakes in English, which was her second language: a great lady – unmistakeably an aristocrat of the *Ancien Régime*, since her father had been a duke with an illustrious name – but with very little hauteur of manner. She didn't care greatly for social gatherings, but when she attended them, she could captivate effortlessly, or so it seemed. But beneath all this, and even as she held her child in loving arms and ordered her grand households with tranquil authority, as though she'd never had occasion to do anything different, she could see the people around her, the ones she did not care about, as potential prey, and dissect their weaknesses. Amelia had swiftly learned to respect her judgement, and listened to her now.

'Lord Thornfalcon loathes the situation in which he has been placed,' the Marchioness said with calm certainty as they spoke of the matter again. Amelia was dressing for a quiet dinner at home followed by tonight's ball, which Sophie would not attend, so they had dismissed the girl's abigail to allow them to talk in private. 'You can see it written on his face.' She had finished arranging the younger woman's hair, weaving a string of pearls through her lustrous dark locks, and stepped back to see the effect of what she had done.

'I should think he must dislike it,' said Amelia. 'Thank you, that looks very well, I think. It is surely most disagreeable – and who should know better than I? – to be the subject of such gossip and be unable to prevent it. But he always remains impassive; we may be reading him wrongly. Perhaps he will think your idea quite mad, and refuse to countenance it for so much as a second.'

'Bah! He is desperate for a way out – desperate to escape all the attention that is being showered on him. He will be delighted, I am sure, and most grateful to you for your providential suggestion.'

'I can easily credit that he would be glad to forgo women flinging themselves at his feet, and falling off horses so that he is obliged to rescue them, and fainting into his arms at balls so that he is obliged to catch them, and all that sort of nonsense. Presumably, such behaviour would have to stop, once we were betrothed, and that must be a relief to him. But what of the great romance with his brother's widow? If he does genuinely intend to marry her, despite all the reasons why he should not, the last thing he will wish to do is to engage himself to someone else.'

Sophie made a rude, unladylike noise of derision. 'If he had wished to do that, he might have done it already, quietly – a marriage of that peculiar nature must always be quiet. That the lady desires such a match, I can well believe – that *he* does, I would not wager a penny on. It is a very pretty, romantic tale, no doubt, and it is no wonder that it should be, since she herself has crafted it in what I must admit is a most impressive way, and made sure that it is spread about. *I* see what manner of person she is, even if others do not. The question is: does he, or is he blinded by love and by desire? And it is very simple, after all – if he wishes to take this grave step and wed her, he will refuse you, and you will be no worse off than before, for I am sure he would not tell a soul.'

Amelia digested this. 'If you are right about her, and he does say yes to my suggestion, she will be my enemy,' she said slowly. 'I will have ruined all her plans – or if I have not in truth, because I have no intention really of marrying him, of course, she will think I have.'

'There is always a price to be paid for anything worth having, I have found. And you *will* have ruined her plans, because even if – when – it is known that you have jilted him and the engagement is at an end, it will hardly suit the nature of her story to marry him afterwards. He will have chosen another, but then been rejected by her, and she will be second choice. It will not seem so much like a great and noble sacrifice a man makes for the woman he adores, but rather a lack of imagination on his part. "Oh, there she is again, I had quite forgot; I might as well marry her." That is not very romantic, and I do not see her as a woman who has ever been second choice in her life, or would stand to be seen by the world as such. I think she is very proud, though it is an odd kind of pride to my mind.'

'That's very bad, then – I would be destroying her life and taking away her future. I can't do that, Sophie! That would be a dreadful thing to do to another woman, and especially one who has already been widowed so young!' Amelia swivelled on her stool with a swish of blue and gold silk, so that she could meet her sister-in-law's eyes, not just catch their reflection in the mirror.

Sophie shrugged in Gallic fashion. 'You would only be destroying her life if His Lordship truly plans to marry her. If he does not, you have done nothing to her; the responsibility is his, and unless she is excessively stupid, she must realise it. And her fantasy remains intact, if she cares for that. The man she adores has chosen duty over love again. It is her tragic fate, and his, to be parted once more. He doesn't love *you*, naturally. Nobody, least of all her, need think it is that sort of marriage – he weds to please his family and secure the succession, not to indulge his own feelings.'

'But what of my terrible reputation?' protested Amelia. 'How does that fit with the story? I doubt most respectable families would be willing to welcome me, and a connection with the scandalous Wyvernes.'

'Your reputation is irrelevant for the purposes of this fiction. Nobody is threatening to declare *your* match publicly invalid, nor brand your future children bastards, no matter how bad the Wyverne name is. In fact, it may even be forgotten in the press of all these other exciting events. That would be a good thing, no?'

'I suppose it would. But I still think Lady Thornfalcon is bound to hate me.'

'Probably she will. But what of it? She cannot hurt you, and if she slanders you, it will be put down to sheer jealousy. And

Amelia, if I have understood your peculiar English laws aright, if Lord Thornfalcon has an ounce of brain in his handsome head, he cannot seriously mean to wed her, however much she wants him to, and even if he wishes to for his own part. He has responsibilities to others than himself, and to his unborn children most of all.'

'Yes, but if he loves her...'

'If he loves her, he will not engage himself to you. He will make this crazy match to the extremely annoying woman with the horrid lisping child, who can call him Papa Dear instead of Uncle. But if he does not love her, he will leap at the chance you offer him. It is not as though your jilting him, when you finally do, will damage him in the least. It will very likely free him from his disagreeable entanglement, and when he is free, he will still be handsome, rich and eligible, with a hero's reputation to boot. Such men will always find suitable brides, you need have no doubt of that. Worry about yourself, not him.'

'I can't believe it's as simple as you make it sound.'

'Perhaps not. But probably he will be at the ball tonight, escorting his sister, and you will have the chance to observe him, will you not? And his brother's widow too, if she is there, which I expect she will be. One disadvantage of the situation she has created – I expect she did not realise it in advance, for it is difficult to plan for every eventuality if one is not greatly experienced in scheming, which I imagine she is not – is the enormous number of ladies of the ton who have been so impressed by her romantic fantasy and his heroic nature that they have decided to throw themselves at him.'

'Literally, in many cases,' Amelia conceded with a mischievous grin. She had seen as much herself, a week or so ago, and so had Sophie, which perhaps was what had put Lord Thornfalcon in their minds.

'Literally, like the lady who tried to tumble down the steps into his arms and only succeeded in breaking her own arm and making herself ridiculous. I don't suppose the widow can be enjoying that sort of thing very much. And she must keep a close eye on him always, must she not? In case one of these most persistent debutantes succeeds in entrapping him and carrying him off, as in the prints, if she does not pay sufficient attention.'

'It's not just debutantes, or all the other young ladies who wish to marry him themselves,' murmured her sister-in-law. 'I understand that many married ladies also have less honourable designs on him.'

'Well, he is very handsome, I suppose, if one does not dislike a man with chestnut hair,' said Sophie, whose own husband was devilishly dark, judiciously. 'Do you? You are dark yourself, of course, so there would be a pleasing contrast, and I can see that you would make a sufficiently pretty pair, you and he.'

'I?' replied Amelia with a little heat. 'It does not matter what I think of him! I wonder you should say such a thing, Sophie! Even if it were to come off – and I must think of how I am to approach him first, and then he must agree to it, which is by no means certain – it does not matter a jot what my opinion of him is. I would merely be using him, and helping him too, I suppose, if what you believe is true.'

Sophie murmured an apology, smiling a little to herself, and rose to leave. 'It is time for dinner,' she said. 'Your grandmother is to join us this evening, as she has had a good day and feels well, so let us not be late – you know how she dislikes it above all things, and it will set her scolding us about the decline of modern manners.'

'You're right.' Amelia jumped to her feet. 'If one is more than one hundred years old, one has earned the right not to be kept waiting.' And then after a moment, grudgingly, 'I suppose he is quite handsome. If, as you say, one does not dislike a man of his colouring on principle. But he is too broad-shouldered and too tall. There is altogether too much of him for true handsomeness.'

Sophie laughed. 'I cannot admit that to be a possibility. There is no such thing as too tall for a gentleman, and as for too broad... He is not a seven-foot giant from a fairy tale, Melia; I am sure he is barely taller than Rafe.'

'I didn't say he was a *giant*...'

Amiably squabbling, the two ladies made their way downstairs to dinner, so that Delphine, the fearsome Dowager Marchioness, might have her dinner at the appointed hour.

5

Amelia looked about her with bright curiosity as she entered the hot, crowded ballroom in Lady Keswick's wake, feeling rather like a rowing boat bobbing behind a frigate in full sail. But it made a difference, she discovered, to have an object for once, to be doing something positive to better her situation – tonight, she was no longer dreading the unwelcome attentions she so often received, or, at any rate, not so much. Tonight, she would see Lord Thornfalcon for the first time since Sophie had proposed him as an answer to her problems. She would try if she could to judge precisely what he felt about the situation in which he found himself, and in particular his widowed sister-in-law's part in it.

She'd seen him before, of course, on many occasions, since his excessive height made him stand out from any crowd, but he'd never been presented to her and she had no sort of connection with him, nor any other member of his family. They had not danced together, therefore, nor ever exchanged so much as a word or a glance. He was presumably ignorant of her very existence, except perhaps as a subject of gossip; they had that much in common, at least. She had most certainly not been one of the debutantes who gushed and giggled if he so much as glanced in their direction. And, it scarcely needed to be added, Lady Keswick with her passion for propriety and deep desire to see her niece respectably married had not contemplated for a second taking a hand in what she termed the disgraceful scramble for the Major's attention.

Inevitably, she and her aunt had discussed the rumours that swirled about the Thornfalcon family at present – it was almost impossible to avoid the topic that was on everyone's lips, and Amelia had deliberately turned the conversation in that direction in the carriage on the way to the ball. She had experienced no difficulty in doing so, curious to know the older lady's feelings on the subject now that she just might have some personal stake in the matter.

'Judith Thornfalcon must detest her son being the centre of such a sensation,' Her Ladyship had said loftily. 'She is not at all strong, suffering cruelly from rheumatic joints, and I am sure she would not be here at all if she had not the child to bring out. Miss Thornfalcon's come-out was supposed to be last year, for she is quite nineteen now, I believe, but they were in black gloves for her husband and her eldest son last Season, and so could not appear. Naturally, her mother does not want to let another year pass and find her almost on the shelf at twenty without so much as making her curtsey to the Queen. I have some acquaintance with Judith Thornfalcon, from my own youth: only a little. And I must add that although I am sorry for what she is undergoing, naturally,' she said, descending rapidly from Olympus and sounding like an ordinary human woman for a moment, 'it would be idle to deny that it makes a pleasant change for people to be whispering about someone else than the Wyvernes for once. Long may it last!'

'Do you think Lord Thornfalcon really will marry his brother's widow, Aunt?' Amelia had asked her, feeling a little guilty for indulging in idle tittle-tattle when she'd just been reminded just how unpleasant it was to suspect oneself thus discussed.

'I hope he has more sense and decency than to do so!' Lady Keswick opined majestically. 'They have always had a good name as a family, before this dreadful start. Why, the current Viscount's grandfather was a friend of my own father's, I believe, and my parent was, it need not be said, a person of irreproachable morals. They made the Grand Tour together. No! I do not choose to credit that this young man, who seems otherwise estimable and has served his country with distinction, even if he is quite unnecessarily good-looking – which always leads to trouble, in my experience – is even contemplating such a dangerous path. No child of mine would ever be so foolish as to consider making such a scandalous choice of mate, I can be sure of that!'

Amelia, thinking of her meek cousins Tom and Annabel, and their even more timid younger brother Peter, none of whom had ever dreamed of taking any action not approved by their formidable mama in advance, and likely never would, was obliged to bite the inside of her lip for a moment before she could say, 'You don't think it romantic, then, ma'am, as so many people seem to?'

In grey and shades of purple, Lady Keswick rather resembled a fancy pigeon, and her chest swelled out like one as she intoned, 'I do not! And if you tell me that you do, Amelia Wyverne, I will be forced to conclude that you have inherited your father's sad unsteadiness of character, and I shall be very sorry to hear it. Very sorry indeed!'

'Well, I don't *think* I have,' said Amelia cautiously. 'I expect it should have shown itself by now if I had. And actually, thinking about it, I don't think I do find it so terribly romantic, ma'am. The law seems to me to be foolish and most odd – forbid a thing, or do not forbid it, surely. What other action is there that only becomes a crime if someone says, "Look, there is a crime!"? And everyone pretends to be terribly shocked and that they had not known all along, when of course they did.'

'I can call several similar things to mind,' Lady Keswick said in oracular fashion. 'But do go on, child. I do not say that you are wrong in principle.'

'If it is true that Lord Thornfalcon and Miss Hall, as she then was, loved each other when young and were separated because of mere worldly considerations, I am sorry for it. But so much has happened since then. Of course I don't have a sister, so I can't be sure, but I do not think I would care to marry my sister's husband, if she died. Whether I loved my sister a great deal or whether I was not close to her at all – actually, I don't know which would be worse. It doesn't seem... quite right. Comparisons would be drawn. Surely. It's not romantic at all, is it, Aunt? It's a little bit sickening. And Sophie thinks that the lady has set the story about for her own ends, which puts quite another complexion on things, if true.'

'Lady Wyverne is a woman of great good sense, as I have previously observed. The French are not in the least sentimental about such matters, I understand.'

Amelia agreed that Sophie wasn't sentimental, and nor was her own grandmother, for that matter, and the carriage had drawn up at their destination at that moment, so that the conversation had perforce been terminated.

Now she succeeded in attracting her aunt's attention, and said on a sudden inspiration, 'Aunt, would you present me to Lady Thornfalcon and to her daughter? I was not previously aware that you had any acquaintance with them.'

Lady Keswick looked at her keenly. 'I shall, Amelia, if you can look me in the eye and assure me that you have no intention

whatsoever of making an exhibition of yourself over the Major in
the quite disgraceful manner—'

'Aunt Millicent,' said Amelia with great seriousness, 'I assure
you, I have absolutely no intention of joining other young ladies
in their silly antics. I cannot afford to, even if I wished to, which I
don't.' This at least was true, she consoled herself. 'I am very well
aware that behaviour which might invite mild censure when
perpetrated by others must have far more serious consequences
for me.' *I should know it – you've told me often enough*, she said
silently. 'But I feel sorry for the family,' she added suddenly,
surprising herself with the truth of it. 'I of all people know how
unpleasant their current situation must be for them.'

'Very well. Your feelings do you credit, child. Let us find them.'

A few moments later – no mere crowd could stand in Millicent Keswick's way, and this one parted before her as had the Red
Sea before Moses – Amelia was dropping a curtsey to a sweet-
faced lady of her aunt's age, who leaned heavily upon an ebony
cane, and her daughter. They were both round-faced and rosy-
cheeked, with delicate, pale skin and abundant chestnut hair.
Their natural strong resemblance to each other was enhanced by
the identical expression of weary, guarded politeness they both
bore on their faces; they looked as though they were both of an
amiable disposition which was being severely tried just now.
*They think I only want to know them so I can scrape acquaintance
with Lord Thornfalcon*, she realised. They must have been positively besieged by ladies wanting to be fast friends with them.

'Judith,' Lady Keswick said, kissing the air adjacent to that
lady's cheek, 'I am glad to see you looking tolerably well, and I
hope you will be pleased to know my niece. Despite occasional
appearances to the contrary, she is *not* a foolish young woman.
This Season, this fact alone may serve to lend her a distinction in

your eyes that she would otherwise scarcely merit. I am sure you will not fail to understand me.'

Amelia grinned in response to this outrageous statement; her aunt was nothing short of magnificent, and for her own secret purposes, she could scarcely have hoped for a better introduction. A set was forming up, and she could see that Miss Thornfalcon had no partner; she could also see that one of her own more disagreeable admirers was making his way purposefully in her direction, no doubt aiming to ask her to dance so that he could squeeze her hand, her arm and any other part of her he could reach, if she accepted him. If she did *not* accept him, she would not be able to dance with anyone at all that evening. The rules were stupid, but they were unbreakable, at least by her. 'Miss Thornfalcon,' she said impulsively, 'would you care to take a turn about the room with me?'

Miss Helena was plainly not as startled as she might have been by this abrupt request; Amelia was aware that it could not be the first of its kind. And this was no place or time to explain at length. 'If we don't go immediately,' she said in low tones, 'Mr Peacock will be upon me in an instant and I shall be obliged to dance with him. I assure you, if you had ever done so as much as once, you would understand why I do not wish to repeat the experience.'

Such a plainly put request for sisterhood was near-on impossible to refuse, and her companion did not do so. In the blink of an eye, they were proceeding at a fair pace towards the far end of the ballroom, away from the crowded dance floor and its ring of observers, and Lady Keswick was somehow presenting the eager young gentleman with a dowagerly barrier that he could not pass without grave discourtesy and a degree of courage he clearly did not possess. She was no more eager for her niece to further her acquaintance with the disreputable young man than was his quarry.

At length, the two girls achieved the relative safety of an alcove, and paused there. Helena Thornfalcon turned to look at Amelia in speculative fashion. 'Well, that was odd,' she said frankly, her grey eyes level, a spark in them that might have been amusement or anger, or some mixture of both. 'Are you always so very determined, Lady Amelia?'

'Only when I have a purpose in mind,' Amelia replied with equal forthrightness. 'And I must tell you directly that, contrary to what I am sure you must be thinking, my purpose is *not* to become bosom bows with you and insinuate myself into your family so that I may the better set my cap at your brother.'

'If that's true, it will certainly be a pleasant change.' Her companion smiled, but there was no humour in it.

'Has it been very bad? I only ask because I am also the subject of gossip, just as your family is, and I too have done nothing whatsoever to deserve it.'

'Oh, goodness, you are, aren't you?' said Miss Thornfalcon, paying Amelia the compliment of not pretending to misunderstand her. 'It's been, and continues to be, quite atrocious for Mama and me, and most of all for my poor brother, and I am sure your own position has been quite as bad for you. Is that why you sought me out?'

'In a way...' Amelia paused for a moment and then said, 'Please don't think me odiously self-pitying, but I don't seem to be able to do anything to persuade the world that I am nothing like my father or my stepmother. It's most unjust, because I never lived with him apart from when I was very small, so I didn't know him at all well. He had no hand in my upbringing, and I've never even so much as set eyes on her.'

Helena grimaced. 'I don't suppose you have ever gone to watch her when she is performing on stage?'

'Making up a family party? We certainly have not! Lady Wyverne has often sent us complimentary tickets for one of the best boxes; my brother Rafe says it is done to taunt us, and my other brother, Charlie, is terrified of her after their only meeting and starts and grows pale whenever her name is mentioned. Rafe says he is sure that she has told people that the conspicuously empty box belongs to the family that has so cruelly cast her out, in order to make herself and us more talked about. It is all a deal of nonsense, and most provoking. But all that is far from the point I meant to make to you. I am irretrievably tainted by association, and I don't think there is anything obvious that I can do about it. And therefore the manner of men who pay court to me...'

'Mr Peacock?'

'He's not the worst of them. They have offered for my hand, so many of them, though of course Rafe has refused them all. He thinks they will grow tired of it, and someone better will come along at last. But I'm not so sure. And I'm not the sort of person who finds it easy to sit idly by and do nothing.'

'Nor I,' agreed Helena with a genuine smile of amusement this time. 'Am I to understand that you have some idea in mind that may help you, and us too?'

It was a pleasure to talk with someone so quick-witted. 'I do, though I must admit it wasn't my idea but my sister-in-law's. And I don't know if it will work, or if your brother would agree to it. But I think it might help him – in fact, I am more confident that it will help him than that it will help me. I sometimes think that my situation cannot be mended. I don't know if you can understand this, but I think perhaps you can – I'd rather do something a little rash that I've chosen for myself than let others organise my life for me. I don't mean my family, I mean...'

'Life. Fate. No, I do understand, I think, because I see something similar happening to my brother. So tell me – do not be afraid that I will think ill of you, whatever you say. I can see that in a quiet sort of a way you are desperate, and we are too, so what can I do but sympathise and listen? Perhaps it might be considered odd, for us to be so open with each other so quickly, but we are both ill at ease and worried, and possibly that creates a bond between us faster than many hours of inconsequential conversation over the teacups might.'

'I think that's true, you know. Very well. Before I tell you, I promise you, I promise you faithfully, that this is not a ruse to get close to Lord Thornfalcon, and then to trap him. I swear it on my dear brother Charlie's head, though there is little enough inside it in all conscience.'

'Marcus is already trapped,' said Helena with a touch of bitterness. 'I do not see how his case can be much worse. If I think your scheme is crazy, be sure I shall tell you so directly, and we shall not fall to quarrelling over it. Go on!'

'Sophie's idea is that he should pretend to court me, and in the fullness of time, we should become engaged to be married. But it would all be false, of course. I have no true desire to marry him, or anybody just now. It is merely that Sophie thinks – and I cannot put the blame on her, for I think it too – that if I were to be associated with someone as... as good and noble as your brother is believed to be, and I am sure he truly is, my reputation might improve and people might begin to see me differently at last. That's all I can hope for.'

'And then you would jilt him.'

'I would. We would put it about that we had decided we could not agree and had parted amicably. His reputation would not suffer in the least. Mine might or might not, I suppose, but honestly, I do not see how it can be much worse than it is already.'

Her companion was silent for a long moment, and Amelia said rapidly, 'I'm sorry. It is a nonsensical idea, and it was presumptuous of me to mention it to you. I only beg that you will not mention my foolishness to anyone else, even if you do think badly of me. Let us speak of something else. Do you wish to return to your mother?'

'Oh, goodness, no! I think it is an excellent scheme! I only wonder if Marcus will be open to the merits of it. My fear is that he may not, for he is in the worst of humours at the moment, and no wonder.'

A short while later, Amelia and her new friend watched from the shelter of their alcove as Helena's sister-in-law arrived at the ball, accompanied by her mama. They were a little late, perhaps, most of the other guests having arrived some time ago, and there could be no mistaking the stir of interest that ran around the room at the sight of them. Many eyes other than their own were watching avidly as the pair made their way with cool assurance through the throng to greet the younger lady's mother-in-law, who stood with her tall son at her side and must make so public a greeting. Who could question the young widow's right to claim it? They were still her family.

'She does love to make an entrance,' Miss Thornfalcon muttered grimly. 'Honestly, I do not know how Marcus bears it. If I were being made a public exhibition of in such a fashion, I would run shrieking from the room.'

'She is very beautiful,' Amelia said. This was undeniable, but scarcely adequate. Probably, she thought, Lavinia Thornfalcon

was the loveliest person she'd ever seen outside of a painting. She
didn't look quite real; she was a silver-gilt princess from a fairy
tale. Her hair curled just as it should, and was piled up on her
head to show the delicacy of her long neck, adorned with a fine
diamond necklace – lovely, but not ostentatious. Nothing about
her was ostentatious. She was of average height and superbly
proportioned, and she moved with fluid grace; her silver and blue
gown was elegant in its simplicity, the neckline modest but not
outmoded. Not the most captious critic could say that her nose
was too long or too short, or her mouth too big, or her figure less
than ideal in any tiny detail. If someone had told Amelia that the
woman was of the fairy race rather than an ordinary human, she
would not have struggled to believe it. 'Never mind your brother,'
she added after a moment. 'How do *you* bear it? She is unnatu-
rally perfect.'

'I know! She was so even as a girl. No spots for her, no
awkward blushes. She makes me feel that I am some vast, blun-
dering creature who is far too clumsy to be in company, and will
cause a catastrophic breakage of some kind at any moment. I feel
as though she's waiting – ever so patiently – for me to do something horribly gauche, and if by some chance I don't, there'll
always be a next time. I am bound to confirm her silent bad
opinion of me eventually and we both know it. And yet I can't
blame her for her beauty. She has what nature gave us, as we all
do. If I liked her even a little,' she said with devastating frankness,
'I could forgive her for looking like an angel.'

'Why don't you?'

'If you asked her, she would hint discreetly that I am jealous
of her appearance, with just a suggestion of a sad little smile. But
honestly, I don't think I am. I don't trust her, that's the truth. I
think she is false from her topmost curl to the perfect toenails on

her littlest toes. And most of all, I don't think that this great love story that she has spun around her and Marcus is genuine. And it's so excessively unfair to him, and to my poor brother Ambrose. Nobody ever mentions *him* when they're sighing over how romantic the story is. He loved her, and he was barely thirty when he died! How do you suppose Marcus feels, to have all the world believe that he wishes to take advantage of his own brother's death in such a manner? Or my mother, what is she supposed to say? Mama can do nothing but smile at her, no matter what she feels. She will be judged if her face betrays the least hint of disapproval. Everyone is watching her now – look at them. She cannot even show her natural grief for her eldest son. Did you know that many foolish girls, led by Miss Lancaster and Miss Archer, who obviously admire her greatly and find her story excessively romantic, are now declaring themselves Friends of Lavinia, and wearing her colours in support of her cause? As if she even has a cause! Oh, I could slap her!'

'I can't even imagine,' Amelia said. 'I didn't know that – about her supporters, I mean. I have some slight acquaintance with the ladies you mention, though they certainly are not friends of mine.'

These were deep waters indeed, and for a moment, she quailed at what she had so lightly proposed. She would be involving herself in these people's lives, and even if her plan worked, which was by no means certain, they'd all be affected by it. Futures would be changed. Did she dare to do this, in reality?

'Our whole situation is ridiculous and unpleasant. It is making my mother unhappy, which she does not deserve for she has been through enough, and – I believe, though we have not spoken openly of it yet – driving my brother half out of his wits. And that is why I think your idea is a good one. Like you, I have a great desire at least to act, to try to mend matters. And so I think you should call on me tomorrow, and after a little while, I will contrive that you shall find yourself alone with Marcus, and you can put your proposition to him. Let us not delay, in case in the meantime she finds some way to entangle him in her toils even further.'

6

Marcus, sitting alone in his library during the hour at which morning calls were traditionally paid, was a little surprised to receive a note, via one of the footmen, which said that his sister required his presence immediately in the small sitting room. Helena wasn't the sort of person who stood on ceremony; she was an energetic young woman, and if she wished to speak to him, she would generally run down the stairs in a most unladylike fashion and burst in upon him with the words she meant to say already trembling on her lips before the door had closed behind her. So that was strange. Moreover, his mother and his sister both knew that the very last thing he desired to do was to come and take tea with them while a procession of ladies passed through the house and attempted to further their acquaintance with the family. Lady Thornfalcon might tell the butler that she was not at home to most of her visitors, but she couldn't turn away everyone, and certainly not ladies she'd known for many years, or relatives. But that didn't mean *he* had to be present. He couldn't avoid his many admirers in public places or at events to which he was obliged to escort his female relatives, but he was damned if he'd help to encourage them in his own house. He wasn't hiding in the library precisely... Very well, that was exactly what he was doing. He felt hunted.

Still, the small sitting room wasn't the room where visitors were normally greeted, but was the chamber Helena had claimed as her private space, so Marcus felt reasonably safe going to see her there. He tried very hard not to peer anxiously out of the library door into the hall before he opened it fully, but judged from the grins hastily wiped from the other attendant footman's face that he hadn't entirely succeeded. Shaking his head, he made his way up the stairs at a faster pace than he would normally have used, for he had heard the tap of the doorknocker, and knew himself in peril. He was not safe even in his own home. Wasn't an Englishman's home supposed to be his castle? This was obviously untrue. Or if this house in Half-Moon Street was his castle, it was a castle under siege.

Marcus was surprised, and far from pleased, then, when he opened the door of Helena's room and found that she was not alone in it. She had a companion – just the sort of fashionable young woman he was at such pains to avoid. Though they must have been expecting him, since he had been summoned not five minutes since, the expression of trepidation that animated both their features now made him even more irritated than he had previously been. If Helena was plotting something with some foolish friend of hers, it would be the outside of enough. He opened his mouth to utter a reproof which, although it was perforce designed for other ears than hers, and therefore far less blistering than it might have been, would still leave his sibling in no doubt that he was gravely displeased with her, and surprised too at her insensitivity.

He had no chance to share his thoughts. Helena said hurriedly, 'Marcus, I can see from your face that you think I have tricked you into the company of one of the young ladies who has developed a foolish passion for you, but I promise you, the truth is far otherwise. This is Lady Amelia Wyverne – oh, Amelia, I suppose I should have presented Marcus to you first, but you know exactly who he is, obviously, so that would really be the height of folly. Marcus, Lady Amelia is also suffering a great deal from unkind and unfair gossip this Season, as I am sure you have heard, and in looking to find a way to better her own sad situation, she has hit upon a way to improve ours. To improve yours, in particular, and I am sure that if you are honest, you will admit that you are in grave need of it. So I will leave you alone together and she will share her idea.'

And with a whisk of her muslin skirts, she was gone, and the door closed behind her with a significant clunk.

Marcus looked at Lady Amelia silently, and Lady Amelia looked at him. If he'd been inclined to be interested at all in young women of the ton, which he wasn't, he must have admitted grudgingly that she was a reasonably attractive specimen of the breed. She was tall enough that he did not get a crick in his neck staring down at her, and her hair was dark and lustrous, curling fashionably atop her head. Her eyes were an unusual shade of dark blue-grey, sparkling with life, and her face was mobile and expressive, her features fine and her mouth, in particular, well-shaped. Soft. Appealing, even. But he wished her at the devil, all the same.

An awkward little pause grew between them, which at last she broke. 'Lord Thornfalcon,' she said in a resolute tone, 'what your sister says is all true. I have a great deal of sympathy for what you've been going through as a family – though it's none of my business and I don't propose to discuss it at all,' she added hastily, presumably in response to the thunderclouds she saw in his countenance. 'I imagine, if you have had any leisure at all to listen to the whispers circulating around the polite world when they're not busy talking about you, then you must know how *I* am spoken of.'

Marcus became aware rather belatedly that he hadn't uttered a word since he had entered the room, but had been standing staring at his unexpected visitor like a gaby. 'Yes,' he said reluctantly, trying not to growl. 'I have never cared for gossip, and I care for it considerably less now, but moving in society as I have been doing these last weeks, I have not been able to avoid hearing...' And then he said, remembering his manners, 'Will you not sit down, Lady Amelia? I have no real idea what you and my sister are about, but we can at least sit while we discuss it. I assume you must have some serious motive in contriving that we should be alone in this improper fashion.' He knew he sounded like a pompous ass; he didn't seem to be able to help it.

'I suppose your sister might have stayed, for propriety's sake,' she replied, seating herself gracefully in one of the sofas after she had moved a pile of Helena's books. If she saw his words as a reproof, it didn't seem to disconcert her greatly. 'I have nothing to say to you that I have not already told her, but I understand that you are expecting a great many callers today...'

'Today and every day,' he said grimly, sinking into an armchair opposite her.

'So that she does not wish to leave your mother alone to entertain them. I will be brief, then. You know, sir, that my reputation is... tarnished, because of my father and my stepmother.'

'I have seen that lady upon the stage,' he told her, interested, rather against his will, to know where she could be going with this tale which at present was unfortunate, certainly, but no affair of his. 'My friend Jeremy dragged me to see her as part of my recovery, or so he said. She makes a powerful impression.' Rosanna Wyverne was not the greatest actress who ever trod the boards, far from it, but she was a striking presence: beautiful and arresting, whether despite or because of the rumours that circulated about her poverty-stricken early life and her long marriage to the notorious Marquess.

'Does she? I have never so much as set eyes on her. My family have always gone to a great deal of trouble to keep us apart, trouble which they might as well have spared themselves, given that my reputation is no better for it, as far as I can tell. You do not know me, but I assure you, I have done nothing to deserve the things that are said of me.'

'I must sympathise, since my mother and sister are also suffering through our current notoriety, even if they are not subject to gossip on their own account – as in your case, the stories that circulate about my family and hurt them so have nothing whatsoever to do with any actions of theirs. I cannot quite say the same myself.' He winced; he had not meant to say anything of the kind to her, and was not sure why he had said even that much when he had intended to be completely silent upon the matter. 'Will you give me the word without any bark upon it, ma'am, and tell me why you are here?' An edge of frustration roughened his voice still, and he heard it and cursed inwardly. She had done nothing – yet – to deserve harsh speech from him.

She swallowed visibly, but said bravely, 'Very well. My idea – it was my sister-in-law's plan, but I have adopted it and must own it – is that the only way I can redeem my reputation is to be courted and eventually betrothed to someone of unimpeachable reputation. Unlike myself.'

Her voice was very small as she spoke those last two words, and he felt a spasm of pity for her, but it was lost almost instantly in his growing anger. 'So you intend that I should wed you, then, Lady Amelia, and redeem your reputation in that rather startling manner?' he said icily. 'I must congratulate you; none of the other ladies who have been... so kind as to interest themselves in me recently have actually gone so far as to propose marriage to me with such boldness. Not in so many words, and not to my face. Some of them have proposed other things, of course. But I confess I had not expected a young woman of birth and breeding to offer herself to me in such a blatant fashion. I suppose I should say I am honoured, but you will forgive me if I do not feel able to deal in false coin just now. I must of course refuse your very generous proposal.'

He had had no intention of letting any part of his anger and bitterness – which was little enough in all conscience to do with her – bubble up within him, but once he had begun speaking so unguardedly, he had found it impossible to stop before he had vented just a small part of all the emotions that were boiling inside him in volcanic fashion. At least he hadn't sworn at her, not quite. When he realised what he'd done, though, how unnecessarily cruel and unforgivably rude he'd been, he was ashamed. He'd never made a lady who was almost a stranger to him cry before; it was a new low. Women – chiefly Lavinia, of course – generally had to know him more intimately before they were reduced to tears by his words or actions.

'Oh!' she said, and he realised with surprise that the crystal drops that sparkled on her long, dark lashes were tears of frustration rather than maidenly distress. 'Oh, you are a provoking man, and so self-righteous! I wonder so many ladies wish to... to entangle themselves with you. I am sure they would not if they knew you even a little better! Will you not at least hear me out before you give me a dressing-down I have not in the least deserved?'

'I'm sorry,' he said stiffly. 'I was intemperate. But what am I to think?'

'Perhaps not always the very worst, on so little evidence?'

He grimaced. 'A hit, a very palpable hit! Go on. I shall not interrupt you again.'

'We shall see if you can manage it. I don't have the least desire in the world to marry you, I can assure you, but I am suggesting a false engagement. One that shall last a little while – long enough, at all events, to persuade the world to think a little differently of me than it does at present, and then be terminated, at my instigation, naturally, but by amicable agreement on both sides.'

'Why me?' he asked bluntly. The idea was completely crazy, but he had promised to listen, and he would.

'Because of your reputation,' she returned in the same level tone. 'Because you are known to be so very noble and good and...'

'Nauseatingly virtuous and high-minded.'

She grinned at him unrepentantly. If his heated speech had thrown her off balance, it had not been for long, it seemed. She had brothers, he recalled irrelevantly. Perhaps that accounted for it. If he had ever spoken to Lavinia so...

'All of that. And a hero, too. Who would ever imagine that such a person could be interested in someone like me, from a family like mine?'

He chose not to address this. 'I don't see that it could possibly answer.'

'Your sister thinks it might.'

'My sister is a silly little goose. She wishes nothing but good for me, and I am sensible of it, but she has no knowledge of the world.'

'Well, perhaps I am a silly little goose too, and perhaps I am also naïve, but I think it could work. As I said to her, I can more readily see that it could help you in your awkward situation than me in mine. My problem may in fact be insurmountable. But at least I'd be doing something positive. I feel so helpless at present.'

'I can certainly sympathise with that,' he said with feeling. *Helpless* was the perfect word to describe his current situation.

'I suppose the question is,' she said lightly, still meeting his eyes with a bright challenge in hers, 'not whether my plan has any chance of success, but whether you actually want to be rescued.'

7

Amelia had been nervous at the prospect of speaking with Lord Thornfalcon, and alone too, but she had been obliged to own that, as his sister had impressed upon her both last night and on her arrival in Half-Moon Street, she couldn't really expect to enter into such an extraordinary arrangement with a gentleman without having some private conversation with him first. Their engagement, if it ever happened, would be false and temporary, but there would inevitably be some sort of relationship between them, though it would be an odd connection and not what the world imagined. And so she had not objected when Helena had said firmly that she intended to leave them alone together, and had done so.

He'd been shocked, of course, and had taken her up wrongly, though she had soon set that to rights and he had then apologised for his hasty speech. She didn't really blame him – it was apparent that he was labouring under a great deal of strain, and she understood that men could sometimes be foolishly reluctant to pay heed to ideas that originated with women. But in the end, he had listened intently enough, a frown creasing his handsome brows. She had meant all along to try to persuade him – her brothers could have given witness to the fact that she could be extraordinarily persuasive – but she had lost patience with the idea when it came to it, and gone straight to the heart of the matter.

Did he want her – or anyone – to set him free, or was the bond with his old love, destructive and dangerous as it was, simply too strong to break?

He was silent in the face of that stark question, and she feared she had overstepped the mark once more and would be obliged to endure another stinging reproach. She could well imagine how his men and junior officers would go to great lengths to avoid incurring his displeasure; he might have been wrong in what he said to her, entirely mistaken in her intentions, and he had been merely lashing out in pain at the object before him, but all that did not render him any the less formidable. And now she had encroached on ground far more personal, without any invitation or excuse, except that her question was the only one that signified. If he really desired to marry his sister-in-law, Amelia was wasting her time, and might as well go home before her good name suffered any further damage from this scandalously unchaperoned meeting.

Against her will, and much to her displeasure, she found that she was trembling slightly. But she would not apologise or back down, having come this far.

He said after a long moment, 'I suppose that is a reasonable question.'

'And?'

'I shall not speak of my feelings with you, except to say that they have been lacerated by what I have undergone since I returned to England and came into society. I do not intend to marry *anyone* at the present time, it is the furthest thought from my mind, and nor do I expect to change my fixed purpose in the foreseeable future. You will forgive me if I decline also to be more specific, or to mention any names in connection with your question. I think I have been plain enough.'

Amelia could not fail to notice that he still hadn't precisely answered her. How stiff he was, though he was sitting to all appearances relaxed in an easy chair. She could not wonder that the caricaturists chose always to portray him in uniform; he seemed to be wearing it mentally, as if he needed it. And perhaps this was all the answer she could expect, and all she needed, since it told her that even if some part of him, or all of him, longed to marry the woman he had once loved, and probably still loved for all she knew, he did not mean to do so. It was not necessary to ask his reasons, since they were sufficiently obvious.

She said gently, pitying him despite his stature and his strength, and hoping she was not showing it too plainly, 'If you did begin to woo me – to make pretence of wooing me – and then asked for my hand, the ladies who pursue you so would have to stop. Surely they would. There would be an explosion of gossip, at first, at this new and startling event, and perhaps it would be disagreeable for a time, but then it would subside and people would forget their romantic follies.'

'I wonder if they all would?' he muttered.

She could give no answer to that, and like him, she would not mention names – a name.

His brow lightened after a moment and he said, regarding her intently, 'I must be sickening for something. A fever, perhaps. I should send you on your way and call my mother's quack to come urgently. I find myself on the verge of agreeing to your madcap scheme, even though there is a voice in me that screams that I must not, that I will live to regret it.'

'If you are hearing voices,' she said tranquilly, 'you should definitely call for the doctor, and take his physic, however nasty it is.' She had won, she thought, but she was clever enough to show no hint of triumph. Her heart was beating unaccountably fast, she now realised – she had been engaged in battle this half-hour, with a worthy opponent, and she had won.

8

A question that had never yet been discussed was whether or not Lady Amelia should tell her brother Rafe, who was after all her guardian, the truth about the course upon which she had embarked. There was no need to commit just now – Lord Thornfalcon had not yet commenced his wooing, which presumably would take some time – but a decision must be reached sooner or later. Rafe would probably disapprove strongly, she thought, and call the scheme crazy, which would be unpleasant. She had no desire to be at odds with him. But on the other hand, when Lord Thornfalcon's attentions began to be obvious, she didn't think she could bear to have Rafe labour under the delusion that he'd been right all along, and that patience had been all that she had needed until an eminently suitable husband presented himself. He'd then be hurt and confused when the engagement was inevitably broken off, and it seemed unfair to put him through all that unnecessary turmoil. It was so hard to choose. Perhaps it was cowardly, but she'd decide later.

She and Helena had agreed that they would be fast friends;

this was no particular hardship, since they'd liked each other on sight and seemed to share a basic impatience with the currently imperfect way society was organised. She would spend time innocently in Helena's company, as any friend might, impeccably chaperoned by her aunt and by Helena's mother, and Lord Thornfalcon would gradually (but not too gradually) come to be sensible of her many attractions. He would then show a growing interest in her. It would all be enormously subtle, they'd agreed between the three of them. Lord Thornfalcon hadn't evinced any great enthusiasm for the plan, but he had agreed to it, which was what mattered.

Unfortunately, subtlety did not appear to be the currency of the world they moved in. The Dowager Lady Thornfalcon had in unexceptionable fashion invited her old acquaintance Lady Keswick and her niece to accompany her family to the theatre one evening; she had a private box. It was meant to be a quiet sort of a beginning. Though Amelia had as yet had no conversation with Lord Thornfalcon's mother on the topic, she knew that she had been admitted into the secret by her daughter, and had been delighted with the scheme. Amelia had been given to understand by Helena that her distrust of Lavinia was only exceeded by her mother's, so the Dowager could scarcely fail to seize on anything which seemed likely to thwart the woman's plans. Lady Keswick, naturally, remained in complete ignorance, and – Amelia hoped – always would. Her displeasure was not a thing one incurred lightly.

The theatre was noisy and full of activity, and as Amelia took her seat, she could see nothing to concern her about the audience, who were greeting each other and gossiping at full volume, as normal, from the boxes to the pit to the rafters. Nobody was paying their party any particular attention, absorbed as they all were in their own affairs. But when she looked around her as the buzz of voices subsided a little, she made a most unwelcome discovery. She might not be the object of general interest, but she was still being observed. She was not placed next to Lord Thornfalcon – not on their first outing in company – and now she was very glad of it. 'Your sister-in-law is in the box directly opposite,' she hissed to her companion.

'Oh, goodness me,' said Helena in response, wielding her fan so that it covered her mouth. 'Let me see. Oh, so she is, and she is glaring at you with excessive fierceness! I must greet her or it will present a most odd appearance. Mother, there is Lavinia, with her parents and her cousin Mr Wilkinson.'

The whole of the party, apart from Amelia, bowed and nodded cordially at the group opposite. It was impossible for them to do any less, and even Lady Keswick was obliged to incline her head in majestic recognition. Amelia, who could not greet someone to whom she had never been introduced, looked down at her lap and wished herself otherwhere. It was true that the lovely woman opposite had shot her a most unfriendly look on first seeing her, though her face had now returned to its habitual cool perfection and she appeared to be conversing with her companions with well-bred ease.

'I do not see why she should shoot daggers at me in such a fashion,' she whispered to Helena. 'Is she really so madly and indiscriminately jealous that a friend of yours cannot even accompany you to the play without provoking her ire?'

'The problem is, she is always angling to come with us, even though her parents have a perfectly good box of their own, as you can see. Mama is forever putting her off, because it would be so unpleasant for Marcus to be in such proximity with her – you can well believe that she would manoeuvre into sitting next to him, and she would make such a performance of it that nobody would have any eyes for the stage at all. On the one occasion when we were obliged by her shameless behaviour to invite her or be blatantly rude, Marcus developed a sudden head cold on the very day of the expedition and did not come with us. She was quite white with fury when she realised, though she covered it with smiles and attentions to Mama. So the mere fact that you are here, and he is too...'

'Shh, girls!' said Lady Keswick in penetrating tones. 'The piece is about to begin, and I have a great dislike of people chattering when they should be paying attention.'

Amelia saw very little of the play, and could hardly have said afterwards what it had been. Shakespeare? Sheridan? Though it was a foolish conceit, she felt as though the younger Lady Thornfalcon's eyes were burning into her across the auditorium as the woman sat, assessing every tiny detail of her own dress and appearance, and finding each one of them wanting. She had thought her cornflower-blue silk gown and simple pearls quite pretty, and suitable for the occasion, but now all at once, she doubted herself and found them sadly dowdy. Blue was Lavinia's colour, and suited her so much better.

There was no possibility, she thought, of intercourse between the two boxes during the interval, since ladies did not generally roam about the theatre, and that was a mercy. She had already seen enough of Lord Thornfalcon's painfully correct manner towards his sister-in-law to be confident that he had no intention at all of making his way across to see her. Such an action could only serve to light a fire under the rumours that were already circulating, to the edification of all observers and the delight of the Friends of Lavinia, some of whom were no doubt present tonight. But she had underestimated the widow, as she soon realised.

A friend of Lord Thornfalcon's lounged in from an adjoining box as soon as the curtain had come down, and was presented to her: a Mr Jeremy Gastrell. He was a slight, rather carelessly dressed gentleman in his early thirties, with a mobile, comical sort of a face; he rather resembled a friendly frog from a children's storybook, and she liked him instantly, even before he said, 'I am a little acquainted with your elder brother, Lady Amelia – we were at Oxford together. It is good to see that he has left his Buckinghamshire fastness and comes into society more now that he is married. It cannot have been good for him to stay so solitary, and he can only be congratulated on finding such a pearl of a wife despite never exerting himself in the least in the matter. I should find it hard to credit if you told me now that he had attended an assembly or a party and met her there, like any ordinary person might. But then he has always been an enigmatic sort of a fellow.'

Amelia smiled at the accuracy of this. 'Sophie is a distant cousin of ours,' she explained. The wonder of it was that it was even true, though the relationship was very tenuous indeed. 'She came to stay with our grandmother to keep her company and converse with her in French, and Rafe was instantly taken with her. So you are quite correct, sir; he did not even need to leave the house in order to find a bride.'

'You see! I knew I was right. But I am very happy for him.'

The gentleman, whose manners were very easy and confiding, was enquiring politely about the health of Amelia's little nephew when another visitor arrived. Rather to her surprise, she heard Mr Gastrell make some exclamation of disapprobation under his breath, and when she saw that the new arrival was the person who had been pointed out to her as Lavinia Thornfalcon's cousin, Mr Wilkinson, she thought she knew why. This was confirmed when she caught her companion's eye. Gastrell gave her the ghost of a wink and said very low, and outrageously, 'It seems we have a spy come in our midst, ma'am. I am sure I can speak freely to you, for you have the air of a sensible person, or indeed you would hardly be here in company with the Thornfalcons.'

'You think his cousin sent him...?' Her voice also was pitched little above a whisper.

'Of course she did. I assume you are not at all acquainted with the lady? You cannot be, or she would hardly have needed to send her lapdog over here, wagging his little tail, to sniff out what you are about.'

Mr Wilkinson did indeed have an air of being on a mission, and was plainly anxious to be presented to her. He was currently conversing with her hostess and Lady Keswick, but kept shooting little glances in Amelia's direction.

'She must know who I am without asking, even though we have never been introduced. I find most people do even though I have never exchanged two words with them,' Amelia said with a touch of asperity.

'Well, you are in the same case as my poor friend Marcus, then. But why are you here? That's the question she'll want answered.'

'Miss Thornfalcon is a friend of mine,' she told him repressively. 'I presume a young lady is allowed to have friends, if her guardians find them unexceptionable, without first seeking her sister-in-law's approval. It seems to me that such loosely connected persons as she might with advantage mind their business.'

'You presume altogether too much,' he said, shaking his head comically. 'And as for minding one's business, it must be clear enough what her business is. You are not at all the sort of person Lavinia wishes to be spending time in the Thornfalcon household, I assure you. But here he comes to speak to you and earn his juicy bone. Bow-wow, little doggie!'

She was struggling to suppress giggles as Lady Thornfalcon said, 'Lady Amelia, may I present Mr Wilkinson to you? He is a distant connection of our family by marriage.' *Not nearly distant enough just now*, her expression said.

'Lady Amelia is a new friend of mine,' Helena said, as Amelia dropped a correct curtsey and Mr Wilkinson bowed, goggling at her all the while as if he had been tasked with memorising every detail of her appearance and manner and found the task arduous. 'And what is so particularly pleasing is that Lady Keswick, her aunt, whom I see you know, is a friend of Mama's of many years' standing, so that we may all be comfortable together. Is that not a pleasant coincidence, sir?'

'Oh, quite, quite,' replied Mr Wilkinson rather fatuously. 'Here's to friendship, what? Auld lang syne, and all that. Should auld acquaintance be forgot? I should dashed well think not.'

It seemed from the contortions of his face that he might be inspired to burst into song in illustration of his point, in case they had failed to understand his literary reference. To forestall that unwanted eventuality, Mr Gastrell said, not unkindly but most firmly, 'I think I hear the orchestra tuning up in anticipation of resuming. We shall not trespass on Lady Thornfalcon's hospitality any longer, shall we, Wilkinson?' And he bowed himself, and his reluctant companion, out of the box, with another sly wink at Amelia as he left.

'I see my old friend Jeremy has been charming you, Lady Amelia,' a deep voice said near her ear, making her start. 'I might have imagined from the way you had your heads together that you had known him since you were a child in short petticoats, and confided all your schoolroom secrets to him, had I not long experience of his ability to make one feel rapidly at ease in his company. It is an extraordinary skill, and one few people share.

Certainly, I do not, as our first meeting must have made you all too aware.'

Amelia could not doubt that Lavinia would be observing them closely from the other side of the theatre as they spoke, and if the woman had been jealous at her own mere presence, she would not care at all to see her conversing with Lord Thornfalcon in such a civil manner. But had he not the right, even the duty, to be ordinarily polite to one who was his guest? Who was this woman who thought to control the actions of a man to whom she could have no real claim? Unless, of course, there was some intimate connection between them of which Amelia knew nothing. She should not be so naïve as to ignore that possibility, since Lord Thornfalcon had, unsurprisingly, not shared any secrets with her, except for saying that he did not mean to marry. And if that were still entangled in some fashion, how would Lavinia react when it became clear that her wild suspicions of Amelia were not, in fact, without foundation?

'I liked Mr Gastrell very much,' she said with a fair assumption of ease. 'He knows my older brother quite well too, he was telling me. That's quite a rare thing, for Rafe had not been used to mix in society at all until he inherited the title.'

'And who can blame him for wishing to stay at home in peace?' he said with emphasis.

She could not be comfortable, she found, conversing with him under such close observation. Their situation was more awkward already than she could have imagined. 'It is time we took our seats,' she warned him. 'This has been enough, surely, for a first attempt, sir. It is too soon for your attentions to grow any more particular.' Indeed, she feared very much that others than Lavinia were watching them now, and taking note. She could almost feel the first faint stirrings of interest from the people around her.

Lord Thornfalcon moved away in obedience to her words, but as he went, he said, for her ears alone, 'Come, Lady Amelia, you will find yourself obliged to be braver than that before we are done, and endure a great deal more. And,' he added barely above a whisper, so that she almost thought she might be mistaken in what she heard, 'so shall I!'

9

Marcus found that the proposition that had been put to him by Lady Amelia, and his acceptance of it, had improved his state of mind a little, and gave him the sensation of having won a precious breathing space. This was in one sense an illusion, of course. He knew that Lavinia would make him pay, one way or another, even for the young lady's innocent presence in his mother's box at the theatre. But their opportunities for private conversation were limited now, and even Lavinia was not so far lost to all sense of propriety that she would appear at his home at midnight, banging on the door to demand to know what he was about. He was sure he might expect her soon enough in a slightly more orderly fashion, accompanied by the child she used so often as her excuse for visiting, though once they were alone in his chamber, she would no doubt commence flaying him alive. Yet on this occasion, her very unreasonableness worked against her; since he might as well be hung for a sheep as a lamb, he suggested to his sister that they call upon Lady Amelia later that afternoon and ask her to come walking in the park with them, as it was a fine day.

'You really are resolved to go through with this?' Helena asked him with a slight frown. She had put on her best green velvet pelisse and matching bonnet, and accompanied him out of the house without protest, but she seemed uncertain now.

'I am determined to do it,' he said. 'And if I am, I do not see why *you* should suddenly experience doubts. It seems perverse of you, Nell. You were a great enthusiast for the plan just a day or two ago.'

'I was, and I remain so. I do believe it has a chance of success. But I saw Lavinia's face last night; she was quite furious, though she concealed it, and as yet you have done nothing really to make her so angry.'

'Do you think I am a coward?' They'd never discussed the matter in such plain terms before; perhaps it was time.

'No,' she shot back. 'Of course I don't. I think you are in a horribly difficult situation, and Lavinia has no intention of making it any easier. Quite the reverse, in fact. Before this, she was enjoying herself enormously. I have seen her almost preen to be the centre of attention, and yet such attention. I could shake her!'

'I've told her in plain words that I will never marry her, you know. And more than once.' It mattered to him that his sister trusted him in this.

'But she doesn't believe you?'

'She doesn't want to believe me, and so she refuses to do so. I shouldn't discuss her with you though, Nell, tempting as it is to relieve my feelings. It isn't honourable.'

'It may not be, but I do not give a button for that and nor should you. After all, she is making me suffer too. It's not precisely enjoyable for me and for poor Mama, with Ambrose dead less than eighteen months, to watch her making a cake of herself – to put it no more strongly, though I might – and of you.'

He could not deny the truth of what his sister said. 'Perhaps this may indeed be a way to stop her, to force her to accept that whatever happens, I will not wed her. The only way that is open to me, if she refuses to believe me when I tell her so. I can't engage myself really to marry someone just to drive Lavinia off – it would not be fair to any woman to expose her to such unpleasantness for my sake, and there is no space in my head or my heart even to consider the matter properly and find a bride for myself. How could I really think of wooing any woman, situated as I am? This pretence is all I am capable of. But it *will* be unpleasant, you know, much more unpleasant than you have any idea of yet – it cannot fail to be. I hope Lady Amelia is prepared for it.'

She tucked her hand in his arm. 'She says she is. Well, we will all face it together.'

Marcus was surprised, and not particularly pleased, though of course it could not signify, to find his old friend Jeremy comfortably ensconced in Lord Wyverne's house in Brook Street when he arrived there with his sister. Mr Gastrell greeted the Major with his usual amiability and glibly explained – though of course he had no need to justify his presence to anyone, least of all Marcus – that he had thought it only proper to call upon the Wyvernes directly after he had made Lady Amelia's acquaintance the evening before.

'Thought I should pay my respects to the Marchioness,' he said. 'Should have done so long before this, but she is gracious enough to forgive me for my lack of manners!' And he kissed his fingers to the Wyverne ladies in a fashion that made Marcus suddenly itch to trip him up, or otherwise make a fool of him and shake his damnable suavity.

Lady Wyverne indeed appeared charmed by Jeremy, as women so often and so unaccountably were, and smiled on him graciously; Lady Amelia seemed no less taken with him than she had the night before. And somehow – Marcus had not the least idea how it came about, and certainly had not been consulted on the scheme, or he'd have vetoed it – they soon found themselves a party of four strolling together in the park. Marcus was aware that he was frowning, and could not seem to help it.

It was the hour of the fashionable promenade and a fine, sunny afternoon, so the place was extremely busy. Ladies took the air in barouches and landaulets, or were driven by gentlemen in dashing, high-perch phaetons; some bolder ornaments of the ton drove themselves and made a fine show, no less skilled whipsters than their male counterparts. But there were also sufficient throngs of pedestrians to make the paths almost crowded. Mr Gastrell and Lord Thornfalcon were obliged to greet many persons with whom they were acquainted, though neither Helena nor Lady Amelia had more to do than return a nod once or twice. But many more who did not speak to them watched them avidly as they passed.

They could not walk four abreast, and Marcus counted himself fortunate to outmanoeuvre his sly friend and take Lady Amelia's arm, so that Jeremy squired Helena, whether he liked it or not. Marcus didn't give a fig if Gastrell didn't like it; in fact, he hoped he didn't, because he was damned if he wanted his insinuating friend playing his flirtatious tricks on either young lady. Curse him, he was fair and far off if he thought he could trifle with either Marcus's sister or... whatever Lady Amelia was to him. There wasn't a word for what she was. Not yet.

He only became aware that he was still behaving like a bear with a sore head, despite his victory, when Lady Amelia said, amusement in her voice, 'It's perfectly true that you probably don't need to speak to me at all to set tongues wagging about the mere fact that we are in each other's company, sir. And certainly, I am not asking you to do anything as extreme as to *smile* in my general direction, or make any sort of polite conversation. God forbid. But I had no notion that being wooed would be so excessively dull and silent, I must admit. Next time, I shall bring my sewing, or a good book.'

He looked down at her, still frowning. She was smiling at him with a most unwelcome gleam of intelligence and understanding in her fine, dark eyes. 'Am I being dull?' he asked. He couldn't deny that he had been largely silent. No doubt Jeremy – in the unlikely event of being accused of such a thing – would have turned the pert words away with a quip that won his companion over. But he was not made that way.

'Terribly dull. And your constant scowl is most off-putting. I'm sure Mr Gastrell would be a far more amusing escort. Look at him, making your sister laugh.'

Marcus gritted his teeth, observing that what she said was quite true. 'No doubt he would! But then he is a practised cicisbeo, and I am not. Yet if I am to woo you, madam, it will scarcely serve our purpose – or do your precious reputation any good at all – if you should be seen flirting with him, or any other such light sort of fellow, day and night.'

He half-expected her to accuse him of jealousy, a claim he would have repudiated with unflattering promptness and emphasis. But no, he had underestimated her.

'It's true,' she sighed. 'I am sorry it should be so, but there it is. There is to be no flirting at all for me, since it is plain that *you* would never engage in such an enjoyable activity. I suppose I must resign myself to tedium and your gloomy looks. Unless you should care to tell me interesting details of your military experiences, of course, and all the brave actions in battle of which we hear so much.'

'I should not!' he said, revolted. 'I think you must be

confusing me with the coxcomb I appear to be in the da—in the cursed public prints.'

'It is just that I have observed – though my experience is somewhat limited, I admit – that gentlemen often do enjoy talking about themselves at great length. And you don't seem inclined to ask *me* any questions, so what is to be done?'

'I do not need to ask you any questions at all to discover that what you are, Lady Amelia, is a shameless minx.'

'It has been said,' she admitted, a fugitive dimple peeping for a moment in her smooth cheek. 'But look! Here is my brother Charlie, one of the people who has said it, wandering about aimlessly. Let me present him to you, sir.'

Lord Charles Wyverne was a slight, dark young man of decidedly dandiacal leanings, and it was fortunate that his sister had appeared directly before him, because his shirt-points were so high as to render his peripheral vision almost non-existent, as if he were a horse with blinkers. Nor could he easily look down, so that it was as well the path was level and unobstructed. It seemed unfair that he should choose to inflict upon the world a startlingly garish purple and gold waistcoat that he alone was unable to see. But he was plainly an amiable young man, and seemed genuinely pleased to encounter his sibling, and delighted to be presented to Lord Thornfalcon, his sister Helena, and Mr Gastrell. When quizzed mischievously as to what he was doing alone and on the strut, so finely arrayed, he admitted naïvely that he was showing off a new coat, and had set out with a friend, but had lost sight of him. His new companions could scarcely wonder at it. 'Do you need us to take you home, Charlie?' his sister asked with false solicitousness. 'You may take my arm and I shall guide you, and not let you stumble. I'm not sure you're safe out on your own.'

He didn't seem to take offence at being teased; presumably, he was well used to it. 'You don't understand fashion, Melia, that's the thing. These shirt-points of mine are all the crack – can't expect a mere female to appreciate the finer points of what's the rage among the more discerning fellows.'

'No,' she said, 'I don't understand it at all, it's perfectly true.' But she nobly refrained from asking either of her other male companions, who could both see their own feet without any trouble, if they did either, and so Lord Charles joined the party, taking his sister's other arm without further protest.

On the one hand, Marcus thought, since the whole of the haut ton appeared to have decided to take the air this fine afternoon, one couldn't be enormously surprised to encounter any members of it in particular; on the other, there did seem to be some sort of malign fate in operation once again, since it was not five minutes later that they bumped, in his case literally, into his widowed sister-in-law and her small family party.

Lord Thornfalcon was fully recovered from his bayonet wound and the debilitating fever that had followed it, and restored to excellent physical condition, or he might have been knocked from his feet when he was violently accosted by a diminutive whirlwind in the shape of his niece. She must have run at him from some considerable distance, for she had picked up speed and momentum, so that when she crashed into him and seized him about the legs, he staggered at the impact, but providentially did not fall. She clung to him like a monkey and looked up, saying winsomely, 'Uncle Marcus! I am so happy to see you! You do not come to visit us, though I wish you would, and it has been an age since we stayed with you. I hope you are quite well?' He could hear, faintly, passing ladies who had happened to observe the scene cooing over the young Miss Thornfalcon's adorableness, and her obvious and deeply touching affection for her uncle.

As a child about Priscilla's age, Marcus had had an expensive mechanical toy bought for him by his fond godmother: a soldier in a red-painted metal coat, who had marched across the room and crashed satisfyingly into furniture and walls, but only, of course, if its owner had activated the mechanism and pointed it in the chosen direction. Priscilla had long since reminded him of this toy, since she seemed to have as little will of her own as the automaton, but went where her mother told her, and said exactly what her mother had primed her to say. She was an apt pupil, there could be no doubt, but she was still just a child for all her calculated tricks. Though it took a strong effort of will for him not to recoil from her whenever he met her, he tried hard to conceal it. 'Good afternoon, Priscilla,' he said now, unable to insert any enthusiasm into his voice, wishing she would let go of him. He would welcome her childish affection for him gladly, however difficult the circumstances, could he only credit it as genuine.

'Priscilla!' said Lavinia in tones of gentle indulgence, approaching in an altogether more ordered fashion and smiling up at him, a vision of silver-gilt loveliness that could still make him blink, despite everything. 'I know you are excessively glad to see your dear uncle after so long, and I cannot blame you for it, but it is not at all ladylike to run, you know, nor to seize him in such an unmannerly fashion. I pray you, remember that your noble uncle sustained a grievous injury in his nation's service, not long since! I am sorry, Marcus – I hope you will pardon my poor child's natural enthusiasm. She is so very fond of you, and of course, we cannot forget that she has no papa now to love her.'

There weren't enough passersby who could overhear to make an actual audible sensation – though it was truly surprising how Lavinia's silvery voice carried – but Marcus felt rather than heard a stir run through those who could. There was another low sound too, which he thought was his sister, making rude gagging noises behind him. And at his side, Lady Amelia was stifling something, possibly giggles.

'I'm here too,' Helena said. 'Possibly you did not notice me, Priscilla, in all your excitement. Good afternoon, Lavinia. Am I not to receive a hug from my niece? I assure you, I am quite braced for it. Luckily, I have not undergone any battle injuries in recent months, so you need not hold back on my account.'

The child, who did not appear to be chastened by her mother's arch reproof, no doubt because she had been warned in advance to expect it, shot a questioning look at Lavinia, and at some unspoken sign, embraced Helena with markedly less vigour than she had employed upon Marcus.

'Helena,' said Lavinia, with corresponding coolness. 'I am glad to see you looking so well. Will you not introduce us to your friends?'

'Gladly,' said Miss Thornfalcon crisply. 'Lady Amelia Wyverne, Lord Charles, may I present my widowed sister-in-law, Lady Thornfalcon? Mr Gastrell you know, I think, Lavinia. And here are Lavinia's parents too, Sir Lionel and Lady Hall.'

Shaking the hand of the man who had, along with his father, contrived to separate him forever from the woman he had loved, Marcus could only admire Lady Amelia's sangfroid as she and Lavinia curtsied to each other, and as she accepted with every appearance of well-bred ease the Halls' notably tepid greeting.

When he had been free to marry, and Lavinia had, Sir Lionel had disapproved of the idea, because of his lowly standing as a second son. But now that sense and reason and above all his own personal distaste forbade the match, though the law was infuriatingly equivocal, the baronet appeared to have changed his mind. Or had had it changed for him by his daughter. But then, Marcus was no longer just a soldier, but a viscount now. The houses that

Lavinia had occupied as a married woman – the title, the land, all of it – were now his, and could be hers again. What a marked difference it appeared to make, to Hall and his wife both. No more than their daughter did they appear to relish the sight of him conversing and walking, however casually, with an eligible young woman. Lady Amelia might not be as lovely as Lavinia – after all, who was? – but she did not share her disadvantages, and they must be painfully aware of it.

After a little interval of rather stilted conversation, Priscilla began demanding to accompany Marcus and Helena home, so that she might see her dear grandmama, and spend some time with her. One might have imagined from her impassioned pleading that they shared a deep bond, which was not the case, or else that the Dowager's health was in so poor a state that she could expire at any moment, which thankfully also was untrue. But when the Halls' insistence was added to hers, and Lavinia prettily begged that they be allowed to come, unless it should be a great inconvenience, it was impossible to refuse. And so the party separated, Jeremy assuring Marcus that he need not trouble – he would escort Lady Amelia home with the greatest of pleasure. Marcus might have responded that this was scarcely necessary, since she had the perfectly adequate company of her brother, but with an effort, he restrained himself. Whatever his friend was about – perhaps it was just idle mischief – this was no time to get to the bottom of it.

Helena's silent but satirical presence made any sort of private conversation between Lord Thornfalcon and his sister-in-law impossible; there was also the child. Priscilla had insisted on walking between them and swinging on both their hands, while shooting melting glances up at each of them in turn, as if to say, *Are we not a pretty little family? Imagine if we could always be together so!* Despite his discomfort, he could not help but feel a stab of pity for her; it was true that she had lost her father, and he could not doubt that Ambrose had been a loving parent. But Marcus knew that most of the people who saw them together were probably thinking as she was, and wondering too if there was any deeper significance in the grouping that they made. Had His Lordship made the decision to risk all for love at last?

10

It was much later, and the house was quiet. Lavinia had dined *en famille* with Marcus, Helena and their mother, hours ago, and spent a quiet enough evening in their company. It happened that they had no engagements to call them away, and if Lavinia had previously committed herself to attend some event, she had missed it without the least compunction. She had kept up a flow of easy conversation all the while, showing a pretty deference to her mother-in-law and even making Helena smile in reluctant amusement once or twice, reminding Marcus of how charming she could be if she put her mind to it. She stored a fair quantity of clothes in her former home for herself and for her child, and was therefore as immaculate as ever. As beautiful.

He had undressed, his main concern as ever to prevent his valet from suspecting that anything was at all out of the ordinary, and sat in his dark-grey silk banyan in one of the large armchairs by his bedroom fireplace, staring into the empty space. It was too warm for a fire, and would be warmer yet in a short while. He could not delude himself that she would fail to come, for this illicit interview was the only reason she was present in the house tonight.

It was almost a relief when the door opened; as with a battle, the thing itself was always easier to deal with than the waiting beforehand. Lavinia had her hair down, reaching almost to her waist, and it fell in a lovely, shining curtain over the delicate silk and lace of her peignoir. This garment was respectable enough, but she had not fastened it, and as she moved he caught glimpses of her much more flimsy nightgown beneath. Against his will – always against his will, now – his blood stirred at the sight of her. And she knew it, counted on it. Later, she would seek to inflame him, to overturn his self-control, but not yet. First, she would speak her mind and make him pay for his offences, real or imaginary.

'You have been seeing a great deal of Lady Amelia Wyverne, have you not, Marcus?' Without being invited, for they had passed far beyond that, she came and sat in the chair opposite him, and the robe slipped open, revealing more of the flimsy night-rail and the warm skin beneath it. Nothing she did was ever accidental. He'd learned that recently, though he should have realised it long ago.

'She is a friend of Helena's,' he said shortly.

'So I am told. But you should not take me for a fool. Do you mean to woo her?'

'I first met her less than a week ago, but if I did, Lavinia, it would be no affair of yours.'

'I would have thought that her reputation might have put you off. The thought of her father and her stepmother and all the shocking things they are rumoured to have done should be enough to make one shudder, and avoid the whole pack of them like the plague. Was not the actress whore the son's mistress for years while she was the father's wife? The whole world knows as much. Come, Marcus! The Wyvernes are the last family in England that a man with a name as proud as yours should wish to ally himself with.'

'Not the last,' he replied steadily. 'And I must ask you not to slander them. Whatever the rest of her family may or may not have done – I don't know and I honestly don't care – Lady Amelia is innocent of all of it, and you shall not smear her name.'

Her crystal violet eyes filled with tears as she looked at him. She let them fall. How could anyone so beautiful be guilty of anything ugly? 'You are so cruel now,' she said brokenly. 'You were not always so. But to compare me, and my poor parents, with such a disreputable family... to speak to me in such a cold tone of another woman, as though you hated me. What have I ever done to deserve such cruelty from you? What have I ever done but love you, that you should throw our past back in my face when none of it is my fault?'

'Lavinia, you are right. I cannot blame you for failing to resist your father's pressure, and my father's, when we were little more than children, for I did not resist it myself. Our marriage was impossible then, or so I believed and you did too, or said you did, and it is impossible now. That at least is not in question. No matter what you say, no matter what you do, I will not wed you. Must I repeat it incessantly, every time you force this sort of painful meeting on me? And *you* accuse *me* of cruelty. Hear me now and believe me at last: *I will not do it.*'

'You will not be honest, will you, even now when we are alone? We were more than children,' she said, low and seductive. 'Much more. Must I remind you of it?'

In a moment, the peignoir would slip from her bare shoulder. It always did. 'I remember everything, Lavinia, and with distress, but I still will not change my mind. Even though we did what we should not have done, we were innocent and loved each other, and so I cannot truly regret it. We stopped once it was clear that you must marry my brother, did we not? So that at least I cannot reproach myself for. I did not betray him. I do not reproach you either, for anything you did then, so many years ago. It is your actions now that I question.'

'We stopped, Marcus, but not straight away. Not quite straight away. If you remember everything, as you say, then you will remember that. I certainly cannot forget the night we were both so terribly distressed, and sought comfort from each other. The night when we conceived our child.'

The terrible thing was, she'd told him this before, to his enormous shock, and he still wasn't sure he believed her. Understandably, he supposed, no mention had ever been made by anybody of Priscilla's parentage being in doubt when Ambrose was alive. There had been no frantic letter sent to him in Spain, no word from Lavinia – no communication at all from her in eight years, in fact. She could have written to him with perfect propriety as his sister-in-law and enclosed any sort of message for his eyes only; she had not.

It was not even as though he'd counted on his fingers and wondered; if Priscilla was supposed to be an eight-month child, nobody had ever said as much in his hearing. Ambrose had never shown the least sign of doubting his wife, or his brother, in any of his frequent, affectionate letters. She'd sprung the news on him when he'd returned, when his wound had almost healed and he could no longer avoid her, since she had free run of the house, both here and in Somerset.

The rumours she had caused to be spread about him had carried no hint of this. Of course they had not. Their early love had been painted as chaste and pure. The fact she always taunted him with – if it was indeed a fact – cast quite a different complexion on the story, and set her in quite a different light, and him too. The Friends of Lavinia might reconsider their support, might pull back in horror from their idol. Her reputation would suffer, and the child be branded a bastard. He'd no longer be the noble, self-sacrificing hero either, but God knows he did not care for that.

'Lavinia, I will not insult you by questioning your truthfulness. It's not as though I enjoy making you weep, though I know you think I do. But the plain fact is, if Priscilla really is my child, she had much better not be. Ambrose accepted her as his, and if it is a secret we alone share, we should take it to the grave together, if you have any concern at all for your child and her future. It does no good to anyone to set any of that in question. Can you not see? If I married you fifty times now, it would not make *her* legitimate again. She would always be an object of scandal, almost of incest, and you too. I wish you could bring yourself to admit that I am right, however cold you think me.'

'You do not love her, or me. I would never have believed you could be so heartless.'

'You have reason to know that I am not. I care for her as a niece, though indeed I do not know her very well, which is neither my fault nor yours, but a matter of circumstance, so you need not upbraid me with that as well. But I do not like – you know this already, so I may as well not waste my breath – Lavinia, I do not like the way you set her as a messenger between us. I do not like the way you put words in her mouth. Let her keep her identity as my brother's legitimate daughter, and let her be an innocent child. Childhood is short enough, and adult life sufficiently hard. Do not drag her into this twisted thing that lies between us. Do not continue to make a public spectacle of her. It cannot be good for her.'

'It cannot be good for you, you mean.' Her silvery voice had an edge to it now.

'None of this is good for me, and I don't understand why you seem to believe that it is good for you, or for Priscilla. What's past is gone forever. You would be much better marrying another man, if that is what you want. You could make a new life for yourself with a man who would adore you and treat you like a queen. I am sure you would not lack for highly eligible suitors if you would give up this ridiculous story of our great lost love.'

That was when she stood and let the peignoir slip, and the night-rail fall to the floor after it. Naked, she stood and looked down at him, confident of her power.

'No,' he said. 'No, my dear, I will not. You need not prove how enormously desirable you are – I know it already. But you must really think me a fool if you imagine I will risk everything for another night with you. If it is true that you have one illegitimate child already, it would be sheer madness to risk making another. And Lavinia, if you force me to say it again, *I will not marry you.*'

'You can't tell me you don't want me.'

'I am sure I will never be able to say that if I live to be ninety. But I can resist you, and I will.'

'Are you sure?'

She stepped forward.

11

Amelia could only speculate on what had occurred between Lord Thornfalcon and his sister-in-law when she all but forced herself and her daughter into his home after their encounter in the park. If he still loved Lavinia, her behaviour could surely only cause him pain. But whatever lay between them, which, she reminded herself, could be none of her business, it clearly had not shaken his resolve to begin his public wooing of another lady without loss of time. This became apparent at the next assembly they both attended, which was at Almack's that Wednesday. He claimed her hand for the first dance, before anyone else had the opportunity to do so, and for the supper dance too. Amelia saw a speculative gleam in her Aunt Keswick's eye, and knew she would be having a conversation with her on the subject before long. Her aunt had also darted a swift glance of interrogation at her old friend Judith, and must have perceived the expression of tranquil complaisance that her features bore as she and her son stood chatting civilly with the Wyvernes. If Lord Thornfalcon was indeed interested in Lady Amelia – and perhaps it was too soon to say for certain if he was – Lady Keswick might reasonably assume that his mother at least had no objection to it.

The same could not be said of everyone. The Friends of Lavinia were present in force, standing together in little groups, bearing their silver and blue colours as badges of allegiance. Amelia saw Miss Archer and Miss Lancaster standing prominent among them – young ladies who seemed to have conceived an instant dislike of her last Season, though she had no idea why that should be so, since they did not know her at all. They had never made any secret of the fact that they gossiped about her with great glee, and now that they had taken up Lavinia's cause, their enmity could only grow.

When she took Lord Thornfalcon's outstretched hand and accompanied him to the dance floor, she thought she heard a sort of low hissing from behind her, just at the edge of her hearing. It wasn't a pleasant sound, but she did not turn to see from whence it came; she was sure that she'd have seen nothing, apart perhaps from some angry, disapproving faces, which was no great novelty after all, and should not distress her. Had her partner heard it too?

'I suppose this sort of thing was what you were referring to when you said that I might need courage,' she said to him when the steps of the country dance brought them together for a moment, then apart, then together again: a frustrating situation in which to attempt to converse.

'Not really. I cannot blame you for not liking it, but I don't see what they can do to hurt you.'

'Other than gossip about me? But you will say that I must be accustomed to that.'

'I know it is hard, but I suppose we both should be by now.'

She could only acknowledge the truth of this. If things seemed worse for her than they had been before, she only had herself to blame. She'd wanted to make things happen, and already there was no denying that she had. And Lavinia's supporters might be noisy and conspicuous, but they were not the true arbiters of society. She hoped.

'What's next?'

'I believe I take you driving in the park. That will be a true statement of intent. And tell me, ma'am, have you been persecuted by the unwelcome attentions of over-eager suitors this evening?'

'We've only just arrived.' It was true, but as the evening wore on, she began to see a difference. Almack's had always been one of the safer places for her during this Season and the last; it might be notoriously dull as far as entertainment went, but the fearsome patronesses denied vouchers to many of her more disreputable admirers, and thus protected her from insult somewhat. Still, Mr Peacock, who was the son and heir of a baron, was here, and one or two others of his kind, and yet they did not approach her on this occasion. Others did, men of an unexceptionable nature for once; her dance card was soon almost full, and Lady Keswick was visibly delighted. This, it was plain, was at last the Season she had envisaged for her niece.

Amelia said as much when she and Lord Thornfalcon were reunited for their next dance. There was no hissing this time; perhaps the Friends were regrouping and considering their next move. It would be idle to hope that they had accepted the situation so easily. 'You were right, sir, though I do not know how you knew. My hands remained unsqueezed, nobody has slobbered over them yet, nor even attempted to look down my bodice. If the change comes from a mere dance or two with you, I must thank you for it.'

'Is that the sort of thing they do?' he asked her. His face was quite grim, unsuited for the bright lights and cheerful sounds of the ballroom, but then he never had the most cheerful of miens. Perhaps he had been different once, she thought.

'When they're not trying to get me alone on a terrace, or in some quiet corridor. There is little chance of that here, of course. The patronesses would not stand for it, and they are not to be trifled with. And so my brother Rafe and his wife were not obliged to accompany us tonight.'

'I can see why you resolved to do something to improve your unendurable situation. And if it's helping already, I am glad. At least some good has come out of all this.'

'And *your* situation?'

He was silent for a few moments, frowning still as they parted and came together again. He was an excellent dancer, though his expression was scarcely such as to convince any of his many admirers that he was halfway to falling in love with her and dizzy with the joy of it. But his focus on her was intent, nonetheless. Nobody could doubt that he was listening to her with the utmost seriousness. She could be quite sure that Lavinia, who didn't seem to be here, would hear of it tomorrow from a dozen directions.

'My situation remains unchanged for now, as far as the attentions I am receiving are concerned. A young lady fell from her horse in the park early this morning, just in my path, and I was obliged to pick her up; luckily, she was not seriously hurt, for she was a very poor horsewoman to be playing off such dangerous tricks, and might easily have broken her neck. She was not at all happy that I refused to accompany her home, but left her groom to do it. There will be nothing worse than bruises to show for her adventure, and perhaps she at least will not trouble me again. But have you seen the latest print?'

'I must confess that I have not.'

'My friend Gastrell was at pains to show it to me this morning; he appears to derive some pleasure from the exercise. It features our trip to the theatre. No, do not worry, you are not to be recognised in it, but an enormous number of young ladies are attempting to clamber into my box from the pit, while I stand there besieged as usual; they climb on each other's shoulders in their eagerness. I dare say you can picture it. The action on the stage has quite ceased, and the actors stand in consternation. Perhaps I might be amused by it, were I not the subject. It seems to me a deal of artistry and skill expended in a worthless cause.'

Amelia did not ask His Lordship if the print featured his sister-in-law, looking on in disapprobation at the scene; it seemed likely that it did. She still did not know him well enough to feel confident of discussing the matter with him, especially not tonight when he was looking so forbidding and unapproachable.

They ate their stale cake and drank their lemonade together, under dozens of unfriendly pairs of eyes, which did not conduce to the flow of easy conversation, and shortly thereafter, she and Lady Keswick prepared to depart.

'I shall be sternly quizzed about you in the carriage; you may be sure of it,' she whispered to Lord Thornfalcon as they took their leave of each other. He was so serious tonight that some sudden mischievous impulse prompted her to tease him for a reaction. Did the man's face never soften?

'I would rather face a cavalry charge by cuirassiers than be interviewed by your aunt,' he responded with the first gleam of humour she had seen from him all evening. 'She terrifies me; with that great beak of a nose, she might easily be Lord Wellington done up in a diamond parure and long gloves. Good luck!'

She was smiling to herself still as the door closed on them and the vehicle rattled into motion. Making Lord Thornfalcon betray amusement, possibly against his will, felt like a small triumph, though she wasn't certain why it should.

'Well, Niece,' Lady Keswick said majestically, 'it seems that the Major is growing somewhat particular in his attentions. I believe that you only made his acquaintance a few days ago, and yet here we are, proceeding with some haste. The first dance, and then the supper dance, and at Almack's too, which is so vulgarly – but I must admit with justice – termed the marriage mart. He is of a ripe age to marry and presumably a man of some worldly experience, so I must assume he knows what he is about, to take such actions in such a public place. But do you?'

'What do you mean, ma'am?' Amelia was playing for time, for she had a fair idea of what these words of caution signified. But she must tread carefully here.

'It is right that you should be reserved on such a delicate subject, and I do not criticise you for it. Your behaviour so far in regard to him has been unexceptionable.' Amelia felt a pang of guilt at these words of praise, which she could hardly think she deserved, but said nothing in response beyond a murmur of thanks. 'Hmm. Keep your counsel still, if you wish. But if Lord Thornfalcon means to offer for you, and your brother approves it – which I cannot doubt he would – you will do well to think seriously before you accept him.'

'It is a good match, in worldly terms,' she said equivocally.

'Yes, of course it is, child, and not just because of his title. You are not a fool, and you know that you would not care be one of those women who can call herself Viscountess but has nothing else to show for it but a draughty castle in the middle of nowhere. And I do not speak only of his wealth. They are a good family, an excellent connection, as I believe I have said to you before. I know much to the young man's credit and nothing to his discredit, apart from this mawkish story that his brother's widow is putting about, and the tawdry gossip that it has engendered. But it would be foolish to ignore the whispers, nonetheless.'

'He cannot intend to marry her, ma'am, surely. We have discussed this before, and his actions this evening alone suggest that he does not. You must be correct in thinking that there is a great deal of nonsense in all the gossip, as there so often is.' It was impossible, Amelia found in this moment, to do anything other than converse with her aunt on the topic of her possible marriage with the utmost gravity, quite as though it were all real and not pretend.

'Indeed. I hope he is not making use of you to send *that woman* a message, for though his position is undeniably awkward and one must sympathise with it, that would not be the behaviour of an honourable man.'

It would be rash to underestimate the older woman's shrewdness. And what to say in response? 'I do not think that he would do so. Why me? He must know that my reputation is... more fragile than that of other ladies. Given that, it would be cruel to trifle with me, and I have no reason to think him cruel.'

'You do not know him. Do not forget that. I am not sure a woman knows a man until she has been married to him for five years, or ten, and then, of course, it is far too late to mend matters without a great deal of trouble.'

Amelia blinked at this unexpected cynicism, which shed an unfortunate light on her aunt's own marriage, or perhaps on her view of the world.

'But I agree. I think we can expect him to call on Wyverne in a short while. Though I am not in general a believer in hasty engagements, these are not circumstances in which I would recommend a protracted courtship. If you feel you can overlook the stories that are put about concerning his improper relations with his late brother's wife, and it seems to me from what you have said that you can, I would advise you to marry him as soon as it can be arranged. It will be safer that way,' she finished cryptically.

'You question Lady Thornfalcon's intentions? Obviously, I don't mean his mother.'

'Quite obviously you do not, child. And I have said enough, I think.' Lady Keswick would not be further drawn, and soon Amelia was at home, in bed, pondering the events of the evening, which kept her from sleep for a surprisingly long time.

12

As he had promised, Marcus called upon Lady Amelia the next afternoon to take her driving, and happened to encounter her brother Rafe as he was entering the house. They greeted each other cordially, of course, and he felt obliged to explain why he was there, feeling devilishly awkward as he did so, like one of his own young cornets or subalterns. He received a rather penetrating look in response, from dark blue-grey eyes that greatly resembled Amelia's own. Though he flattered himself he was learning to know her a little, so that he could read the fine nuances of her myriad changeable expressions, with her brother, he could not claim such insight. He had no idea what the man might be thinking.

Lord Wyverne was a man of much his own height, but of a rather less massive build. He was as dark as both his half-siblings, but a very different character from his younger brother: a Corinthian rather than a dandy, in immaculate but casual sporting dress, and practical top-boots rather than gold-tasselled Hessians. 'Come into my library for a moment,' he said affably enough. 'My sister will only keep you kicking your heels in the hall.'

This was an invitation that could not be refused, and Marcus soon found himself seated opposite the Marquess in a comfortable, book-lined room much like his own. If it had till fairly recently been the previous Lord Wyverne's private den, it showed no sign of his occupation, apart perhaps from a fine modern painting of Danae in her shower of gold (and not much else) about the mantel. Marcus dragged his eyes away from the piece, which disconcertingly somewhat resembled the current Marchioness in face and form, and concentrated upon the man opposite him.

Lord Wyverne was toying with some ornament on his desk, and said rather abruptly, 'I received a note from Lady Keswick this morning – I was about to say, from my aunt, but she is not my aunt though she is Amelia's; she was my first stepmother's oldest sister. We are a somewhat complicated family,' he added with a reluctant grin of brief duration. 'At any rate, she wrote to me in aunt-like fashion to tell me that in her opinion, I might expect to receive an offer for Amelia's hand from you soon enough. I wish I might show it to you, for she has a high opinion of your character, and expresses it in such stately periods as must be a matter of wonder and admiration. I dare say I have never received such a letter before.'

Marcus opened his mouth to speak, but Lord Wyverne interrupted him before he could begin. 'I didn't call you in here to interrogate you as to the nature of your intentions. I am sure Her Ladyship might easily be wrong, though I would not choose to be the man to tell her so. What I wanted to say to you was that if by chance you should be considering my sister as a prospective bride, I hope you will not allow yourself to be deterred by any gossip you may have heard – damn it, must have heard – about the Wyverne family. If you are a man of sense, which you appear to be, it will be obvious to you already that Amelia has had no part in anything disreputable, and if indeed there is some Wyverne "taint" that comes from my late father's mode of life and the last woman he married, it has less than nothing to do with her.'

'Of course I know that,' Marcus said readily. This at least was an answer he could give honestly. 'Only a fool would not see it directly upon meeting her.'

'I'm glad to hear it. I can only say that there are a great number of fools in the world, some of them are scoundrels too, and many of them have asked me for her hand in less than flattering terms and been sent away, each of them with a flea in his ear.'

'I know,' Marcus could not prevent himself from replying. 'She has told me so, and I was very sorry for it.'

'Has she indeed? That's... interesting. And if you should know all this, believe as you do and yet still be reluctant to ally yourself with such a notorious set of relatives, I hope you will accept my solemn assurance that the stepmother who is still living – as half of London will attest, having seen her half-naked on the stage with their own eyes – was never my mistress. I know the world believes she was, but she was not. The rumour originated with her and is entirely false.'

'You do not need to tell me such private things, Wyverne. Even if the worst of the rumours were true, it is none of my affair.'

'Well, I could put two very different interpretations on that statement. But you note I do not ask you, still, if you intend to offer for Amelia. I do hope you appreciate my forbearance.'

Marcus smiled with a little effort. 'I was about to say that I too have been the subject of most unwelcome gossip – I still am – and so I would not be the first one to rush to judge a man because of what some chattering idiot told me about him. I also know,' he added with feeling, 'that life is damned complicated, and one's actions can often bear a construction that is most discreditable, without there being so much as a grain of truth in it.'

'God knows I can understand that,' Rafe said soberly.

'But though you do not ask, despite your brotherly right to do so, I will tell you that I do mean to offer for your sister.' In the moment, he was unexpectedly affected by his own words, sham though it all was, and perhaps this was what brought surprisingly raw emotion to his voice when he said, 'I think the man who wins her love will be a lucky man indeed.'

'I think so too.' There was a brief silence between them, then Lord Wyverne added, 'I turned away all the others without consulting her, because it was plain that they would have brought her swiftly to ruin and misery. I should not dream of telling my sister whom to marry – only of hoping she will listen when I beg her not to tie herself to a rogue, an imbecile, an inveterate gambler, a fortune-hunter or a libertine. Thornfalcon, if she tells me one day that she wishes to take you, I shall be happy for you both. But it must be her choice. She has not so much as mentioned your name to me, you must understand.'

It was horribly awkward, to have a man be so open and confiding and reveal so much that must cause him embarrassment, when the declaration Marcus had just made was not genuine, so that he was here entirely under false pretences. He felt low as a snake, and was glad when the door opened to admit Amelia, in smart red bonnet and pelisse, with a poorly concealed expression of trepidation upon her animated little face. They both rose at her entrance, and her brother said smoothly, 'I was just asking Lord Thornfalcon a few questions about the possibility of buying a commission for Charlie; you know he has mentioned the idea more than once, and it is not good for him to be idle on the town now that he has left Oxford.'

Her brow cleared instantly and she smiled on them both. 'I do not know if Charlie would enjoy soldiering as much as he appears to think, but naturally Lord Thornfalcon would be the perfect person to ask. He must have a great deal of experience of what it takes to make a good leader of men.'

'And I am happy to be of help. I see no reason why Lord Charles should not do well. I have observed that his manners are easy and he does not set up his back when he is teased by others, which counts for more than you would imagine. Fellows with a short temper and a great sense of their own consequence are the last people we need, and often struggle to make a go of it. Of course, being too amiable can also be a problem, but that is usually the case when the boys are very young and unformed in their personalities and too easily influenced to unsteady courses. He is perhaps a little older than the general run of new officers, but that may be for the good. I too did not join as a mere stripling; I was almost eighteen. He is twenty-one or so, is he not? It is no great age, after all. We are not the navy; we do not take up mere children, or if we do, we should not.'

'I am glad to hear it,' Lord Wyverne said seriously. 'You do relieve my mind...'

In this pleasant manner, Marcus and Amelia extricated themselves from the mansion after a little more conversation, and it was only when she was seated beside him high up in his phaeton, which had once been his brother's, that she said doubtfully, 'Is that really what you were talking about?'

'No,' he replied in low tones. 'It was a ruse, I think, meant most kindly – to avoid making you feel uncomfortable or pressurised by walking in on a serious discussion regarding the future. But we cannot discuss it now.' His groom Williams was in attendance behind him, solid and imperturbable and impossible to miss. Although it was not entirely unheard of for a gentleman to set down his servant so that he could converse privately with a young lady – there being a limited amount of mischief that even the most eager and inventive of couples could be expected to get up to in broad daylight in an open, high-perch vehicle – Marcus thought he should have more of a care for Lady Amelia's good name than others might, and therefore would not be seen with her in public unaccompanied by any sort of chaperon. It would not help her fragile reputation at all if he were to be anything less than perfectly correct in his treatment of her. Perhaps when they were officially betrothed, it might be different. But no – the relationship was to be of brief duration, he must remember. He would not wish to leave her worse off than she had been before she met him. That would be poor recompense for her trust in him.

'It is very frustrating always to be obliged to converse in front of others. I know my brother has been quizzing you, and it is the outside of enough that there is no way in which you can tell me the details of it.'

'If we are discreet... He had an extraordinary letter from your aunt this morning.' They were speaking in little more than whispers, and though Marcus was driving, paying due attention to his horses and keeping his eyes alert and fixed on the road and the carriage traffic around them, he was doing it largely by instinct and could not have said much about their surroundings if he'd been asked.

'I see. I suppose it is no great surprise. And is he displeased by its contents?'

'I am sure you could see that he was not. He wished to share certain matters with me, not ask me any questions. To assure me that if I had heard certain unpleasant rumours that might influence my decisions, they are absolutely untrue.'

'It's dreadful that he should be obliged to say as much to you, or anyone. He is a very private person, as perhaps you could see.'

'I told him had no need to tell me anything of the kind. But he wanted to. And I answered the crucial question he was too considerate to ask.'

'In the affirmative?'

'Naturally. He said he would not attempt to influence you now, though he did before – but that if you came to him and gave him news, he would be very happy.'

She digested this, and said very low, 'I do not like deceiving him at all. I should have been braver and told him the truth before now. He is the best of brothers and guardians.'

'I can see that he is. I felt like the basest creature in existence when I lied to him by omission. Should we tell him how matters really stand?'

'I can't decide. My fear is that if we did, he would be hurt and distressed at my behaviour, and perhaps even dislike the scheme so much that he would forbid me from seeing you, or something of that nature, and I don't want that.'

He didn't want that either. 'Then we have no option but to continue as we are. Maybe things will be easier...'

'When matters are made public. Do you think so? Truly?'

13

If Lord Thornfalcon had really thought that public recognition of his courtship of Lady Amelia would make either of their situations immediately easier, it was soon clear that he'd been wrong. Their appearance driving together in the park had drawn stares and glares from many of the people who had seen it.

The caricaturist produced a fine piece – for those of a mind to appreciate it – to commemorate the event, which showed His Lordship in his phaeton with a gang of ladies chasing it in a wild pack, ripping their flimsy garments as the horses reared in terror. For the first time, Amelia herself appeared, quite recognisable to anyone who knew her, her bonnet flying away and her long, dark hair coming loose. She was shown clinging on to Marcus's broad, uniformed chest and begging him in an uncurling ribbon of desperate speech not to let her fall, lest she be torn to pieces. His reply was somewhat less than gallant:

O, my dear Lady A, I promise you I shall not, for if they catch us, they will rend me limb from limb too!

And the superscription was:

An Heroic Wooing

Lavinia was nowhere to be seen in this instance, which was the only small mercy.

Mr Gastrell, meeting his friend at White's late the next afternoon, was quick to show him this work of art, in his self-appointed role as daily gadfly. The cheerfully vulgar print lying between them on the table, he raised an eyebrow in enquiry and said casually, 'The fellow seems to think your intentions are serious.'

'I can see that for myself,' came the short response.

'Honestly, old man, it's a mystery to me why so many fine, young women persist in making spectacles of themselves over you when you barely have a civil word or a smile for any of them – or for anybody at all, come to that, these days, even your oldest and most devoted friend – save for Lady Amelia. It is not surprise that the caricature johnny has taken good note of it.'

'Is that so?' Marcus was aware that his manner was menacing and his tone terse, but Jeremy did not appear to be intimidated; he was still smiling wryly and would clearly not be put off. 'Very well, then – if you must know, damn your eyes and your impudence, yes, I do mean to offer for Her Ladyship. Her brother has told me that he will not oppose me, but it must be her decision. I have not asked her yet, but I will without delay. It is monstrously unfair to leave her thus exposed to insult. I wonder if she has seen this latest atrocity.'

Mr Gastrell whistled and looked sharply at him. 'Matters have progressed so far, then! And I cannot doubt that she will accept you when you offer. You are the catch of the Season, naturally, but she is a fine match indeed. I shall be congratulating you soon, old fellow!'

Marcus looked at him squarely. 'It had occurred to me once or twice that you might have some interest in that quarter yourself. Was I mistaken?'

'Completely,' said his friend cheerfully. 'I won't say it hadn't occurred to me that I might test the waters to see if you were serious, and how you'd feel about a little opposition in the field – but it soon became pretty plain to me that you were. Which was vastly interesting news. So I left off immediately. You must have noticed it. Never let anybody say that I need telling a thing twice. No flies on Lady Gastrell's firstborn, dear old boy.'

Marcus had always thought his old companion had never looked at a woman seriously in his life, but passed from one flirtation to another – to put it no more strongly – like the proverbial bee in a garden of bright and tempting flowers. But he was not sure he believed him now in his disavowal of any serious intention towards Amelia. Of course he must claim as much, since Marcus had just informed him that he was about to offer for the lady in question. He hoped Jeremy's heart was not seriously wounded; what a coil they would be in, if it were. He could hardly let him know that the wooing was all for show, and yet if he did not, he wronged his friend gravely. 'If you are gammoning me in this fashion because you really care for her, Jem, I am very sorry—'

'Gammoning you? I'm telling you I never did, you complete gudgeon. Not a pin. I'm telling you too – now that it seems you're over your old infatuation and have moved on, not before time – that there's only ever been one woman for me, ever since I came home from school with you as a callow stripling and set eyes on her for the first time. I lost my heart to her then, so surpassingly lovely as she was, and somehow, I have never found a way of getting it back. I knew I could never have a chance with her when she was yours, I wouldn't have dreamed of such a thing, nor when she was married to your brother, of course, but now...'

'Lavinia.'

'No, your aunt Susan! Of course Lavinia, you beetle-headed old idiot. Always Lavinia. I must confess, I don't always like her very much, especially not at the moment, but I love her and it seems there is no getting free of it.'

'I'm sorry. I truly am, Jeremy.'

'Nothing to be sorry for, man. She loved you first – she loves you still, for all I know. She certainly gives every sign of it. But I can continue to be patient. What I'm hoping is, it's come to be a sort of habit with her, and she simply doesn't see any other way to be. And she's rather painted herself into a corner with this tale she's spun about your great and noble love. Such a hero as she's made you – I scarcely recognise you. She's in desperate need of help and doesn't know it, my poor angel. I have to find a way to persuade her that my love is just as great and noble, if not more so, being secret and unrequited for so long. I have every confidence I can pull it off. Have you ever known me to fail in anything I set out to do?'

'Good God, Jem, I'm so cork-brained. I swear I never had the first idea.'

'Well, I didn't mean that you should. Mum as an oyster, that's me.'

'And you would wish to marry her, and bring up the child...'

'Ghastly brat,' said Mr Gastrell cheerfully. 'Needs taking in hand. But you forget, I have a dashed houseful of younger brothers and sisters. I'm not scared of young Miss Thornfalcon. I'm quite sure she's sound at heart.'

Marcus was silent for a moment, wondering if he should tell his friend what Lavinia had claimed about Priscilla's parentage. It might be true – that was the worst of it – in which case, her suitor should know it, but if it wasn't, it showed Jeremy's idol in no very flattering light. Nor him, for that matter, though he could not regard that in such a moment of seriousness. And as for Lavinia's continuing attempts to seduce him...

Mr Gastrell said abruptly, 'I don't want this to come between us and our long friendship. I'm a selfish sort of fellow, you know me – I want it all and the moon too, all tied up in a bow. So understand me, Thorn, for I mean this – I won't ask you about anything that happened in the past, nor blame either of you for it. We all have our little histories, don't we? If *she* should choose to tell me anything, if things between us were ever... I should be honoured beyond measure by her confidence. But I won't hear anything from you, now or ever, even if you should want to tell me, which, old man, I should hope you don't. A lady's good name and all that.'

The decision had been taken from him, then; he could only be glad of it, and bless his friend's unexpected tact.

Marcus reached out and clasped his hand strongly. 'I hope I shall be wishing you happy too before long, Jem. I can't give her to you or help you to win her; that would be the action of a damned coxcomb, for she's not mine to give. I don't... It's impossible to speak of it, but I hope you will achieve all the good things you deserve and live a long and happy life together. And I can't think of a better father for Priscilla – my poor brother would be delighted if he could know of it. He was devilish fond of you too, you know, in his quiet way.'

'Steady,' said Mr Gastrell, some obstruction temporarily making his speech a little hoarse. 'We have said enough, I think, dear old boy. More than enough. Can't have us weeping over each other like watering pots in White's, of all places. Not at all the done thing. Brooks's, of course, who knows what they get up to there? Would you care for a glass of Madeira, Thorn? I know I would.'

14

Amelia was sitting with her sister-in-law when Lord Thornfalcon presented his card the next day. It was not even close to the hour for paying morning calls, so she looked at Sophie in some surprise.

'Thank you, Kemp, please send him up directly,' Lady Wyverne told the butler. When the door closed behind him, she said tranquilly, 'I expect he has come to offer for you, just as we planned. I shall leave you alone. Such matters do not require an audience, in my experience.'

Her heart beating unaccountably fast, Amelia said. 'Oh! I suppose it must be that. It seems perfectly ridiculous, when it is not real. But perhaps he feels he must make a show of it.'

'He can hardly announce to the world that you are engaged without telling you first,' said Sophie reasonably. 'That would not be at all convenable. Yes, it is false, and yes, you know he means to do it, but it is only common courtesy to tell you when and make sure you are in agreement. And for the sake of the servants and so on, it would look most odd if you had never had any sort of private interview. I am sure Kemp is a secret romantic at heart and is even now most interested in what might be occurring. If I cared for propriety, which you know I do not, I could console myself with the knowledge that Rafe has approved this suit, for he has told me so. I do too, I told him in return. I said nothing of its not being genuine.'

'Hush!' said Amelia, agitated. 'My mind is not easy about Rafe, I know I should tell him, but... He, Lord Thornfalcon, will be here in a moment. Do I look well enough to receive him?'

'What can it matter?' asked the Marchioness, amused. 'Did you not just say that it was all a sham? But yes, of course you do. That dark-red bodice becomes you excessively, and you have been in high bloom these last few days. Perhaps I should not leave you alone, but stay here as a stern duenna. Who knows how far His Lordship's concern for verisimilitude will take him? If he tries to kiss you, Melia, you can always stamp on his foot. Or have you a pin about you?'

Provoked by her sister-in-law's teasing, which she considered to be in poor taste, Amelia feared that her colour was as high as that of her scarlet gown when she greeted His Lordship a moment or two later. Sophie received him graciously and gave him her hand, which he bent over and brushed with his lips with a fair show of enthusiasm, considering that he could not have been expecting such antique formality. Then Lady Wyverne took herself out of the room without another word, smiling infuriatingly all the while, and shut the door firmly behind her.

They were alone, and stood looking at each other in silence. It was not their first private interview, of course, and the previous one had not been so very long ago, but somehow, this felt different.

At length, he said, 'I thought I must call and speak with you. Have you seen the latest print?'

She shook her head wordlessly.

'It features you – our carriage drive together. It isn't saying or implying anything to your particular discredit, but you are quite recognisable in it, and so... The purpose of this exercise we undertook was not to damage your reputation but to enhance it. Therefore it is time, I believe, to announce our engagement, so that I may give you some protection. If you are not thinking better of it?'

'Why should I be?' she prevaricated. Now that it came to it, she felt almost a sense of panic. It had seemed like a light, easy sort of thing to do, almost a game, and now it did not. Especially if this man was still in love, or otherwise involved, with someone else whom he could never marry.

'It is a grave step.' His face reflected his words, and no wonder.

'It would be, if it were real,' she shot back. She was all on edge, irritated by Sophie and now by him, though she knew that there was no sense in it. He was only doing what she had suggested he do. He was playing his part to perfection, and she must do the same.

'It is still a grave step, for all the world will believe it is real.' In her distraction, she'd not invited him to sit down and now he crossed the room to her side and stood uncomfortably close. It was because he was so very tall and broad, she thought. Because she certainly was not frightened of him. 'You were right, it seems, that your scheme was more apt to help me than you. It has already done so, and I am sensible of it. I am not sure you are able to say the same.'

'That's not entirely true. The men – I will not say gentlemen – do not harass me so, as you have noticed. They are scared of you, I think. That is an improvement.'

'I pray it may not be only temporary. Perhaps our engagement should be a long one, so I can offer you some protection from them, at least for the rest of the Season. I wish I could send them all to the devil for their foul impertinence.' His words were fierce but his tone was gentle, and she found herself blinking away a fugitive tear at the care he showed for her. This virtual stranger. He took her hand, the lightest of touches; he did not clasp it tightly. 'Thank you,' he murmured. 'You are very brave, Amelia, and I honour you for it.' He raised her hand to his lips, as he had done with Sophie's a moment or two ago. A butterfly kiss, no more, and with no greater significance than a graceful show of thanks. Surely.

Her hand had been kissed before, and more than once, gloved and ungloved – before the pins and the stamping shoes, she had suffered that indignity a dozen times, and hated each one. This was just the slightest of caresses, a mere brush of the lips across the sensitised skin, and yet at the sudden intimacy of the touch, flesh to flesh, she shivered as she had never done before. Not in revulsion, this time.

He might easily have misinterpreted her movement. Slight as it was, he must have felt it, for he still held her. He might have released her and stepped away with a word of apology. But he looked down at her and his green eyes darkened. His expression was serious, as it generally was, but not grim, not now. If anything, he seemed almost dazed, his featured open and softened in a way she had never seen before. 'It has been almost eight years, Amelia,' he whispered, 'since I kissed a woman. Or wanted to.'

'Do you want to now?'

'I must confess I do.'

'I've never been kissed,' she said with disastrous honesty. 'Not once. It is most frustrating that my bad reputation is entirely undeserved. When men have tried, I have stabbed them with pins. Hairpins. Long ones.' Why had she started babbling of hairpins when he spoke of kisses?

'Do you have a pin on your person now? Just in case?'

'No.'

'Would you care to go and fetch one? I can wait.'

Was he *joking* with her again? That made it twice.

'No,' she said, not joking, and with a boldness that surprised herself, put her hands either side of his face. Then she pulled his head down so that she could kiss him. Her first kiss would be one she chose for herself – he could give her that, if nothing else. It seemed important, suddenly, to claim this moment.

Apparently, it wasn't something you needed to learn to do. Kissing. Or she didn't, with Marcus, in any case. You could just do it by instinct and it could be good. So good. His strong arms came out to hold her, and she melted into them in irresistible impulse and wrapped her arms about his neck, where they seemed to belong. His lips were not immobile under hers; they were warm, responsive, delicious, and she tasted them with unbridled delight. It was plain to her that he liked it too. They tasted each other, and lost themselves in it, entirely absorbed in pure sensation.

It could not have been a concern for the proprieties that prompted Sophie to leave them alone together for only a very few minutes, for she had none. It might have been an imp of mischief that caused her to return so quickly, or perhaps pure, uncontrollable curiosity. Or it could have been that her formidable and unwelcome visitor overwhelmed all her best efforts to keep her out. Sophie was a powerful woman too, but she was young yet, and inexperienced, socially, compared with a dowager at the height of her powers. She could perhaps have stopped Lady Keswick by the use of ruthless physical violence, but in no other manner. 'Amelia, here is your Aunt Keswick to see you,' she said with forced lightness as she opened to door. And then, 'Oh, *merde!*'

15

Marcus could feel that Amelia would have sprung instantly away from his embrace when they were so rudely interrupted, but he let her go only slowly, reluctantly. Their goose was cooked. It was not as though there was much point in pretending that they hadn't been locked in each other's arms when they plainly had. He said, with what he thought was reasonable composure for a man with a most inconvenient and damnably persistent erection, 'Lady Wyverne, Lady Keswick, I trust you will both pardon me. The fault is all mine, but Lady Amelia has just consented to be my wife, so perhaps on this occasion, I may be forgiven.'

'Do you have her brother's consent to address my niece, sir?' the Dowager asked awfully. He had not been called 'sir' in a way that intimidated him so much since he had left school; he could only be glad that Lady Keswick, unlike his schoolmasters, didn't appear to be currently in possession of a cane or strap. It was hard to know what she might do or say next, but he was still standing on his feet, so it could have been worse. He'd been wounded in battle and survived it. He could do this.

'I do, ma'am,' he responded readily. 'He was good enough to

give it a day or two ago, when we discussed the matter. I have his permission. So I am not quite lost to all decency, I assure you.'

'Hmm,' she huffed enigmatically. And then she said, 'Well, it is highly irregular, but one must make allowances, I suppose, for natural ardour and... so forth. Congratulations, Lord Thornfalcon, you have shown good judgement in your choice of bride. I am pleased for you too, Amelia. And you will recall, child, I am sure, the advice I gave you a little while ago about the inadvisability of long engagements. What I have seen today in this room makes my opinions even more pertinent. Don't you agree, Lady Wyverne?'

The Marchioness appeared to be imperfectly stifling mirth, but she responded promptly enough. 'Of course I do, Lady Keswick. You are always so wise. I am sure you will recall that my own engagement was of extremely short duration: only as long as was needed for the banns to be called, in fact.' Though Marcus supposed that this was true or the lady would not have said it, he didn't find it to be a particularly helpful comment in the circumstances, and from a glance at Amelia's horrified face, he thought she must be feeling the same. A moment ago, he'd suggested a protracted engagement, and she'd tacitly agreed, or at least raised no objection. A betrothal lasting several months – to the end of the Season and beyond – would benefit both of them, surely. But now matters appeared to be getting out of hand with alarming speed.

Lady Keswick nodded in majestic agreement. 'Three weeks is a perfectly adequate length of time, I consider, if there is no impediment to a marriage. And if there is some impediment, three years will not be long enough. I trust, Thornfalcon – since we are to be related, I am sure there can be no objection to me addressing you thus – that there is no such impediment. It would have been unwise and unkind in you to offer for my niece's hand, let alone subject her to your incontinent embraces, if matters were otherwise.'

The appalling old besom means Lavinia, he realised. Lavinia might be said to be a pretty substantial impediment – she'd certainly think so herself.

'No,' he said rather hollowly. 'There is no impediment. And I am confident my mother and my sister will be very glad when they hear the news.'

If he had hoped to draw her away with this red herring, he was to be disappointed. 'Judith has always been a woman of tolerable good sense,' Lady Keswick said, 'except when she married your father, of course, Thornfalcon, for he was a man who would neither be driven nor led, but I suppose the match was made by your grandparents with worldly considerations in mind, so one cannot blame her for it. I am sure she will agree that your betrothal need not be of unnecessarily long duration. For several excellent reasons.'

I'll wager she would, thought Marcus, one of the reasons subsiding at last, to his great relief. He had once, when dazed and lightly wounded as a young soldier in Portugal, been a helpless passenger in a wagon overloaded and poorly managed, which had escaped from the control of its incompetent driver and terrified horses – mercifully for the poor beasts, at least, the traces had broken – and careered down a hill at enormous speed to crash into some obstacle at last and overturn in great noise and confusion. Bones had been broken, and heads cracked. He had just the same sensation of utter powerlessness and impending disaster now, though he wasn't sure if Lady Keswick was the hill or the wagon. Or the wall at the bottom.

Rather surprisingly, the unpredictable Lady Wyverne came to their rescue; his new fiancée, most uncharacteristically, had still not uttered so much as a word. 'No doubt you are right, ma'am,' she said cordially. 'We are all most grateful for the kind interest you take in Amelia's well-being. But perhaps such an important detail is more correctly a matter for Lord Thornfalcon to discuss with Amelia and with my husband, who is after all her guardian, at a more convenient date.'

It was as neat and elegant a set-down as he'd ever seen given, and Lady Keswick did not so much as blink as she digested it. She had good fighting bottom, he'd give her that. It must be years since someone had been bold enough to take her on and best her in such a fashion, let alone a slip of a Frenchwoman. He had not been in the way of seeing any of the famous boxing matches of recent years, since he had been abroad about his duties, but he had a feeling that he and Amelia were now privileged to witness a bout as worthy of celebration as Cribb versus Molineaux.

'You are quite right to reprove me, Lady Wyverne,' the older lady said with magnificent carelessness. 'It is none of my affair, of course, as *a mere aunt*.' Only a complete nodcock would believe that she meant these words with any seriousness. 'I only wished to offer the benefit of my many years of experience of the world.'

'I would not dream of reproving you, ma'am,' Sophie replied. 'I am sure that nobody would ever think to describe you in such an impertinent manner. You do yourself so much less than justice.' She appeared to be enjoying herself, and it was possible, Marcus thought as he watched, fascinated, that the two mighty combatants – the wily old champion and the cocksure young challenger for the title – had already forgotten that he and Amelia were still in the room. Perhaps they could sneak away and leave them to it. Perhaps they could take up where they had left off. He became aware that he was holding his betrothed's warm little hand – he wasn't sure if he had taken it just now without realising that he was doing so, or if she had slipped hers into his in unconscious search for comfort. Probably it didn't matter which. He squeezed it in silent communication, and she returned the pressure.

But she had plainly had enough of whatever it was that they were all caught up in. 'I'm sorry, Aunt,' she said, pressing his hand again and then discreetly letting it drop. 'I know your words were prompted by nothing other than loving concern for me and for my future, and I will always be grateful for it. But Sophie is quite right – we shouldn't discuss such matters without Rafe's presence. He *is* my guardian, after all. It must be for him to decide what is best for me, not anyone else, until I pass into the authority of my dear husband, of course.'

This was doing it rather too brown, Marcus thought. She was looking perfectly meek and saintly now, long, dark lashes lowered to hide those bright eyes, which were probably gleaming with mischief, could he but see. She had very much the appearance of one who was submissively willing to do whatever her wise male relatives might command, however unreasonable it might be. But she was not generally anywhere near so biddable, and her aunt must know it. He became aware of a great bubble of laughter welling up inside him; he felt strangely intoxicated, he realised.

'Hmm,' Lady Keswick said again, her voice heavy with scepticism. '*The authority of your husband*, indeed. I wish I might live to see it.'

'Surely you of all people can't mean that, ma'am,' said Sophie sweetly. Since the late Lord Keswick had been well known to live under the cat's foot, this too was a shrewd hit.

Lady Keswick's bosom swelled in indignation, and she lost her self-control in spectacular fashion. 'I can see that I am being disgracefully mocked,' she pronounced. 'I do not know what young women are coming to these days. You both deserve to be soundly spanked.' She gathered the folds of her gown about her in high dudgeon, and was clearly about to leave on this surprising statement, which Marcus thought was both interesting, as suggestions went, and unanswerable, but Sophie, game as a pebble, would not let her opponent have the last word. Not on her own home ground.

'Perhaps you're right,' she answered ambiguously. 'You so often are. I will go and find Rafe directly!' And she held open the door for her adversary, winking at Amelia and Marcus as she obliged her to leave the room, and followed close behind her. The last they heard as the door closed was the Dowager protesting that the engaged couple should by no means be left alone, after what had so recently occurred, and Sophie's outrageous reply: 'I thought you wanted him to spank her? I find you most inconsistent, ma'am!'

16

A more awkward situation could hardly be imagined, Amelia thought. The interruption they had lately suffered had been bad enough, but this was much worse. She knew she was scarlet with mortification again; she felt hot all over.

Marcus said thoughtfully, 'Did you know her late husband? I was never acquainted with him, and I'm not sure how long it has been since his death. Perhaps she is a widow of long standing.'

'No, it has only been two or three years, so I did know him. He was an extremely shy, gentle sort of man, and left the direction of all his affairs to my aunt. But they appeared to be deeply fond of each other, nonetheless. Everyone said he was henpecked, and that it was a sad thing, but I thought they were very happy in their own way.'

'Hence, perhaps, the spanking,' he murmured. 'One should not jump to rash conclusions, of course, about who...' And then, 'Oh! I should not have said that. I do beg your pardon. What an extraordinary time we have been having. You have been sorely tried this afternoon, I think, my poor Amelia!'

'Say rather, poor Aunt!' She couldn't, she hoped, be blushing any more than she had already been. 'I have never seen her so utterly routed – I would not have believed it possible. Perhaps Sophie has been practising set-downs in private for just such an occasion. I am only sorry Rafe and Charlie were not here to see it.'

'So am not I,' he replied. 'Our audience was large enough, I think. Any more and we should have been obliged to sell tickets and refreshments.'

She said resolutely, 'That was all my fault. You would not have been put in such a situation if I had not kissed you, and I am sorry for it.'

'Are you?' he said. 'You will have me thinking that you did not like it, which would be a sad state of affairs indeed. Perhaps we should do it again, just to be sure.'

'You are every bit as bad as Sophie, or Aunt Millicent,' she said crossly. 'I had always been used to think you an excessively serious sort of a person, even a gloomy one, and now when you should be sober, you will not leave off joking me. You know perfectly well that I liked it. But I still should not have done it.'

'Would it have been better if I had begun it? But you can claim I did, if you wish, because it was I, was it not, who mentioned kissing first? I tempted you beyond what you could be expected to bear. You're only human.'

'You did not... *tempt* me! How can you be so ridiculous?' She could have stamped her foot in frustration.

'What was it, then?' he asked. 'Perhaps simple, natural curiosity? That is understandable, I suppose. You had never been kissed; now you have. I hope it was satisfactory, as a first experience.' He did sound a little more serious now, as if his question mattered to him, but she could not regard it. Such things should not be spoken of. If ladies and gentlemen began revealing their deepest thoughts to each other, where might it end?

'How is this helping my reputation?' she shot back defensively, eager to move the subject to slightly safer ground. 'If we continue on this path, I shall soon be just as bad as people think me!'

He sighed, and the novel, amused brightness of his expression seemed to dim. 'Yes,' he said. 'You're right. It is I who should apologise to you. I should not have allowed it.'

This made her unaccountably angry too, even though he was only agreeing with her, which had been what she'd wanted. 'Well, that would scarcely have made me feel any better, if you had pushed me away!'

'I had no desire at all to push you away. I would rather have pulled you closer still, and probably would have if we had not been stopped. Perhaps it is as well we were. Shall we agree that the kiss was mutual, and leave it at that?'

The kiss. *The kiss*. The Kiss. Her brain insisted on capitalising it, on illuminating it as though these were the first words of some precious manuscript, as though it had great significance when surely it had not. Not to him. A man who hadn't kissed a woman in eight long years was probably desperate and would snatch at any opportunity he was given; hence, perhaps, his giddiness now. God knows she had given him an opportunity. She'd grabbed hold of him, practically forced herself on him – what could the poor man have done, thrown her in the fireplace? For him, it had been a matter of merest proximity – that was all. She'd never kissed anybody before, and he'd almost forgotten how, it had been so long. What a sad pair they were. Though they were not really a pair at all, of course.

'Very well,' she said firmly. 'It shall not happen again.'

'It does seem a pity,' he said irrepressibly. 'But you're probably right. You'll just have to restrain yourself in future. Or I shall have to borrow a pin or two from you.'

'You are the most provoking man who ever lived,' she huffed. And then, unforgivably, 'No wonder nobody ever wanted to kiss you in eight years!'

'Oh, I didn't say that,' he said, and suddenly, he sounded a little sad, though that surely couldn't be right. 'I didn't say that at all.'

17

A marriage has been arranged and will shortly take place between the Honourable Major Lord Thornfalcon, of Half-Moon Street and Thornfalcon Manor in Somerset, and Lady Amelia Wyverne, sister of His Grace the Marquess of Wyverne, of Brook Street and Wyverne Hall, Buckinghamshire.

Marcus looked down at the note he had written out several times for insertion in all the usual newspapers. He folded the final one and sealed it, stamping his crest into the red wax. It would have been more conventional to have said that Amelia was the daughter of the late Lord Wyverne, but neither she nor her brother had wanted that. It was understandable.

He'd gone to see the Marquess, with Amelia, on that extraordinary and very long afternoon, to tell him formally of their engagement, since it seemed that everyone else in the world knew already. They found Rafe, with his wife, in his library, and he'd had the sensation that they too had interrupted something intimate, but he was a great deal less perturbed by that than he would have been a few hours earlier. He'd been tempered in the fire, he thought. Mere considerations of embarrassment could trouble him no longer (though he discovered soon enough that he was entirely mistaken in this). What an extraordinary family they were, the Marchioness not least. *And that was definitely her in the picture of Danae over the mantel.* Who were these people? And that was even before he'd met Amelia's grandmother.

Delphine Wyverne, he'd thought at first, was considerably less terrifying than Lady Keswick. She didn't look intimidating at all, so tiny, old and fragile as she was, as though a stiff breeze would blow her away. But God almighty, she was sharp. She looked him up and down quite shamelessly when he was presented to her, taking her sweet time about it, as if to emphasise how very much of him there was to see. When she had looked her fill, she said, with a familiar twinkle in her eye, ignoring him completely and addressing Amelia, *'Mon Dieu, ma petite, quelle figure d'homme! Vous avez vraiment les yeux plus gros que la b...que le ventre!'*

Marcus had something of a facility for languages – he could swear with great fluency in Spanish, Portuguese and even rough French – and he suspected that this was another innuendo. Or not even that. A statement of fact. Something about eating? Good God. He felt he was blushing furiously for the first time in years. Amelia's obvious deep embarrassment didn't help at all. 'Grandmère! He might understand you!' she hissed in furious French. He could have got the sense of that easily enough even if he hadn't spoken a word of the language.

'Bah!' said Madame La Marquise, unabashed. 'I dare say he does – what of it? Good God, is he not a fully grown man by anyone's standards? If you are to marry into this family, young man,' she said in perfect English, addressing him at last and dispensing with all the usual courtesies, 'you must put any thought of embarrassment aside. Better you do it directly. It will save a great deal of trouble.'

'I'm beginning to realise that, ma'am,' he said with feeling. 'I'm already a different person from the one who arrived here. Was it just a couple of hours ago? It seems much longer. So much has happened.'

The younger Marchioness gave an unladylike little snort of laughter. 'It certainly has. And Lady Keswick made the most extraordinary suggestion earlier, which I am sure you will appreciate when you hear it, madame.'

Amelia covered her face with her hands at this and muttered despairingly behind them, 'Is there no way to make it stop? Could I burn down the house, perhaps? Would that do it?'

'Yes, leave off, both of you.' Lord Wyverne appeared also to be amused, but plainly had a little more sense of decency than his wife or his grandmother. 'You are putting Amelia to the blush, which is undeniably entertaining, but our guest is also mortified, and you will be well served if he makes a run for it and is never seen again. If I were him, I would seriously consider going abroad to escape from this houseful of lunatics. I have had a serious conversation with Lord Thornfalcon on a previous occasion in which I believe I convinced him that the terrible Wyverne reputation is largely undeserved, and now you are undoing all my good work between you.'

'Lady Keswick was the chief culprit,' said his wife unrepentantly and not entirely truthfully. 'She began it, Rafe. I have never been so shocked in all my life, I assure you. I will view her in an entirely new light from now on.'

'I too,' Marcus said before he could stop himself. Spending time with this family was like being drunk and tossed in a blanket – it was enjoyable while it was happening, or parts of it were, but he had an uneasy feeling he was bound to regret it afterwards.

They had pressed him in hospitable fashion to stay to dinner and celebrate, but he was bound to refuse. 'Lady Keswick knows of our engagement,' he said. 'I don't suppose she will run about the streets shouting it aloud as if she were selling ballad sheets.'

'I wouldn't bank on it,' muttered his betrothed. 'She'll have us married before the end of the week if she gets her way.'

'But it is not right that she or anyone else she may tell should know before my mother and my sister do. If they came to hear of it through some officious person's tittle-tattle, they would be deeply hurt, and rightly so. I must tell them straight away.'

The Wyvernes were obliged to admit the justice of this, and so he took his leave; it was only right, he thought, that his family should be kept informed that matters had progressed to the point where they were now to be made official. There would be a great outpouring of gossip and exclamation, and they must be prepared for it.

Amelia accompanied him out into the hall to say farewell, and he saw the confusion he was experiencing reflected in her face. They could not speak frankly – the footmen stood waiting to open the door for him, faces carefully blank – so he was forced to content himself with taking her hand, not for the first time this day, and lifting it to his lips. He was trying very hard, and failing, not to recall what *that* had set in motion, and how wonderful she had felt in his arms.

But he should have known already that he could not touch her without consequences. Once more, he brushed her bare skin with his lips, and once more, what should have been an insignificant contact, a mere formality, set every part of his body tingling with awareness of her. Her hand trembled in his grasp, and he did not know, dared not imagine, if she felt it too. If they had been alone... But they were not alone. It was fortunate that they were not. This inconvenient physical connection, if that was what it was, could not signify anything, and must be overcome.

'All will be well,' he said softly, scarcely knowing what he was saying. He wasn't sure if it was true, but he hated to see her unhappy. She smiled at him uncertainly but made no response, and they parted. He strolled home deep in reverie and blind to his surroundings.

His mother and sister had indeed been delighted at the news; there was no need for pretence here, for they knew everything. Almost everything.

'I'm excessively glad,' Helena said in her blunt way. 'I don't care if it is real or not. It will put a stop to all this nonsense of women falling off horses and pretending to be my best friend in the world when they scarcely know me. Lavinia – not to mention Priscilla – will have to start behaving like real persons rather than characters from a sensational novel.'

'I wonder if they will?' sighed Lady Thornfalcon. 'I am delighted too, naturally, my dears, but I confess that Lavinia's behaviour still worries me. Only conceive how furious she will be when she hears. She will be shamed by this, or believe she is, and I fear from my knowledge of her character that she will not care for that at all.'

'Jeremy told me that he thought she'd painted herself into a corner and would not be able to get out of it without aid,' Marcus remembered. He was drinking a glass of brandy before dinner – this was not his usual habit and probably not a good idea, but after the day he'd had, he felt he could justify it as medicinal.

'And he is the man to help her?' asked his mother with quick interest. 'I confess I had sometimes suspected as much when you were boys together.'

'Well, I most certainly had not. And he's my oldest friend.'

'Men!' said his female relatives in chorus, rolling their eyes.

'But you can't rely on him to save you,' Helena continued thoughtfully. 'It would be highly convenient for us, without question, if he swept in and carried her off over his saddlebow like young Lochinvar. It would be most uncomfortable for her, of course, and scandalous, but I cannot be expected to regard that. How delighted we would all be to be rid of her. But as Mama says, Lavinia has gone too far down the road of your great love story to merely say, "You're right, it never would have worked, I wish you very happy." And there are those stupid Friends of hers, too. I hope Amelia will have a care – I hope you will have a care of her too, Marcus.'

He had admitted that she was right to be worried, and now, as he looked at the pile of notes before him, he wondered if it would make things better or worse if he told Lavinia of his betrothal to her face, before she heard of it from some other source or read it in the paper over the breakfast table. No doubt the direct approach would be the decent thing to do – but did it not also imply that she had some special right to such delicate information? It seemed to lend some credibility to the illicit bond she was determined to entangle him in; anyone who heard of it would be bound to think so. Even to seek a private interview with her – which he had never done once since his return to England, or indeed since her marriage – was dangerous. He couldn't involve his mother – that would add insult to injury. Could he insist that *her* mother be present when they spoke? But surely, she would find that humiliating, as if she were a child and not an independent woman. There didn't seem to be a solution that could defuse this devilish situation without pain and bitterness.

At length, he decided that the bolder course would be the better. He had an uneasy feeling that his choice was not motivated by anything resembling courage, but rather by a desire to know for sure that Lavinia knew, rather than be left wondering if she had heard yet. And if she were furious, he might bear the brunt of it, in private, rather than whoever happened to tell her, in God knows what public place. Though this was probably a vain hope.

He called in Berkeley Square late that morning, and was fortunate, if that was the word, to discover her at home. Finding her sitting reading with her child and her mama, he was reminded that his anger and frustration at her behaviour made him unjust to her sometimes; she loved Priscilla, and spent a great deal more time with her than many mothers of their station in life.

'Uncle Marcus!' lisped the moppet in ecstasies, and flung herself at him as she often did. He was prepared this time and barely staggered, allowing himself to be drawn over to where she had been sitting so that she could show him her books, and the geographical puzzle she had been working on. With no audience to observe them, or for her to play up to as she had been primed to do by Lavinia, it was possible to have a much more natural sort of conversation with her. Perhaps Jeremy was right, with his greater experience of children, and she was more than the mechanical puppet he'd thought her. She must be, he realised. He had been unjust to her too. She was an innocent victim of this situation, and he must never forget it.

But he was aware all the while of Lavinia and her mother beaming complacently at the pretty domestic picture they presented as they sat together, and aware too that his sister-in-law could not refrain from sending significant glances in his direction whenever Priscilla said anything especially adorable. What the sharp, violet-blue glances signified, of course, was, *If you married me, you could spend every day with your child like this.*

At length, he said with a slight, strained smile, 'Lady Hall, I must have some private conversation with Lavinia, if you do not object. A mere family matter – it will not take long, I promise. I hope you will understand and permit it.'

Of course she would permit it. She would permit a deal more than that if it led to a marriage. She whisked Priscilla away, protesting, and closed the door firmly behind them. Screaming could soon be heard, faintly, from the corridor.

'She loves you so,' Lavinia said soulfully, apparently unsurprised. 'It is only natural that she should be overset when you see her so rarely, and now arrive out of the blue to raise her hopes. It is unsettling for a child to live in such uncertainty.'

'I did not create the uncertainty – you did. Lavinia, you must know that I am not here because I have finally relented and decided to marry you. I cannot allow you to continue with that delusion for a moment longer. I am sorry I am not closer to Priscilla, but it is unreasonable of you to expect me to seek out that closeness when it seems to me that all you want from it is a public show...' She began to speak and he overrode her. 'A public show designed to manipulate me into offering for you, when I have told you a dozen times that I never will.'

Her eyes flashed blue fire. 'Then why are you here?'

'To tell you that my engagement to Lady Amelia Wyverne will be announced tomorrow or the next day. It did not seem right to me that you should hear it from another, or come across it unawares. It is no baseless rumour – it is true.'

Her face was perfectly still – cold, lovely and unreadable. 'How kind of you to visit me on purpose to tell me,' she said acidly at last.

'That is indeed what I came to do.' He rose from his seat.

'And that is all you have to say?'

'What more is there to be said? We loved each other once, but that was over when you married Ambrose. That is the plain truth.

I know the marriage was not of your choosing, but the past cannot be rewritten. You have called me a coward often enough, but that would only be true if I wished to marry you and did not dare. Lavinia – I cannot say it any more clearly – I don't want to. I do not know if I would laugh at all the difficulties in our path if I loved you; I don't know because I don't love you. It can make no difference to you whether I marry Lady Amelia or another, or nobody.'

'I notice you do not think to tell me that you love *her*.' She had risen too, and they stood facing each other like adversaries.

'I will not discuss her with you. It would be unconscionable to do so. She is not your enemy, Lavinia – I pray you, do not make her one.'

'And what if I tell her that Priscilla is yours? That I was in your bedchamber, naked, just a night or two ago? That you still desire me – I know you do – and will never be free of your obsession with me, even if you try to deny it? That you betrayed your own brother to lie with me because of it?'

'Tell her if you must. I don't suppose I can stop you. I have no idea what her response would be, though I wouldn't be so sure that she would believe you without question. But think of your daughter, and do not take another step towards telling the whole world something that can only hurt her. You seem to hate Amelia – do you really think it wise to entrust her, or anyone, with this secret? Such things once said cannot be taken back, however bitterly one regrets them afterwards. The storm of gossip that you have unleashed may yet turn and strike you down too, and your innocent child – Lavinia, can you not see that?'

She slapped him then, hard.

He stood and took it, saying nothing in response, then walked from the room, and from the house. If he had his way, he would never return.

18

The news was out. And it wasn't too bad, Amelia told herself. Of course the Friends of Lavinia were shocked and furious, enraged even, but then they'd hated her already. There was an ugly little scene one evening when, in the press of people waiting to enter Almack's, someone – she could not have said who – had trodden heavily upon the flounce of Amelia's gown, in such a way that a rip quite a foot long had marred the silk, exposing her petticoat; the tear was so extensive that it could not easily be pinned up, and she'd been obliged to admit defeat and go home, her evening coming to a premature end. It might have been an accident, of course; someone might have stumbled into her – but she didn't really believe that. It was a petty sort of revenge, if that was what it was, and she did not speak of it to anyone, least of all Lord Thornfalcon.

Marcus's own admirers seemed more sanguine; he was betrothed and out of their reach, and they appeared to accept that and move on. It was not as though he'd ever given a single one of them any encouragement. The incidents of damsels falling from their horses at his feet or down flights of stairs into his arms ceased entirely. And – she could not fail to notice – her unwelcome suitors deserted her en masse, as she had hoped they would.

The printmakers fell upon the announcement as on a gift from heaven; this was only to be expected. The ladies of fashion were depicted going into mourning for their lost hopes, and tore at their hair and at their dark but insubstantial garments. Marcus was now the Hero of Brook Street and – rather prematurely shown marrying a simpering Amelia, despite the efforts of several determined ladies, including a frantic Lavinia, to prevent it – the Hero of St George's, Hanover Square. *Farewell, sweet ladies!* proclaimed the unscrolling ribbon of text. And then the prints ceased, at least for a while. There was nothing more to be said, and other targets for satire.

The reigning arbiters of the ton, who had never had any time for all this childish nonsense, showed almost unanimous approval of the union. Perhaps they took their cue from Lady Keswick, with whom Amelia and Sophie were reconciled over a highly awkward tea at which many insincere things were said on all sides. After tea came ratafia. A mutual though unspoken agreement was reached never to allude by so much as the blink of an eyelash to the unfortunate events that had occurred on the day of Amelia's betrothal, and the heated words that had been spoken then.

The prospective bride could only be sincerely grateful for her aunt's magnanimity, never doubting that the Dowager was genuinely fond of her and wished her nothing but happiness. That formidable lady had been in her youth in attendance upon the Queen, at a most difficult time in the late 1780s when the King had first been seriously unwell, and more than twenty years later continued in intimate correspondence with the long-suffering monarch. This privileged access enabled her to obtain and spread – with Her Majesty's gracious permission, naturally – the interesting intelligence that the Wyverne/Thornfalcon match had the royal blessing. The Queen had been understood to say, the German accent she still retained despite so many decades in England lending pungency to her words, that if the sins of the fathers were indeed always to be visited on their innocent daughters, it would be hard to know who would ever escape censure. This must be a reference to her own young granddaughter Princess Charlotte, now fifteen, and to her eldest son the Prince Regent, whose reputation would hardly bear examination. He was currently still making a cake of himself over Lady Hertford, latest of many irregular liaisons. So open criticism of Amelia's forthcoming marriage, or of Amelia herself, took on almost the appearance of disloyalty – not to the Regent, who was widely disliked, but to his daughter, who was the object of almost universal affection as the sole future hope of the nation.

It was unfortunate, Amelia mused, that Lady Keswick could not have exerted her considerable influence rather earlier, perhaps even last Season, so that such a grave step as a false engagement, with all the complications it entailed, had never been necessary in the first place. But maybe that was unfair – the Queen had spoken kindly to her on her come-out, as had her daughters, and they had received Sophie graciously too, even though her past was obscure in places. With this clear sign of favour, they had both obtained vouchers for Almack's, as they easily might not have done. Maybe more could not have been expected of Charlotte at that time. The poor lady had enough family troubles of her own. Amelia could only hope that when the engagement came to an end, as it must, the Queen would not be too seriously displeased. Lady Keswick – who would undoubt-edly be very annoyed indeed – might be forced to intercede again, and her niece might have to beg her to do it. It would all be highly disagreeable. But that must be a worry for another day.

The plan had worked, then. All that could have been hoped for from the audacious scheme had been achieved. Why, then, did Amelia feel so ill at ease, as the days passed in a whirl of social events at which so many people smiled on her and spoke to her cordially for the first time?

It was the kiss. *The kiss*, et cetera. She must admit it to herself even if she would go to the stake before she said as much to others. It had been so brief, so rudely ended – but she simply could not put it from her mind. She lay in bed and relived it every night, from the moment when he first brushed the back of her hand so softly with his lips to the moment Sophie's voice had cut off their embrace, though he had not released her for a second or two. He had held her so tightly as they'd kissed – he had most memorably said that if they'd continued, he would have pulled her closer yet – and she had liked it. Loved it. His arms had been strong and his chest broad and muscular under the layers of fabric that had separated them. Her nipples had hardened against him, and hardened again whenever she dwelt on the moment. She had shockingly buried her hands deep in his silky, auburn locks, and she could feel its texture under her fingers still; she'd liked that too, and wondered if he had. His lips had opened under hers and his mouth had been warm and inviting. She thought his tongue had just crept out to caress hers, and hers – shockingly – had known to come and meet it. She'd wanted to climb him like a ladder and wrap herself about him. He was strong; she was sure he could cope with it. She even remembered the smell of him – fresh linen and orange spiced soap and clean man – and the feel of his skin, a little rough, against hers.

He had left her wanting more. She was tantalised almost to screaming pitch by wondering what might have happened next.

Her imagination provided her with several suggestions as she lay in her lonely bed – not her cold and lonely bed, because it could grow quite hot, she found.

And when she was in Lord Thornfalcon's company, when he took her gloved hand in his to help her into or out of a carriage, or when she danced with him, moving together in a rhythm that bewitched her... Well, he had been right, damn him. All her senses were in turmoil, because, yes, he tempted her. She had no idea if she tempted him, if he relived the moment too, and remembered how she felt in his embrace, and it wasn't at all a helpful thing to think about. Nor was the notion that between the two of them, with her unassuaged curiosity and the frustration that she must assume came from his eight years unkissed, they were like a powder keg primed to explode. The truth was, she wanted that explosion, however dangerous it might be. What had she unleashed in herself?

It occurred to her, and once she'd thought of it, she could not shift it from her mind, that if for some reason they were shut up in a room together again now, or even a closed carriage, they'd find themselves in each other's arms as they had before, and if this time there should be no interruption, there was no knowing what might happen. This new Amelia was *hungry* for him. She did not want to stop at kissing; she did not want to stop at all. She had felt his lips on hers, exploring her mouth, they had brushed the skin of her hand all too briefly, and she could easily imagine them pressed to the pulse point in her wrist, her neck... Even more shockingly, she who had seen no more of his bare flesh than his face and hands, and did not suppose that she ever would see more, could vividly imagine him without his jacket, his waistcoat, even his shirt. She could imagine her lips on his warm skin too – his strong throat, his chest... She could imagine touching him. She wanted that. It frightened her how much she wanted it.

But – she could not afford to forget this again – they were not truly betrothed and were not, despite Lady Keswick's best efforts, going to be married in a week or two or three. And was it not just as well? He might, for all she knew, still have strong feelings for another woman. Probably he did. Their engagement was nothing more than a sham, and their marriage was never going to happen. He was not going to come to her bedchamber in fulfilment of all her fantasies and smile at her – that rare smile of his, like the sun breaking through a cloud – and tease her and fall into her arms, pressing his body to hers...

She thumped her pillow and turned it over to see if the cool other side of it would soothe her fevered nerves. It didn't.

Perhaps Amelia was distracted then, and that explained what happened. Perhaps if she'd been paying attention, she might have prevented it, and saved herself all manner of trouble and distress.

19

There was a sad crush at the ball that evening in one of the grandest mansions in Mayfair, and Amelia was uncomfortably aware of the pressure of bodies around her. She could not help but fear for her silk again, and hope that she would not see another gown ruined. It was an uneasy sensation, to suspect that people who did not wish her well might easily be close enough, in this crowd, to reach out and touch her, and cruelly ironic that their enmity was based on a false belief. Privately, she was quite as miserable as any of them could have wished.

It was a coming-out ball: one among many, of course, but more lavish than most. Sir Humphrey Aubertin's guests waited to be announced at the top of a broad but shallow staircase that swept down into the enormous ballroom, so that the people already present could have the pleasure of examining them thoroughly and judging them as they entered. The powdered and liveried major-domo who called out their names seemed to take great pleasure in the task, Amelia thought, and would not be rushed. Each party of people must descend the ten or twelve stairs completely before he would proclaim the names of the next group who stood with varying degrees of patience beside him at the top. He dragged out each syllable for longer than one would have believed the human throat could manage; he could have been an operatic tenor. It was all very proper, no doubt, and impressive, but it meant that a dangerous pressure built up at the head of the stair, of persons who had been admitted to the house but could not yet enter the ballroom because of this bottleneck.

And so, as the functionary intoned, 'His Grace the Marchioness of Wyverne, Her Grace the Marchioness of Wyverne, Lady Amelia Wyverne, Lord Charles Wyverne, the Honourable Major Lord Thornfalcon, the Honourable Miss Thornfalcon...' it was impossible to say who exactly in the crowd behind her reached out and pushed Amelia very hard in the small of the back. Sophie later said that she had the distinct impression it was a woman – a slim hand, fast and sure.

It hardly mattered. Amelia knew she was going to fall. Nothing could stop her. The steps were marble, highly polished, and her new silk dancing slippers with their thin, smooth soles could gain no purchase on them. She was toppling over – she could see the horrified faces of her brothers Rafe and Charlie, and Sophie, and Helena... but then strong arms seized her and held her. Marcus. Who could it be but Marcus?

He couldn't prevent her from falling – she had too much momentum already from the push, and his desperate leap and the weight of him had only increased it. But he wrapped her tight, and with reactions faster than such a big man should have been capable of, he angled their entwined bodies deliberately so that his broad frame bore the brunt of the first contact with the unforgiving stone. They hit, with a jarring impact, and then tumbled down the rest of the steps, still joined, and came to a stop at the bottom, tangled amid a confusion of feet, which

belonged to the guests who had preceded them and who had had
no time at all to leap out of their path.

Amelia was not badly hurt – Lord Thornfalcon had made
sure of that – but she was shocked, and all the breath had been
driven from her lungs by the bone-shaking impact and, not least,
by the tightness of his grip on her and his weight as they rolled.
She couldn't see; her face was buried in his chest. But she could
hear a clamour rising around them. There had been screams, she
thought hazily, but not from her.

He let her go, and she almost moaned at the sudden absence.
Opening her eyes, she saw that a dozen willing hands were reaching
out to help him to his feet, voices high and deep exclaiming in shock
and admiration. But he wouldn't go; he ignored them all. He was
kneeling beside her now, careless of what must surely be his own
grave injuries, taking her hand with great gentleness and saying
urgently, 'Amelia! My dear, can you hear me? Can you speak?'

'I'm fine,' she whispered, her head spinning. 'Fine. You saved
me, Marcus. You must be hurt, though.'

'I'm not. I dare say I shall feel bruises tomorrow in a dozen
places, but at present, I am perfectly well. If only you are not
injured.' His tone was neither amused nor grim, but tenderly
concerned, as she had never heard him.

'I promise I'm not... They'll have to make a print of this, you
know,' she said, arming herself with humour. 'The Hero of
Grosvenor Square.'

She tried to struggle to her feet without his aid, but he would
not suffer her to do so, and although she would never have
admitted it, she was thankful for his support, and thankfulness
was just one of the many emotions she experienced when he
insisted upon sweeping her up into his embrace and carrying her
away from the scene of her humiliation. The feel of his strong

arms under her thighs, and his solid chest against her shaking body, did not make her any calmer.

A short while later – too short – she found herself lying on a sofa in some unfamiliar chamber, surrounded by people fussing over her. Various parts of her hurt, though she could not have said which, and the brightness of the chandeliers made her wince. Sophie, paler than she'd ever seen her, was engaged in bathing her forehead in lavender water – where had that come from? – and making a sad mull of it; Helena was chafing her hands with equal incompetence. Had chafing anyone's hands ever actually worked?

'Stop,' she croaked. 'I'm fine. Is Marcus well? Where is he?'

No doubt if Lady Keswick had been present, she'd have reproved her for using his first name again, and pointed out that if they'd listened to her, they'd have been wed already and none of this would have happened. But fortunately, she wasn't, so nobody thought to scold Amelia, for which she was grateful.

'He is fine, or says he is,' his sister said with fond exasperation. 'But I am sure he will be black and blue tomorrow.'

'I should think he must have broken half his ribs,' Sophie put in. 'But you have seen that he is standing and talking and declaring emphatically that he has taken no ill from the fall. He thought you might appreciate a little peace and quiet.'

And so she might, if people would stop talking so much.

'He's gone to fetch you some brandy. Apparently, nobody else could be trusted to do it. He's in shock, in my estimation. And Rafe is having the carriage brought round, but people are still arriving, and so there is a great confusion in the streets. Am I babbling? I'm babbling. I'm sorry.'

'I was pushed, wasn't I?' Amelia said quietly. 'I felt it.' She became conscious that she had a crushing headache. She felt as though she had been thoroughly kicked by a horse. A very large, angry horse that hated her and wanted her dead.

They did not answer immediately, but looked at each other. *Now* they decided to be quiet.

'Yes,' Helena said reluctantly at last. 'We think you must have been. You weren't moving at all – none of us was – so how else could you fall? And Sophie thought she saw a hand reach out and shove you. But it wasn't Lavinia. It can't have been – she was already in the ballroom.'

'Just one of her Friends,' she said tiredly.

'Presumably. Unless you can think of any other deadly enemies you've made.'

Amelia chuckled weakly. 'Thank you, Sophie, that's a great consolation. As a matter of fact, I can't.'

The door opened and Marcus entered, bearing, as promised, a glass with some golden liquid in it. Amelia became conscious that she must be enormously dishevelled, though her skirts had been smoothed down over her shaking legs by one of her attendants. Rather than him. *I'm a little hysterical*, she thought. *If Aunt Keswick were here, she'd throw a jug of water over me.*

He crossed swiftly to her side and offered her the brandy. She shook her head, and then regretted it. He was dishevelled too, his hair disordered and his cravat a wreck, but he didn't look any the worse for it. Not in her eyes, at any rate.

She tried to speak in a normal, conversational tone to him, and was uncomfortably aware that she did not succeed. 'I am quite well, sir, and do not need brandy. But thank you! Did I say that before? I don't think I did.'

'There is no need to thank me. If all those ridiculous rumours weren't swirling round about me, you'd never have had to undergo such an ordeal.'

'So it was your fault all along,' she said, closing her eyes again.

'And there I was foolishly blaming the creature who gave me a good, hard push.'

The door opened once more – *so much for peace and quiet* – and Rafe entered. He smiled to see that she was speaking and more or less in her right mind. He was pale too, but his habitual self-possession had come to his aid. 'I hate to interrupt this touching scene,' he said, surveying them all with a comprehending eye, 'but the carriage is ready; Charlie is waiting by it lest someone should attempt to steal it or sabotage the horses or anything of that dramatic nature, and if you feel well enough, Melia, I am of the strong opinion that we should go. I have had enough of this house, if you have not. I can carry you, for you should not walk.'

'No,' replied Marcus with extreme and rather thrilling decision, 'I shall carry her. It is my right.'

And so Amelia was able to experience the highly agreeable sensation of the Major's strong embrace once again. He lifted her as if she weighed nothing, his arms under her thighs, and – was she not unwell and shaken, so that it might be excused? – her hand crept up and rested against his chest as he bore her out of the room. She could feel his heart beating strongly, though she feared her own was racing. He took her through the crowded entrance hall full of gaping strangers, down the steps and out to the carriage, where he set her down tenderly on the seat and stepped back. It was a large house; the way could easily have been longer and she would have made no objection. *Next time I fall and he carries me*, thought Amelia, still not quite herself, *I shall make sure to do it at Blenheim, or Wyverne, or Buckingham House.*

'I beg your pardon?' he said.

'I did not speak,' she replied with dignity, and closed her eyes again.

'I will come and see how you do tomorrow.'

'Yes, yes,' Rafe said with a touch of impatience. 'Go away now, man. Look to your own hurts. If you can walk without wincing for the next sennight, I will own myself surprised. But I expect we shall be seeing you disgustingly early tomorrow morning nonetheless.'

They did not speak much in the carriage. Rafe and Charlie sat in the backward-facing seats, and Amelia half-lay, half-sat uncomfortably with her head in Sophie's lap. Marcus and Helena would make their own way home, she understood.

'Some other guests realised you were pushed,' Rafe said levelly. 'I heard them speaking of it, and our host Sir Humphrey mentioned it to me with great concern. Otherwise, I might have hoped to pass it off as an accident...'

'That's right; I am so clumsy, it is widely known,' Amelia said with some revival of her normal spirit.

'Of course you are not. You might have feigned a sudden dizziness, or some such, if we alone knew what happened. But others than Sophie saw the hand that shoved you.'

'I do not suppose that anyone could identify the culprit.' This was Sophie, anger kindling in her voice now that the shock was passing off.

'No, my love. But there were several of those so-called Friends behind us. It would be easy enough to put names to them. They will all fall under suspicion indiscriminately, I dare say.'

'I have no interest in attempting to identify her, whoever she was. I certainly observed nothing, and I do not see what purpose it would serve. She has only to deny it, and who could prove anything against any one person amongst others?' Amelia was trying hard to be brave, but she was still shaking.

'You could have cracked your head and died of it,' Rafe said, his voice controlled as ever but with powerful emotion underlying it. Charlie, otherwise speechless this long while, muttered in agreement. 'Or broke your neck. It is attempted murder. Do not try to tell me that it is anything less. Only Thornfalcon's quick reactions made sure you were not seriously hurt. We owe him a great debt, all of us.'

'You're right, Rafe, I could have died, or been seriously hurt, and so could he, Marcus, or any of us, or some innocent bystander we knocked down at the foot of the steps. An elderly person, a woman with child. And for what? A fantasy. A piece of foolish gossip.'

'Hush now,' Sophie said soothingly. 'You need to rest. We can talk about all this tomorrow. One thing I know is that I would not care to be the person who did this, if Lord Thornfalcon found me out.'

20

Rafe insisted upon her taking something to help her sleep, and Amelia did not protest, suddenly bone-weary. She woke late the next morning, aching all over but very aware that she was whole and essentially undamaged, when someone who probably did not even know her to speak to had not intended that it should be so. She had a great appetite for breakfast, which Sophie fetched for her on a tray, and stayed to watch her eat. She brought Louis in for a while too, though he was sleeping, and Amelia held him, looking down at his perfect, serene little face and blinking away unexpected tears.

Thinking that she ought to get up, she found this wish firmly vetoed, and compromised upon the sofa in her chamber, and a dressing gown. She was drowsing there over a book a short while later when Sophie came back into the room rather abruptly and said, a crease between her brows, 'You have a visitor. Not him...' Amelia was apparently excessively easy to read. 'I would have brought him straight up, and damn the proprieties. We have of course said that you are not at home to visitors – and at this hour of the morning, who but he would expect you to receive them? A great many bouquets have come... But Amelia, it is Lady Thorn-falcon. Not his mother. The younger Lady Thornfalcon – Lavinia.'

'She is here?' She had heard the words, but to believe them was another matter.

'Yes. She offers no explanation, as if it is perfectly normal to call upon a stranger – an unwell stranger – at eleven in the morn-ing, but she is here.'

'Please tell me she hasn't brought her daughter with her,' Amelia said with a feeble attempt at humour.

Sophie snorted. 'She has not, but there is no reason in the world why you should see her. I can easily send her about her business. Or if you desire to know what she wants, I can stay with you.'

'No. No, I should speak to her. And alone, so that she will feel able to be completely frank. I've had enough of whispers. Have her sent up, Sophie.'

'Are you quite sure? She may be coming to take advantage of your weakened state – to abuse you.'

'As long as you don't let her push me down the stairs... though she'd have to drag me there first.'

'I will happily push *her* down myself,' was the fierce response. 'Shout and I will come, and send her tumbling as she deserves.'

A few moments later, Lady Thornfalcon was shown into the chamber. Lovely as ever in her blue and silver – and Amelia did not feel so very lovely herself this morning – she entered with an air of great composure, and seated herself without being asked in a chair beside the sofa. Amelia said nothing, but looked at her with naked curiosity. *Let her speak first*, she thought. *She doesn't deserve that I should make it easy for her. Or even show her any ordinary courtesy.*

'I was sorry to hear that you are ill, Lady Amelia,' the woman said after a moment. She didn't trouble to sound as though she meant it.

'I'm not ill. Just bruised and shaken. One of your Friends – I hope you can hear the capital letter – pushed me down the stairs.'

'That cannot be proved. I'm sure you imagined it.'

'I didn't. I felt it. And my sister-in-law saw it.'

Her unwanted guest waved her hand airily. 'A Frenchwoman. They are known to be excitable.'

'Would you care to say that to her face, and test the truth of it? She's in the next room, and will come if I call. Oh, and others saw it too – other guests at the ball. They were speaking of it last night, my brother told me. You can be very sure they will be speaking of it this morning. As will many others.'

'I am confident you will not encourage such preposterous and irresponsible gossip.' The widow was a little pale, perhaps, but still calm.

'You of all people dare say that to me, madam? I thought you might be coming to apologise, but that's not why you are here, is it?'

Something ugly flashed in those lovely, limpid eyes. 'I have nothing for which to apologise. I have done nothing.'

'Just set all these rumours about Lord Thornfalcon's supposed devotion to you and desire to marry you in motion, encouraged and fed them, so that foolish people believe them, and now have acted on their belief. If the culprit could be identified – and I agree, it is unlikely that she will be, if she keeps her nerve and stays silent – she might be charged with attempted murder. Certainly with assault. I expect she is a very young and silly person. You feel no responsibility at all, truly?'

'People have been greatly affected by my sad story. I cannot be blamed for that.' She shrugged her elegant shoulders, a complacent little smile curling her perfectly sculpted lips, and Amelia felt a wave of almost visceral dislike pass through her.

'I'm still not quite sure why you came, but I think you should go now,' she said wearily.

'I won't. I came to tell you the truth, so that you know the man who you have so recklessly decided to marry. He is not free to take you. He is mine. He has always been mine and always will be. And my child is his.'

Amelia absorbed this revelation in silence; if it shook her, she would die before she showed it. 'Then I am sorry for you,' she said levelly after a moment. 'To keep such a dangerous secret must be a constant burden. I wonder that you should have thought to tell me when I have no reason at all to like you. How do you know I won't shout it from the rooftops? And I don't think you can be right in the other things you say, because he *has* asked me to marry him, you know.'

'I should have known no Wyverne would be shocked by what I have just revealed,' the woman shot back viciously. She was a little disconcerted, Amelia thought, that she had not been shown a stronger reaction, or any reaction at all.

'What do you want me to say? I'm not the one with the illegitimate child. If I were, I expect I'd keep very quiet about it. For her sake, if nothing else.'

'There is more.'

'I thought there might be.'

'I go to his chamber. Even now. A few nights ago, the latest time. Just before your sham of an engagement was announced. He knows I will come; he waits for me. I was naked in his chamber, as so often before, and he looked at me and desired me. We lay down together and did things you can't even imagine, you foolish little girl. I have known how to give him pleasure any time these ten years. Because he is mine and I am his.'

'Why do you think he asked me to marry him, then?' Amelia asked, preserving her calm though her heart was pounding. She had pride; she would not show any sign of agitation. Could any of what the woman said be true? And why should *she* care if it was? It would be different if her engagement were real, or the bond between them genuine. All they'd done was kiss, even if she'd wanted so much more.

'Because he is afraid.' Lavinia was contemptuous. She had risen, and stood looking down at Amelia.

'Afraid of you? Because you're mad as a hatter?' Amelia jumped to her feet, suddenly feeling that she didn't want to be alone with this person a moment longer, nor sitting while she was standing, and tugged sharply at the bell-rope beside the fire-place. But it would take a while for her maid to answer it... She opened her chamber door and called out, glad to hear that her voice did not waver, 'Sophie! Lady Thornfalcon is leaving.'

'I will show her out myself,' said the Marchioness, appearing instantly from wherever she had been lurking like a jack in the box, with a light in her eyes that suggested that Lavinia would do well to watch her footing on the stairs.

The widow looked at her contemptuously, then returned her disturbingly intense violet-blue gaze to Amelia. 'Oh, my poor child,' she said unexpectedly, though there was no hint of soft-ness in her tone. 'I should have realised it before. No wonder you accepted his offer – you're in love with him. Of course you are. But believe me, you're wasting your time. He can never be yours, because he's mine, body and soul, and always will be.' And she swept off down the broad staircase with magnificent unconcern, disdaining even to hold the gilded metal banister, careless whether Sophie followed her or not.

'I will see her out,' the Marchioness said quietly. 'I will not push her, much as I am tempted. And then I will come back to you, *ma petite soeur*.'

21

Sophie had coffee brought up by a maidservant, and insisted that Amelia drank some of it before she uttered anything but commonplaces to her. It was easy to see that she was French; any Englishwoman would have resorted to tea in such desperate straits.

'She told me that the child is his, not his brother's, and that she still lies with him,' Amelia told her baldly once they were alone. 'That she did so only a few days ago.'

'She certainly lies,' said Sophie robustly. 'Possibly even to herself. You have no reason to believe any of this. And it is easy enough to see why she says it. You are a great threat to her.'

'We both know that I am not – that the engagement is not real.'

'Isn't it?'

'It isn't meant to be.' Amelia was in a sad state of confusion, as she had been for days. It didn't occur to her for a moment to deny the truth of what Lavinia had said about her feelings.

'It wasn't real at first, Melia. But things change. Emotions do.

Yours, obviously – I had become aware of this already, as had Rafe. There seemed no reason to tell him that the engagement is not genuine, because it seemed to me quite possible that it is. Or that you wish it could be.'

'I am so obvious? Oh God, I am. All London must know it. Even my aunt knows it – that's why she said what she did about long engagements.'

'I cannot say if you are, that is the truth. We know you well, after all – even your aunt. But I do not see why you should be so downcast. His feelings have changed too, quite likely. He saved you last night, at great risk to himself.'

'He's a hero; he does that. It's probably second nature. It doesn't mean he... he cares for me. He's never said he does, or even hinted at it. It could be perfectly true that he is still... intimate with her, you know. She is so very beautiful, they have a history that binds them together, and she wants him so badly.'

'He kissed you, though. That must mean something, even if it is not love. Of course I should not be giving you the impression that a man needs to love you to kiss you, or even that a man may only desire to make love to one woman at a time.'

'I know all that! But I kissed him first,' Amelia confessed, blushing. 'Do not tease me, Sophie, I beg you. He told me then – before I leapt on him, you understand – that for his part, he had not kissed a woman in almost eight years.' *Nor wanted to,* her memory added. 'I had not thought him a liar, I confess. Perhaps I was foolish to be so trusting.'

'Goodness, eight years,' Sophie said, blinking a little. 'It is a fortunate circumstance we came in when we did, probably, though for a certainty it seemed a little awkward at the time. But then, *ma chérie,* if you do believe he was telling you the truth, he cannot have been – I cannot think of a respectable word – he

cannot have been dallying with that creature a few days ago. Can
he? Unless – I am so sorry, and thank heaven Rafe is not here to
know that I am saying such shocking things to you – unless they
fall to it straight away upon meeting, like dogs in the street.'

Amelia had seen dogs in the street; the picture was unpleas-
antly vivid. 'Well... I suppose not. Don't you? And yes, I did
believe him. I still do. He seemed... like one in daze. He is usually
so controlled, but then he wasn't. It affected me, the difference in
him. And so I kissed him.'

'Naturally you did. And you have had no opportunity to do it
again? Even though I left you alone on purpose and dragged
Lady Keswick away, protesting?'

'We were both too embarrassed by her. But he was joking me,
and saying he wanted to do it again. Asking me if I had liked it.
All manner of foolish teasing.'

'I would not think him the type. He seemed perhaps a little
intoxicated? I don't mean he was really inebriated, you understand. But... not quite himself?'

'Yes. I don't think either of us was quite ourselves.'

'That's a good sign,' said Sophie with decision, smiling as at
some private memory. 'Well, we shall have to give him, or you, the
chance again, that is all. It is no good you always meeting in
public. He said he would call today – I am sure he wanted to let
you sleep, and will be here directly now the hour is somewhat
more reasonable. Do you wish to receive him here, or
downstairs?'

'Downstairs,' Amelia said quickly. 'I mean... here, if I am
completely honest.' They both refrained from looking at the big
four-poster bed so emphatically that they might as well have
mentioned it aloud. 'But downstairs. I cannot be like one of those
girls who is always flinging herself at him. My God, Sophie, do

you think he thinks that already? Do you think he thinks I meant to trap him all along? Oh! I can't bear it!'

Sophie said consolingly, 'You would not say such foolish things if you had been able to see his lost expression as he carried you, not knowing if you were seriously hurt. And you must recall how vehemently he insisted on taking you out to the carriage in his arms, though he could quite easily have let Rafe do it. "It is my right," he said, so deep. It made one shiver. If he had not cared for you at all, he need not have done it. There are no grounds for despair, but rather for hope. I shall ring for your abigail directly and together, we will choose a suitable gown for you.'

A little while later, Amelia sat in the yellow saloon, wearing what Sophie had assured her was a most becoming muslin embroidered exquisitely with small, colourful flowers. The sleeves were transparent for the most part, and the neckline, though modest, closed with tiny, silk-covered buttons that ran down to her bodice and picked out the spring green of the design. 'Buttons,' said Sophie cryptically, 'are always good.'

'Sophie, I don't want him to... to ravish me! I don't.'

The Marchioness smiled and said nothing but, 'Of course not.'

They did not have very long to wait; Kemp entered in his stately way after only a few minutes and announced that Lord Thornfalcon was here, and would like to assure himself that Lady Amelia was well, if indeed she felt able to see him. Sophie shot a triumphant look at her sister-in-law and after a short period of rather stilted conversation, Amelia found herself alone with her betrothed. Again.

He had brought her flowers, and did not seem to know where to put them at first. But soon they were confronting each other, and – this time – she invited him to sit.

He said soberly, 'I am glad to see you looking so well. But how are you feeling?'

'Fine,' she responded. And then more honestly, 'A little shaken still. But I am conscious that I am very lucky – well, no, not lucky, because I must have been much more seriously hurt if you had not acted so quickly. Luck played no part in it. How are you, sir? Sophie thought you must have broken all your ribs.'

'I too am fine,' he answered, smiling a little now. 'To match your honesty, I am bruised. I have a great mark the size of a dinner-plate across my back, I see from the glass in my dressing chamber, and other smaller ones in all sorts of surprising places.' Amelia tried not to think about Lord Thornfalcon's fine physique naked in front of a cheval-glasses, and what the surprising places might be, and failed utterly in both endeavours. She wondered instead if any of them were places that might benefit from being kissed better. 'But I have taken no real injury, and I am excessively glad that you have not either. And I think it is ridiculous after everything that you should feel obliged to call me sir. My name is Marcus, and you know it, for I recollect you used it last night. Can you not say it again?'

She drew in a breath and blurted out, before her courage deserted her or her imagination led her astray, 'Marcus, then, I am glad you are here, for I must tell you something. Your sister-in-law came to see me this morning.' To initiate such a conversation was painful and difficult, and not in the least what she wanted, but she knew she could not shirk it.

He was silent for a moment, then said with a return of his old grim expression, 'I cannot suppose that she visited you in order to see how you did, or even to apologise.'

'No. First of all, she seemed to be trying to induce me to say that I had an accident rather than that I was pushed; the truth of the matter she would by no means admit, at least in the beginning. When I insisted upon it and challenged her with her responsibility for what happened, she denied playing any part. She was odiously smug about it all. So I asked her to leave, and *then* she told me what I think she had all along come to say: that you were hers, you always would be hers, that her daughter is your child, and that you still... are intimate with her.'

'Good God,' he said, very low. 'Such malice. And then what? Let us have it all out in the open at last.'

'There is little more to say. I think that she was disappointed that I did not react by shouting and screaming at her – of course, she does not know that our engagement is not real, and so she thought I would be deeply affected by what she told me. And then we exchanged a few more compliments, and she left, and Sophie exercised genuine heroism in refraining from serving her with her own coin and pushing her down the stairs.' Lavinia's parting shot Amelia would by no means share with him.

He smiled briefly, without real amusement, but then said earnestly, 'I am so very sorry. It was wrong in me to involve you in all this... hellish mess. Or not to tell you all my secrets at the outset, once I had.'

'I think I involved myself, did I not? Marcus, you don't need to confess anything to me. You must know you owe me nothing. It's none of my affair if you are still—'

'Of course it is your affair. We are engaged to be married. If I were to be involved in an irregular manner with another woman – let alone my own brother's widow – whose affair is it but yours? You say the betrothal is not real, but all the world, including Lavinia, believes that we are to be married. And so I must tell you.'

'Very well,' she said with a fair show of indifference. 'Tell me.' It was her own fault that this interview had taken a dark turn. She might as well have saved her best muslin with its tempting buttons; he wasn't looking at her now, but deep into the past. She could have been anyone to whom he had chosen to unburden himself, she thought. He plainly wasn't thinking about kissing *her* better.

'Lavinia and I were in love when we were both very young, but my father and hers drew up a match between her and my brother. So much of the tale she has spun is true. She is something of an heiress, will inherit Sir Lionel's estates, which are not entailed to the male line. And Ambrose, of course, was my father's heir where I was destined for the army. I cannot claim that anyone in either of our families – except perhaps for my poor brother, who was away at Oxford – was ignorant of our feelings for each other, but it was dismissed as mere calf-love, which in truth perhaps it was. My mother could not persuade my father to change his mind; he was that sort of man, mistaking stubbornness for integrity. But I think I knew even then that Lavinia would not do well following the drum, or living on what little I could give her in some dreary lodgings, or back home with her parents as though we had never been married. So I gave her up – not out of some great noble renunciation to filial duty, as she would have everyone think, but just because... it was plain it could not be. I had no means with which to support a wife, still less children. There was one painful scene when we parted, we were both most distressed, and yes, we lay together that one time, as we had never done before – not quite. So it is possible that Priscilla is my child.'

'You can't be sure?' If she could trust her own judgement at all, she could see that he was being honest, and that it cost him. And really it was still none of her business, as she had told him.

'How could I ever be? If it were a matter of resemblance, that would prove nothing, and in fact, Priscilla is a copy of her mother and nothing more that I can see. I know only that Lavinia never wrote and told me, there was never the slightest hint of anything while Ambrose was alive; I never heard from her or anyone else the slightest hint that his baby was an eight-month child. Lavinia broke the news to me only when I returned home this year, once my brother was gone. So yes, it might be true. Perhaps even she does not know, or does not want to know for certain. But Amelia, the rest of it is all wicked lies.'

'You told me you had not kissed a woman for eight years,' she said with a tremulous little smile. Though it should not affect her, it was undeniable that it would hurt her if that had been a fiction. He had had no need to say it, after all. She had not asked him.

'And it was true. And I said too that I have not wanted to, and that was true as well. If she told you she had been naked in my room, as she said most spitefully that she might do when I informed her of our engagement, you may mark the careful use of words. That is not a lie, but it is not the whole truth either. She has been used to spending nights in my home when she chose to, with the child as an excuse. And late at night, when all the house is quiet, she will come into my chamber and abuse me for my cowardice, and refuse to hear me when I say I will never wed her, and then at last she will undress herself and try to tempt me. It is her last card, and she never fails to play it. She is beautiful and desirable, and I loved her once, but I have always refused her. I don't care if you say it is your affair or not – I need to tell you this. Outrageous that she should come here and abuse you and tell you falsehoods she hoped would distress you. If we were truly betrothed, the damage might be incalculable.'

She gave a little hiccup of laughter. 'I think I held my own. Those scandalous Wyvernes, you know – impossible to shock. Do you bundle her out of the door into the hall and throw her clothes after her, then?' It was an outrageous thing to ask, but she could not help herself. She could not imagine how a man could extricate himself from such an overheated situation.

'Generally, I pick up a book and feign to read it,' he replied with a flashing grin, gone as soon as it had arrived. 'Or a newspaper, if one is to hand. There is something particularly off-putting and insulting about a newspaper. It enrages her sufficiently that she takes her leave, after more abuse of me. I dare not lay hands on her. And not because I fear that I could not then refuse her, I assure you. It's her reaction I dread.'

'She said you were afraid to marry her, though you loved her, and I told her if you were afraid, it was because she is mad as a hatter.'

'She can't have enjoyed that. Lavinia stands very much upon her dignity, which is odd for someone who has created such a vulgar bustle. She came to see me as soon as I was somewhat recovered from my wound, so that my mother could no longer keep her out, and told me to my great consternation that Priscilla was my child, and that I could yet be hers if I only had the courage, and she has held that line ever since. I think her great scheme to persuade everyone we were some modern versions of Romeo and Juliet was in her head even then.'

'Is she not even slightly worried that any children you had would be declared illegitimate?'

He sighed. 'She has been indulged since birth, and her parents are neither of them very sensible. If they do not want to credit that a thing is true, it is not true. And the law, I suppose they believe, does not apply to them, because they are rich and well-connected. It is dangerous folly. My own heir is a distant cousin of mine – a young man not far into his twenties, and a sharp, ambitious lawyer himself. If I were to contract an irregular union with Lavinia, I am sure Mr Thornfalcon, Esquire, would find it weighed heavy on his conscience, such that – after an internal struggle, no doubt, and only once a child was born – he would object in the most public manner. Of course he would – as my heir, he has a stake in the matter, and would claim it was a matter of the good name of the family. And then the marriage would be voided, and who else would wish to marry me after? And my property, unlike Lavinia's, is entailed. He's a few years younger than me; he can afford to wait for such a great prize. If he did not get it at last, his son would.'

'She can hardly be astonished you won't marry her. Very few men would, in such circumstances.' It was a terrible story; she had known the outline, but not the hurtful detail.

'I don't know if I would, if I loved her. I'd like to think so, I suppose, but the damage to my mother and sister, their reputations and their futures... It is an elegant sort of trap, and an unjust one. But I don't love her, not any more, so it is no dilemma for me. My conscience is not easy about Priscilla, and I have an uneasy feeling that I have not treated Lavinia well, though when I look at the situation, I cannot see what else I could have done at any point. But if Ambrose had lived, if they'd had a son afterwards, I doubt I would ever have heard a word about it. And it is not wise for her to be so careless with her daughter's future.'

'She is reckless because she is desperate,' she said, surprising herself. 'Women must protect themselves; we have so few weapons.'

'I know that. And I agree. If she were fighting for her life, for her child, I would respect that. If she were to be cast out into the street, and only I could save her... But she has an ample jointure, she will have her parents' estate in due course, and it will all pass to Priscilla. She does not *need* anything I can give here; she merely wants it. The simple truth is, she has grown accustomed to being the most beautiful woman in any room she enters, and she is addicted to that attention as any poor soul to opium. I have come to realise this over the last few difficult weeks. It contented her for a while to be the lovely young widow who was the object of general pity and interest, but then she came out of her black and society grew bored by her. A new sensation arose to replace her – Byron and Lady Caroline Lamb, or Byron and Lady Oxford, or Byron and the kitchen cat; I know not what. She could not endure that.' He paused for a while and then said heavily, 'I am sure I sound bitter. I do not like myself when I talk about her. To be abusing one woman to another – it is not honourable. I would not have done so if she had not come to you and said what she did. I was obliged to explain, and to be completely honest. It is a weight off my mind. Thank you for listening to me.'

His words were oddly formal, as if he wished to put a distance between them now, and she blinked away a tear. 'You saved my life, or something close to it. I do not think there can be any question of debt from you to me, after that.'

'Nonsense. But I should go – I will have tired you, and you should rest.' He rose to leave, and then said, 'I know ours is not a real engagement, as you wisely said. I suspect if it had been, it would have been much harder for me to reveal all that I have.'

That stung, as it must since it was confirmation that he cared nothing for her, and so it did not matter in the least what he said to her, but she would not let him see how badly it wounded her.

'And if you had been deeply concerned with all she said to you about me, as a real fiancée would have been, it must have hurt you badly, and cast a shadow between us. I am glad you were spared that.'

It was impossible to answer that without revealing more of her deepest feelings than she could bear to, when it was obvious he didn't share them. But she had to make some response. 'I did not believe most of what she said, even before you explained. It was so clear that she had an axe to grind.'

'If only others could see her so clearly.'

And then he took his leave of her, without kissing her hand, and left her staring at the flowers he had brought her, as they wilted on the side table, wondering what in heaven's name she could do. Because she did love him, she had been forced to acknowledge today, but very plainly, he did not return her love. It was no wonder, perhaps, that he had no eyes for her, or for any woman. He might no longer love Lavinia – he had said so, and she could see that he believed it – but he was still inextricably bound up with her. Even if he hated her, he was in some sense still obsessed with her, and her place in his life. There was no space in his heart or in his thoughts for anyone else. The idea of making his engagement to Amelia genuine had obviously never so much as crossed his mind, and if it had crossed hers, she must banish it.

He had grown a little fond of her, perhaps, and was grateful, and liked to talk to her. She amused him, even, and his life at present held small enough amusement. He was attracted to her, as a frustrated man might easily be to an available woman, or at least he had been when they had kissed. But that was all, and soon enough, when all this chaos had subsided, she would have to break off this ridiculous sham engagement and set him free, though it was the last thing she wanted. They couldn't pretend to be engaged forever, or even for many more weeks; as well as being obviously impossible, it would be unbearable for her. Soon, it would have to stop.

Sophie was so careful not to interrupt whatever she thought might be happening in the yellow saloon that eventually, Amelia was obliged to go and find her, which she did at the nuncheon table. Rafe and Charlie were there too, full of concern for her health. Once she had persuaded them that she was fit to be out of bed and was not likely to go into a decline because she sat on a hard chair for half an hour and ate some ham, they passed a peaceful enough meal. It was not until later that Sophie was able to speak with her alone, in her cosy sitting room. 'I perceive that you remain unravished,' she observed sadly, shaking her red-blonde head, 'and so, I suppose, does he. It is a great pity.'

Refusing to engage in a discussion of how Sophie could possibly know this, Amelia said glumly, 'I felt I had to tell him that Lavinia had been to see me. And after that, there was no question of ravishment. He told me everything.'

'And is she his mistress, as she claims?'

'No. He said she wasn't, and I believed him. He admits that the child could be his, but could just as easily not be. It was just once, he said, before she was married, when they were both over-wrought at being separated. But he said that he does not love her now, and has no intention of marrying her – as we supposed, in fact.'

'Come,' Sophie said encouragingly, 'that is not too bad, you know. He is free to care for you; that is what matters. One cannot be so strict as to overlook a mistake made eight years ago and never repeated since. He is a man, not a saint. It would be most uncomfortable to be married to a saint, I should imagine. Especially for a Wyverne.'

'He is free to love me, but he does not. There is no point trying to deceive myself. Sophie, it may well be true that he no longer has feelings for her. But he is bound up with her in a way that does not allow him to look seriously at any other woman. It has clearly not occurred to him to view me in such a light. He as good as told me that he was only able to confide in me because he didn't care a button for me! I don't see how you can describe that as a hopeful sign.'

'I am not sure that is right. All my observations about his concern for you last night still stand. Melia, I am sure there are men who could share such painful details – and you must agree that it was right for him to share them – then turn around instantly and begin making passionate love to you. But I do not think he is one of them. And he would not be someone to be trusted if he were such a person. "My sister-in-law is trying to ruin my life and drive me distracted with her lies, but hey ho, sweetheart, since you're here, come sit on my lap!" I expect he was distressed at what he was obliged to say to you, and that drove all thoughts or romance from his mind. He is not some smooth Lothario, I think, but someone who feels things deeply, which is to be desired in a man, and certainly in a husband.'

Amelia sniffed and said that no, he wasn't a smooth Lothario, and obviously she didn't want him to be, because that sounded most disagreeable. 'And I said – because you know above all things, I didn't wish him to believe that I was trapping him – that the engagement wasn't real, so that he wasn't forced to remind me of it first. And then he kept repeating it. "I know the engagement isn't real", he kept on saying. More times than were strictly necessary, I thought.'

'Perhaps he wanted to remind himself, more than you,' said the ever-optimistic Marchioness.

'I can't just interpret every single thing he says and does as evidence that he might care for me,' Amelia replied with a deep sigh. 'If I do that, I'll be as bad as *she* is.'

'That could never be!'

Matters were, even Sophie had to agree, at an impasse. Lavinia refused to be discouraged, some unknown person had tried to gravely injure Amelia and, so far, got away with it, Amelia was suffering all the torments of unrequited love, and Lord Thornfalcon's feelings towards her remained unclear, possibly even to himself (this was Sophie's contribution).

But events were moving apace elsewhere. The host of the

fateful ball, Sir Humphrey Aubertin, was a man both proud and hospitable, and, as he had intimated to Lord Wyverne last night, took very strong exception to the idea that one of his guests – and a young lady, too – should be harmed by a person of malicious intent under his very roof. He had not himself seen the hand shoot out and push Lady Amelia down the Carrara marble steps his grandfather had imported at vast expense from some crumbling Italian palazzo, but his trusted major-domo had been close by and had witnessed it, as had several of his intimate circle. He felt as a matter of honour that he was responsible for what could easily have been a most grave injury, and a poor night's sleep – in which the dreadful incident replayed against his twitching eyelids with increasingly more Gothic outcomes – had crystallised his resolve to do something about it. On rising with a very bad head, he wrote and despatched several notes. One of them was to Lord Wyverne, enquiring anxiously about his dear sister's health; one was to Lord Thornfalcon with almost identical contents; and one was to the chief magistrate at Bow Street, with whom he happened to be acquainted. An Aubertin would never shirk his duty, no matter how unpleasant.

Lady Aubertin called on the Wyvernes that afternoon, and was able to report back that the interesting young victim had risen from her bed, but was still pale and shaken, and – if she was any judge – in very low spirits. Even the gift of a basket containing several exotic fruits from Sir Humphrey's famous forcing houses did not appear to cheer her, though she had said all that was civil on receiving them. And if a girl could not be made to smile by a pineapple all of her own, not to mention four or five of the celebrated Aubertin apricots, and a fine bunch of grapes, why, something was seriously amiss. 'I do not think she blames us, though, dear,' she told her husband soothingly.

'Wyverne too was good enough to assure me that he does not,' her spouse responded dolefully. 'Pleasant young fellow, I thought, quite serious, and much unlike his rascally father. But it is a very bad thing, Felicity, a very bad thing.'

The result of all this, upon the next day, was a most unusual visitor at Brook Street: Mr Ezekiel Pennyfeather, one of Bow Street's most celebrated Runners.

22

Marcus went about his daily activities without a great deal of attention. Amelia's fall had shaken him to the core, and his thoughts were whirling in sad confusion. Nobody seemed to think it in the least odd that he should be distracted; his fiancée had suffered a shocking accident, and any man of sensibility must be affected by it. Several sympathetic people told him as much to his face, and he smiled rather stiffly and thanked them, then tried to turn the subject into less painful channels.

Because it wasn't true, any of it. Amelia wasn't his fiancée, they weren't about to be married, and though obviously it was right that he should be concerned for her, as for anyone who'd suffered an accident, their whole relationship was a fiction, and nothing more than that. If he cared deeply, he had no right to. If he could not shake off the overwhelming sensations that fizzed in his veins when he'd touched her, he should. They'd kissed, good God... but *that* he must banish from his mind. If only he could.

He blamed himself. It must be obvious to the meanest intelligence that Lady Amelia had been assaulted because of him. She'd been tattled about before, but nobody had tried to put a period to her existence before she'd tangled herself in his life, a life that was more complicated than she could possibly have known. When she had proposed their arrangement, she had done so in ignorance and, knowing so much more than she did, he never should have agreed to it. He had been criminally irresponsible, and she had paid the price for it.

She had thought that he was merely troubled by gossip, as she was, and that one of those rumours – which, for all she knew, might have been entirely baseless – tied him to his sister-in-law, and her scheme might serve to free him from it. But the truth was far beyond anything she could have imagined. In some respects, her plan had worked perfectly. But inevitably, his deeper and more discreditable involvement with Lavinia, even though it was long since over, had been unknown to her.

She knew now. He burned with mortification as he remembered his awkward, stumbling words when he'd been obliged to tell her everything. Her lovely face, as she struggled to suppress the shock she must have been feeling and hear him out. Her willingness to believe him, when she had no reason to trust him, or any man. Her bravery, when to set him at his ease, she had attempted to make a joke of it. She was a remarkable young lady, an angel, and he'd realised it too late.

Perhaps it had always been too late for them, but he had another reason to curse Lavinia now. It had been her purpose, it was plain, to render him unavailable to any other woman, to mark him as hers forever. How successfully she had done so. She'd put in him a position where, as few men ever were, he'd been forced to confess all his dirtiest secrets to someone he'd much prefer thought exceedingly well of him.

Amelia might pay him the great compliment of believing him an honest man, for which he must always be profoundly grateful, but that was all. Her father had been the country's most notorious libertine, and she had suffered gravely for it, as had her whole family. Only a blockhead would imagine that she'd want more of the same in her own private life. Of course she would not. She deserved so much better. And one might say what one wished about the late Marquess of Wyverne, but he had not brought Bow Street Runners to his family's door, as Marcus now learned from Sir Humphrey that *he* had.

Though she was kind enough not to say so, Amelia must be desperate to end this farce of an engagement. No doubt her brothers, who loved her, were urging her to do so without delay. While she was still tied to Marcus in the eyes of the world, she could not be safe. Next time, she could be killed. The thought was unendurable.

He could not end their connection himself – and though he should want to for her sake, he was painfully aware that he didn't, not in the least – so he could only pull back from an illusion of closeness that could only hurt them both, and hope that after a decent interval had passed, she would speak, and say that it was over. Then she could be free, and safe. That would have to be enough for him.

23

Mr Pennyfeather, calling in Brook Street in his capacity of investigator, was desirous of speaking with all of the Wyvernes who had been at the ball, at once if possible. He sent up a very respectful note via the scandalised butler, who was by no means accustomed to admitting such low individuals into his master's presence. But Rafe only raised a sardonic eyebrow and agreed to the interview, and shortly afterwards, the Runner was received in Lady Wyverne's sitting room by the Marquess, the Marchioness, Lady Amelia, and Lord Charles, as he had requested. Lord Wyverne explained that two other persons, including his sister's betrothed, had also been of their party, and Mr Pennyfeather, making a careful note in a small memorandum book he carried, said that he had been apprised of that, and that it was his intention to speak with the Thornfalcon siblings later that day.

He was a small, round-faced man of crumpled, bashful appearance, not at all the great, burly person Amelia had somehow expected a Runner to be, but he seemed eager and diligent, and was certainly very polite. Once it had been established that only Sophie had seen the infamous hand, for a bare second, and that it had had no useful identifying marks about it that she had noticed, the officer said, 'And so I am obliged to ask – just as a matter of routine, you understand, my lords and ladies – whether the young lady who suffered this terrible assault has any enemies, or persons who might wish her ill. I know it's unlikely, even preposterous, you might say, but I'm bound to enquire as part of my duties.'

Rafe's face was carefully blank, as was Charlie's (though this might be considered to be its habitual state and not any sort of deliberate reaction to the question). But Amelia said, with a quick glance at her sister-in-law, 'There's no point trying to conceal anything. Somebody else will only tell you and you will wonder why we did not. Have you heard of the Friends of Lavinia, Mr Pennyfeather?'

He blinked and said that he had no recollection of the name. 'Some sort of secret society?' he ventured hopefully. 'Something from foreign parts, perhaps? Like those Illuminati?'

He seemed invigorated by the idea that this case, already important, might prove to have an international political dimension, and disappointed when Amelia, with some not enormously helpful interjections from Sophie, explained that they were essentially a loose band of young ladies with vivid imaginations and not enough to occupy their time. She mentioned no names. But when Amelia, blushing, went on to describe, in the most innocuous terms she could manage, the origin of this group of persons and their connection to herself, Mr Pennyfeather perked up again.

'If I understand you correctly, then, this Lady Thornfalcon has got hold of the notion that this Lord Thornfalcon – who isn't her husband, despite a body naturally assuming that he must be, on account of the names – is her property, as you might say? And now he's engaged himself to you, much to her displeasure?

My lady?' This, plainly, was the sort of motive he could understand.

'Yes,' said Amelia. 'I suppose the rest of it doesn't signify – all the "deceased husband's brother" nonsense. He can't marry her and he doesn't want to anyway, but she thinks he should.'

'I am by way of being something of an amateur of history in my own way and on my own time, as is my helpmeet Mrs Pennyfeather,' revealed the officer unexpectedly, 'and I'm sure if the noble lady in question had studied it at all herself, as I recommend to everybody of every station in life, she'd realise that those sorts of havey-cavey goings-on won't do, not by any means they won't, and are bound to end badly. Catherine of Aragon could tell her that, for certain sure. Or Henry the Eighth, come to that! Married his dead brother's wife – lived to regret it. As,' he said thoughtfully, 'did she, no doubt.'

Amelia appeared much struck by this novel perspective on the problem. 'That's very true,' she said, and the Runner beamed at her approvingly. 'But justice obliges me to say that Lady Thornfalcon herself could not have pushed me, because she was already at the ball, down in the ballroom, and I dare say a dozen persons could vouch for her presence.'

'Ah,' said Mr Pennyfeather sapiently, 'it's very fair of you to say so, and reflects well on your good heart, but that's where history comes in again, if you don't mind me saying, miss – my lady, I mean. Nobody ever said that wicked King Richard the Third killed the little princes in the Tower himself, did they? Not in person. But where are they now? Tell me that, eh?'

'Dead, presumably,' said Rafe drily. 'Whatever else we don't know, which seems to be a great deal, we do know that.'

'Yes!' said the Runner with some energy. 'Dead as dragons! But they wouldn't be, if Sir James Tyrrell hadn't been paid to sneak in and bump them off at old Crookback's behest. So clean hands, if I may put it so, don't necessarily mean a clean heart, your grace and ladies. And so it may be here. So it may well be...' He was scribbling furiously in his little book now, as one inspired, and his audience watched him with some apprehension.

'I don't think so,' Amelia said doubtfully. 'Lady Thornfalcon would be very silly to ask some young lady she can scarcely know to push me, and hope that I would be killed by it and that the lady would keep quiet about it afterwards. And I don't think she's silly. I know someone did it – I felt the push – but I think it was an action of the moment, a sudden impulse, not some deep plot.'

'Ah! But then, a young lady can't possibly plumb the deepest darkest depths of the human heart!' said Mr Pennyfeather poetically. He was clearly enjoying himself hugely now. 'History offers us so many examples of wicked women. Thieves, of course, though I am sure you ladies would not credit it, and much worse than that! Marie de' Medici, the poisoner queen, for example!'

'My direct ancestor,' said Sophie cordially.

He looked alarmed, as well he might. 'Catherine de' Medici... No, perhaps not. Lucrezia Borgia, then!'

'More of a distant cousin.' Even Amelia could not be sure if this was true, or a joke at the Runner's expense. Her sister-in-law seemed to have no great liking for this officer of the law. 'Are all your wicked women foreign like me, Mr Pennyfeather? Perhaps English women are not so bad, then, or at any rate, not so enterprising.'

'Oh, I assure you, your grace, they are!' he said earnestly, keen to uphold the achievements of his countrywomen in this field. 'Sarah Malcolm is an infamous name from the last century, and I know of many more from my own experience. Shocking cases!'

'Well,' said Rafe, rising, 'we must leave you to investigate, Pennyfeather. You have been called in by Sir Humphrey, as is his right, and it is not for us to tell you where you must look for your culprit. But I do hope you will appreciate that my sister is the innocent victim in all this, and that dragging her name into some further scandal will not do her any good at all.'

'No, I've no desire to do that, I promise you, sir.' He began to bow himself out, but straightened and said diffidently, 'I must just ask you one last thing before I go: did you happen to recognise any of the people who were behind you at the top of the steps? I'm trying to make up a list, for process of elimination, but it's very slow work.'

They could not help him; they hadn't been looking behind them, but waiting to descend the stairs and chatting to each other. 'Miss Thornfalcon might know,' Amelia said. 'She's very quick-witted, I think.'

'His Lordship, of course, would have been otherwise occupied,' the Runner suggested with romantic emphasis, and Amelia could only assent with as much composure as she could summon. She realised now that if Marcus hadn't been distracted from the people around them by the tender emotions – which clearly he hadn't, for which she ought to be grateful – she most certainly had without realising it. She had been easy prey.

Mr Pennyfeather took his leave, and they all looked at each other with varying degrees of discomfort.

'Well, I have no great liking for police spies,' Sophie said, in case they hadn't observed as much, 'but I must say, although it seems most unlikely that this odd little man will ever find out who shoved you, Amelia, I do not at all dislike the idea of Lavinia Thornfalcon having a few uneasy moments over it in the meantime. That is one good thing, I suppose.'

Amelia shook her head. 'She's altogether too cool. She'll smile icily and remind him that she is a widow and a great lady, and tell him nothing. Because I don't believe she was directly involved at all, even if she really is morally responsible. It would take more than poor Mr Pennyfeather to discompose her, I think, horrid creature that she is.'

Rafe said, 'I wouldn't be so sure. Some of these Bow Street men are very shrewd, and all his chatter about history may just be a smokescreen. It would not do to underestimate him, I believe.'

And he stared rather pointedly at his wife, who shrugged in Gallic fashion, her face implausibly innocent. 'We have nothing to hide,' she said. 'Let the widow and her foolish Friends look to themselves.'

'Quite right!' said Charlie, who had made little contribution to the conversation previously, though he had given all along the rather touching impression, much like a large dog, that he was most anxious to help, if he only knew how. 'Dashed shocking thing. Can't have people running around pushing girls downstairs. Let alone my own sister! Lock them up!'

24

The industrious Runner was as good as his word, and was next to be seen in Half-Moon Street, where he was lucky enough to find Lord Thornfalcon at home, with his sister Helena and his widowed mother. They, like the Wyvernes, had been expecting him. 'Mrs Pennyfeather,' the little man said disconcertingly upon receiving his host's greeting, 'will be fair tickled when I tell her I've met you, sir. She is a great devotee of the latest public prints.'

It was soon clear that Lady Amelia – or someone – had found it necessary to explain the situation regarding Lavinia; this at least spared Marcus the awkwardness of doing so himself and sounding like an utter cockscomb. It could not be helped, he realised, since such matters, however delicate, could not be concealed now that an official investigation was underway. Mr Pennyfeather, with a degree of tact that would have confirmed Rafe in his opinion of him, if he had known of it, made it clear that he knew already that Lady Thornfalcon – the other Lady Thornfalcon – could not possibly be responsible for the assault. 'Not directly, she couldn't,' he added ominously.

It was plain that the officer had indeed spared more than a

casual glance for the prints that featured His Lordship so promi-
nently – he could not prevent himself from shooting sidelong
looks at the Major's tall figure every so often, and then shaking
his head, as if in disbelief that he should find himself inter-
viewing such a notable personage. 'Well then, sir,' he said in a
business-like manner, 'I understand that there's a great number
of young ladies interested in you, setting aside these so-called
Friends of Lavinia, whose concern isn't quite so personal, you
might say. I can't quite make these Friends out, I must say. To get
so agitated about the private life of people you don't know, and
even try to interfere in their personal business, as though they
were characters in a book and not living, breathing humans with
their own opinions... I don't know what the world's coming to.
But let's talk about the other ladies. At least we know what *they*
want, and it's a tale as old as time, if you'll pardon me for
saying so.'

Helena said, smiling, 'Yes – I'll spare my brother the trouble
of answering that, for he finds it all most embarrassing, as I'm
sure you can imagine. The prints are exaggerated, of course, for
dramatic effect, but it's perfectly true that many young ladies –
and not just young ones – have thrown themselves at Lord
Thornfalcon's feet. Literally. Off horses, you know. And swooned
when he was near, so that he was obliged to catch them. But I
think that had mostly stopped, or at least greatly lessened, since
his engagement was announced. Because it was clear to them
that they were wasting their time, to be blunt.'

'Well, we Runners, we appreciate a little bluntness, miss,
when so many people try to spin us fairy stories. You don't think –
any of you – that one of the fainting ladies would have gone to
the bother of hurting Her Ladyship, then?'

'Why should they?' said Marcus tersely. 'I wasn't even slightly
interested in any of them before, man; I'm hardly likely to think

better of it and begin a sordid intrigue with my fiancée seriously injured or even... with my fiancée seriously injured.' He didn't know why it was so hard to put into words what might so easily have happened to Lady Amelia.

'Of course not,' the officer agreed comfortably. 'And a blessing it is that your reactions were so quick, I'm sure, and the young lady took no hurt. You should hear Sir Humphrey talk about it – he paints a very vivid picture, so he does. I wish I'd been there to witness it, for more reasons than one.'

'It was a miracle,' said Helena, much more serious now. 'I can still see it, if I close my eyes. I'm so grateful that you weren't present that evening, Mama; you must have been so shocked and distressed till we realised they were both safe and well, against all the odds.'

Lady Thornfalcon said, shuddering, 'My dears, it still gives me nightmares to think of it. And though the renewed public attention cannot be welcome – and we have had such a deal of it already after all the gossip this spring that I am sure it is a wonder we do not all run away to some remote island – I cannot say that I think Sir Humphrey was wrong to call you in, Mr Pennyfeather. It doesn't seem right that anyone, whoever they may be, should get away with such irresponsible behaviour.'

'No, indeed, my lady,' he said sententiously. 'And it is my duty to speak to everyone concerned, including your daughter-in-law, of course. This is an irregular question, I admit, so I hope you'll forgive me, but how do you think she will be likely to receive me?'

'Coldly,' responded Helena promptly. 'As if insulted that you should dare to interrogate her. Scornfully.'

'I agree, dear,' her mother said. 'But you know, I'm not sure if you realise, officer, how very beautiful she is. She relies on that in all her dealings with people, and she will work it on you, no doubt.'

'There isn't a trick that hasn't been tried on me, ma'am, I promise. And as for those sorts of goings-on, I'm a married man, and not what you'd call susceptible, as Mrs Pennyfeather would vouch. Hard-headed, she tells me I am.'

'If my sister-in-law is not cold – if she tries instead to charm you,' Marcus offered, almost against his will, 'it will mean that she is frightened. But I don't see why she should be. I cannot really believe that she had a hand in this, though there is no denying her ultimate responsibility for the whole furore.'

His mother put in, 'But she will never admit to that, of course. I have known her since she was a child, and lived with her for years while my eldest son was alive, and I doubt she feels a scrap of guilt, or could be brought to understand it. And as for the public attention, which we so dislike, it's meat and drink to her. If you were to arrest her – though I'm not saying you will ever have cause to, of course – she'd play you such a scene as would set your hair on end.'

'Like Anne Boleyn going to the Tower?' Mr Pennyfeather said musingly. 'Screaming, and falling on the floor, and such Drury Lane airs? Well, he that lives longest will see most, as they say.'

Helena, as Amelia had hoped she might, did have some idea of the names of persons who had been standing near them at the top of the steps, having an excellent memory, and gave them to Mr Pennyfeather. She was obliged to acknowledge that several of the ringleaders of the Friends of Lavinia had been among them, including Miss Lancaster and Miss Archer. 'I don't accuse anyone,' she added a little anxiously. 'But these people were definitely there – I saw them. And perhaps they saw others, and you can make some sort of a list when you put it all together.'

'That's the ticket, miss,' he said. 'Slowly and surely does it. Don't you worry, I'm not one to be jumping to any unwarranted conclusions.'

Marcus offered to show the man out; he had a feeling there were things to be discussed between them in some sort of privacy. And indeed, Pennyfeather said, as the door closed and they headed down the stairs, 'You've been having a trying time of it, sir, it seems to me, before even this fresh start. Came home to convalesce, I understand, from wounds taken in the line of duty, and then all this nonsense to greet you.'

'I have a broad enough back, man. But what I can't bear is the notion that I have embroiled Lady Amelia in this cursed situation of mine, and damn near got her killed.' Why was he telling the fellow this? It was none of his affair.

The Runner sighed sympathetically. 'She's a rare, brave one, sir, it's plain to see. Many a lady – and not just ladies – would be making a main fuss if they'd been through what she has. Yelling and carrying on and suchlike. And yet she made sure to tell me that this here Lady Lavinia or whatever she's called couldn't have done it, instead of blaming her as she so easily might have. I'm not convinced Mrs Pennyfeather would find it in her heart to be so reasonable in the circumstances, though she's as good a woman as ever drew breath. But she has a fierce temper, sir, and I won't deny it. No, your young lady is a treasure above rubies, as no doubt you know. And I'm hopeful that I'll get to the bottom of it all, for her sake as much as for the law. The law is an impersonal sort of thing, you might say, but a young lady of that quality... newly betrothed and in love; it fair breaks my heart, and I'm not a soft sort of man by any means. Well, talking pays no toll, so I'll be off, my lord, and good day to you.' He raised his shaggy beaver hat and was gone, most unlikely of Cupids, leaving Marcus staring after him in a brown study.

At last, he shook his head, as if to clear it, and slowly made his way inside.

25

Many people – though probably not Marcus – might have wished to be a fly on the wall at Mr Pennyfeather's interview with Lavinia, but they were all of them obliged to wait in suspense to see if the Runner, who they'd realised wasn't always completely discreet when it suited him, would see fit to tell them of it. They could hardly ask.

He returned to Half-Moon Street the next day, and was shown into Lady Thornfalcon's sitting room once more. Marcus was not present, being out on some business to do with the resignation of his commission, but the ladies received him cordially. He had come, he explained, to show Miss Thornfalcon his revised list, and to see if it sparked any recollections in her sharp brain. 'You might recall, for instance, now you see new names, if any of them were standing closer to you than others. And if some people say they weren't and you say maybe they were, that'll be interesting too. At least I can be tolerable certain *you* didn't push the young lady.'

Helena gave the document great attention, but replied in the end, 'I'm not acquainted with most of these people, that's the problem, so I don't know. But I do know this lady and her husband – at least by sight – and I'm sure they were nowhere near us. I didn't even know she was present, so she must have been some little distance away. I hope that is some help to you.'

The officer gave a sardonic little grunt. 'It's good to have confirmation from you, miss. It's a process of elimination, you might say. To hear them talk, you'd think not one of these people was anywhere near you but ten miles distant, even though the sort of platform affair at the top of the stairs isn't at all large and so they can't all be telling the truth. So it's good to know who I can put some faith in when they tell me where other people were besides themselves, if you follow me.'

'Do you really think you'll get to the bottom of this, Mr Pennyfeather?' Judith asked him. 'It seems to me it's going to come in the end to a group of young ladies and none of them admitting having done it. And if they begin implicating each other in a great state of panic, as I can imagine they might, however will you know which to believe?'

'We have our ways, my lady,' he said portentously. 'But you were right, as it happens, about the other Lady Thornfalcon. Not a word of regret from her about Lady Amelia's fall, and if I'm waiting for her to admit anything in the nature of persuading or inducing someone else to give her a push, I'll be waiting a long time. She's a cold one, and no mistake. Looked at me as though I was lower than a worm, which there's no call for, in my opinion. I have a job to do – at the instigation of Sir Humphrey – and I'm doing it, no more and no less.'

'Of course you are,' Helena said, pouring him some more tea in obedience to a glance from her mother. 'And we at least are very grateful for it, and so I know are Lady Amelia's family, not to mention Sir Humphrey. The fact is, even if she isn't at all involved, I imagine my sister-in-law doesn't actually want you to find out who did the deed. Because if it was one of those silly Friends, I expect she will incur some criticism because of it, at least from sensible people.'

'I dare say that's so, but then you'd think she'd have the mother wit to be a little civil,' the Runner grumbled, giving every appearance of a man who was prepared to hold a grudge for a substantial period of time. And indeed it was hard to see why Lavinia should have chosen to make an enemy of him when she need not have done; it could not help her, even if it was true that he could do her little harm at the moment, apart from passing on his so far unprovable suspicions to the highly influential Sir Humphrey.

Helena told Mr Pennyfeather that Lady Amelia was now considered to be fit to return to society again, and that she and her mother and brother would be accompanying the Wyvernes to dinner at Sir Humphrey's house that evening. 'Do you have any advice for us on how to go on?' she asked him. They understood each other tolerably well by now, she felt. 'Apart, I suppose, from the obvious – do not stand about daydreaming at the top of any flights of stairs.'

'Hmm. On the face of it, miss, it seems unlikely that the person responsible will be so foolish as to try again. Because we do have a pretty good idea by now of who was in the crowd behind you, and if Her Ladyship was to meet with another mishap and one of those people close by – well, her goose would be cooked, as you might say. But still, I can see you're both a mite uneasy, and I can understand why. She's safe enough in a private home tonight. Sir Humphrey has very strong views indeed about these Friends of Lavinia, now that I've made my report to him, and you can be sure he won't be inviting any of *them* to dinner with you. But on a more public occasion... well, let's just say that I've been given access to the young lady's diary of engagements, and we'll be keeping an eye on her, unobtrusive-like, with her agreement and her brother's.'

'I'm very glad to hear it,' she said frankly, and her mother murmured agreement and pressed another slice of lemon cake on Mr Pennyfeather, who was rapidly advancing to the status of confidential family friend.

26

Amelia was unaccountably nervous as she prepared for the dinner at the Aubertin mansion. She had seen Lord Thornfalcon more than once in the last few days, but never alone. He'd called on her assiduously to see how she did, but always accompanied by his sister and sometimes by his mother too. Sophie had naturally been present on these occasions, and once – memorably – also Lady Keswick and Amelia's grandmother. Lady Keswick, as Amelia had feared, was strongly of the opinion that the speedy marriage she had advocated from the first would have prevented the shocking events which had recently occurred. While the Dowager Lady Wyverne wasn't necessarily in disagreement with her, she was on rare combative form that day and chose to take issue with the younger lady, it seemed to Amelia, merely for the fun of it. It had been a clash of titans, Lady Keswick handicapped by her natural reluctance to appear rude to someone past her century, and Delphine held back by nothing at all save her opponent's inadequate understanding of the French language and its riper curses. Once or twice, Marcus's eyes had met hers in unholy shared amusement. But this was all they'd shared.

It seemed to Amelia that he was adhering so closely to the proprieties chiefly as a means of protecting himself. What she couldn't say was whether this was because he regretted the kiss – *the kiss*, the Kiss – or because he regretted his outpouring of deep feeling and of secrets that had so closely followed it. Perhaps it was both. It was, after all, a false engagement, and such personal matters should be shared with a real betrothed, not the stranger who had so rashly entangled herself in his life. For all she knew, he was desperate to be rid of her, and yet was obliged to stay tied to her, at least for a while. Certainly, he had pulled back from any intimacy, taking good care never to be private with her, and even the Marchioness could not claim that that was a good sign.

She did not need Sophie to tell her to wear her best gown. Of course she would, even if only to armour herself with a little courage in her current state of sad uncertainty. But which was her best gown? Every remotely suitable item in her wardrobe had been tried on and discarded, some several times, before with a harassed glance at the busily ticking clock on the mantel, she settled on her first choice. It was deep-pink silk – not the most conventional colour evening gown for young, unmarried ladies, perhaps, but her sister-in-law and her abigail both assured her that it became her greatly and set off her dark hair to perfection. One of its chief attributes was the fact that it was surely a colour that chilly Lavinia Thornfalcon had never chosen in her life; it would be a good long while before Amelia felt like wearing pale blue or silver again. The gown could not be described as particularly low-cut, since she was not a married woman, but its straight column clung agreeably to her body – not that anybody would be able to see a great deal of this while she was sitting down eating – and its puffed sleeves were tiny, so that her arms and shoulders were laid bare above her long, snowy-white gloves.

And now she had to think about jewels... Sophie had offered

to lend her the Stella Rosa – the vast, pink diamond that was almost her sole inheritance from her ancient French family, the now-extinct De Montfaucons. But Amelia had looked at its intimidating size and brightness and thought that it would be wearing her rather than she wearing it. And also it was popularly supposed to be cursed, which was really the last thing she needed just now. So she had put on instead her grandmother's suggestion: something Delphine had inherited from her own long-dead mother and kept close ever since. It was an ancient French Renaissance jewel on an ornate chain of pearl and gold, consisting of two fat, pink enamelled cupids who dangled between them a large, natural barocco pearl. It too was unique and carried a distinguished history, but it wasn't screaming, *Stare at my cleavage!* in quite the same way as the Stella. Nor was it linked to any disagreeable legends, as far as she knew. And Sophie, heroically, refrained from wearing the great pink diamond herself.

She had little chance to converse with Lord Thornfalcon before they went in to dinner. Sir Humphrey was most anxious to show his guest of honour – herself – every flattering attention, and hovered anxiously by her side as they stood in his grand salon. As he was tall, lean and stooped, dressed in old-fashioned grey velvet, he rather resembled a heron with one chick. Lady Aubertin, who was stouter and more obviously formidable, stood guard on her other side, with her shy debutante daughter Philomena at her elbow. Though perhaps they were not aware of it, they were behaving as though they believed that someone might at any moment make a murderous lunge at her from behind one of the Louis XV sofas and they were all three primed to fight them off. Amelia felt a strong desire to apologise to them all for so seriously disrupting the ball that they had gone to so much trouble and expense to arrange, but then reflected that after all, she hadn't asked to be pushed down a set of steps, less still their antique marble steps in particular.

Marcus, conversing with his sister and Sophie at some little distance away across an expanse of Aubusson carpet, was looking handsome and rather forbidding in his severe black evening coat and breeches, but then he always did. And she supposed rather glumly that, as she'd undoubtedly be seated at Sir Humphrey's right hand, her betrothed would be equally honoured by their hostess, and would therefore be at the other end of the table from herself. What was the use in being engaged, even fake-engaged, to someone, if you hardly ever spent so much as five minutes in his company?

She took her host's arm and they moved in stately fashion into a moderately sized dining room, since there were only ten persons present for this intimate meal. They sat down among glowering, murky Old Master paintings, including a huge and graphic depiction of *Jael Destroying Sisera* (with hammer and peg to the ear) which seemed hardly conducive to good digestion, particularly for gentlemen. Brown-haired, pert-nosed Jael, frowning in concentration in a pale-yellow gown that was sadly impractical for her gory task, bore more than a passing resemblance to Helena Thornfalcon, and Amelia, glancing at her, saw that she was transfixed, and perhaps taking mental notes.

But for her own part, she found she had wronged Lady Aubertin, who had, despite appearances, been young once. Amelia was indeed at Sir Humphrey's side, but Marcus was placed considerately next to Amelia herself. Sophie, taking in the situation with her sparkling, dark eyes from directly opposite, smiled brilliantly at her host and began exerting herself to be particularly charming in the French manner. He was soon looking slightly stunned, but pleasantly so, and certainly had no attention to spare for Amelia, or his food. Sometimes, his spoon missed his mouth.

'Are you well?' Lord Thornfalcon asked her without marked originality as she eyed her white soup with disfavour, even with dislike. She imagined that perfect Lavinia had perfected a seductive way of eating soup, but she carelessly had not. Most likely she would spill it on herself. Must she starve, too?

'Yes, thank you, sir. I am quite recovered, and I hope your bruises have faded.' Damn it all, now she had put the picture of him naked in front of his looking-glass back into her mind. Again.

'On the contrary, they are now all the colours of the rainbow, or so I am assured.' He seemed to realise that he had said something that was open to an unfortunate interpretation, and added hastily, 'I braved Jackson's for a bout of sparring this morning, and was ridiculed in quite a shameful way by my acquaintances there. We are accustomed, of course, sometimes to take the exercise shirtless, I should explain. Especially when it is hot – the weather, I mean.'

Shirtless. Amelia closed her eyes for a moment and prayed for strength.

For whatever reason, conversation was not flowing easily between them this evening. An almost palpable constraint had grown up and threatened to paralyse them both into silence, or stumbling commonplaces at best. They both began to speak at once, and entangled themselves in apologies. *This is unendurable*, she thought suddenly.

'Sir...' she began resolutely.

But there had occurred – though indeed they had not perceived it, being entirely wrapped up in their own mutual and intense awkwardness – a natural lull in conversation around the rest of the table, and Sir Humphrey took advantage of it to say to the general company, 'I would like to thank you all for coming this evening. I was not sure if Lady Amelia would care to set foot in this house again after what so shamefully occurred here.'

She murmured a confused denial, and he continued, 'I have been impressed and – I must confess – moved, by Jove, moved, to witness this young lady's courage and her gracious forgiveness. This also applies to her family, who have been the very soul of good breeding in these most trying circumstances.'

It was the other Wyvernes' turn to utter inarticulate noises expressive of modest but civil disagreement, and yet also simultaneously their celebrated good breeding. Amelia, who was feeling slightly feverish, saw Sophie sigh in a soulful manner, as she raised her hand to her not inconsiderable bosom and positively fluttered her long eyelashes at the old gentleman. Rafe, who had been peacefully drinking wine, seemed to choke slightly, and put up his hand to cover his mouth.

'And Thornfalcon too, who nearly lost his bride before the wedding – an absolutely shocking thing to happen in Grosvenor Square, and we really can't apologise enough.'

Marcus, who had clearly been prepared for his turn to come, entered into the spirit of the thing and inclined his head in stately acknowledgement.

'And so, I've been racking my brains, and racking my wife's brains too, to think how I can possibly make recompense to you all.'

'You have called in Mr Pennyfeather,' said Lady Thornfalcon soothingly, possibly in a vain attempt to divert the flow, 'and I am sure we all have a great deal of confidence in him. Not that recompense is needed, of course.'

'Very good of you to say so, ma'am, and he seems a capable sort of fellow, if a little odd. I have hopes he will get to the bottom of the dreadful business, yes. But it's not enough.'

Lady Aubertin, perhaps growing impatient as any woman might after five and twenty years of marriage, said, 'I have been speaking with my old friend Millicent Keswick – I am so sorry that she was not able to be here this evening, but after all, it would have thrown the numbers at table out in a sad way and obliged me to scrape up another gentleman – and she tells me that you are pardonably anxious to marry soon. Quite right! She and I are entirely in agreement as to the inadvisability of long engagements, especially in this particular case. And so we thought we would offer the private chapel here, for the ceremony – so much better than an ordinary sort of church where any vulgar person might wander in off the street to watch, most disagreeable – and Aubertin Priory for the honeymoon. If you obtain a special licence, Lord Thornfalcon, you can be married in a day or so, and put all this nonsense behind you.'

'Really,' chipped in her spouse in a resigned fashion, presumably quite accustomed to being interrupted, 'it's the least we could do. We both agree that Thursday would be perfect. What do you think, eh?'

27

It was a damned embarrassing situation, but it shouldn't, Marcus reflected, be anything more than that. Though it seemed that the universe was conspiring to hurry them to the altar, none of these people – not even the terrifying Lady Keswick who, thank God, was not present this evening – could actually force them to get married this Thursday. Banishing the alarmingly realistic vision of the lady aiming a shotgun at him with deadly intent, he struggled to regain control of the situation, much like the poor fool in Portugal attempting to steer the out-of-control wagon down the hill without loss of life.

'It's excessively kind of you both,' he began, 'but we wouldn't think of trespassing on your good nature...'

Lord Wyverne too had clearly seen the horror and panic on Lady Amelia's face, and added his voice to that of Marcus. 'Sir Humphrey,' he said smoothly, 'Lady Aubertin, it is impossible adequately to express our gratitude, but we have not so much as discussed the date of the wedding yet, nor the venue. All our plans have been overset by the unfortunate events of the last few days. Amelia, I am sure, would prefer to be married at Wyverne

House, our ancestral home, which also has a chapel, while perhaps Thornfalcon might argue persuasively for his own seat, where my sister will after all soon take her place as chatelaine. I shouldn't wonder if that has a chapel too.'

'It does,' said Lord Thornfalcon with emphasis. 'A very large chapel. Enormous.'

'Save the arguments,' Lady Aubertin persisted, 'which one of you is bound to lose, resulting in lingering resentment.'

Her husband nodded vigorously, clearly being familiar with the notion of lingering resentment.

'Accept our offer.'

'I think I must beg a little indulgence from you and consult with my betrothed on the matter, ma'am,' Marcus said firmly. 'In the end, it must be her choice – after all that she has gone through – and I am sure it must be a young lady's prerogative to decide such important matters without pressure, however kindly meant, from her future husband or from anyone else. I would not think to interfere in her bride clothes...'

'Quite right,' said his hostess darkly.

'And I must similarly defer to her in this, and insist that she be allowed some time to make up her mind.'

Amelia's expression was a complex mixture of gratitude – for his averting disaster at least temporarily, he thought – and irritation that he had by this means focused everyone's attention on her. 'Thank you, Lord Thornfalcon,' she responded sweetly. 'It is good of you, and I am sensible of your concern for me, but I believe your first thought was best. We must discuss it together. In private.'

'There's a fine terrace here,' put in Sir Humphrey helpfully. 'After dinner, of course – we seem to have been eating this soup for hours; take it away, Watkins, for heaven's sake, and bring the meat – I'm sure you can go out for a minute or two. Moonlight, and so on. Engaged couple, getting married before the end of the week – perfectly in order. Eh, Felicity?' And he perpetrated something that appeared to be, but surely could not have been, a wink.

'On this occasion, I am sure there can be no objection,' his spouse replied austerely. If she had seen his facial contortion, she did not allude to it.

Lord Thornfalcon could not remember later what they ate, or what, after this extraordinary beginning, they could possibly have spoken of. Lady Wyverne, who seemed earlier to have been flirting with Sir Humphrey for purposes he could not begin to guess at, briskly assumed a more normal manner and conversed in a sensible fashion with both her table companions equally. This left Sir Humphrey free to pay some courtly heed to Amelia, and to take a glass of wine with her in accordance with the quaint old custom. Marcus himself spoke chiefly to Miss Aubertin, whom he'd sadly neglected before: a pleasant enough girl, though shy. Their rather laboured conversation occupied only a small part of his attention and gave him ample leisure to see that Amelia was looking uncomfortable, as well she might, and gulping down her wine rather faster than seemed advisable. He didn't suppose she was used to it; no, it brought a wild-rose flush to her cheeks and a hectic brightness to her eyes. What it boded for their impending private interview – in the moonlight – he did not care to speculate. She wasn't eating much, either, though Sir Humphrey pressed each dish on her with oppressive courtesy.

One of the longest meals he'd ever endured came to an end eventually, and when the gentlemen rose as the ladies left the room, he found himself separated from them in order to escort his betrothed out onto the famous terrace. It wouldn't be quite accurate to say that they were pushed out onto it by their hosts, but they certainly found themselves there by means that he considered mysterious. The door was shut firmly behind them.

It was an undoubtedly lovely scene. The sun had not long set; there were still streaks of bright colour in the sky to the west, and the moon, despite what had been claimed, was not yet visible. Sir Humphrey's mansion had a larger garden than was common for the centre of London; there was indeed a broad terrace with steps at each end that led down to a charming garden, with arbours and winding paths. Large Grecian pots stood at the corners of the balustrade, also filled with flowers that glimmered white in the moonlight. Heady perfume – rose, jasmine, lavender, night-scented stock, recently cut grass – wafted to them where they stood, and a fountain trickled somewhere below them. He'd been oblivious to the weather this spring and early summer, having many other things to worry about, but he realised now that it was deliciously warm. A perfect evening, full of possibilities. Apart from the noise of the water, it was surprisingly quiet and peaceful out here, as though the whole of London were holding its breath and waiting for something. It was intimate. Seductive, even. And a very, very bad idea.

Amelia said with a wild little laugh, 'Do you mind if we stay far away from the steps?'

'Of course not. There's a bench here – shall we sit?'

They did so. The smooth marble seat was perceptibly warm under Marcus's thighs, and he thought that Amelia, in her much thinner garments, must be able to feel it even more. Though on the whole, that wasn't a very sensible train of thought, and one he didn't intend to dwell on. She still hadn't put her gloves back on after the meal, and her bare arms and shoulders were almost brushing his coat, since the bench wasn't very large, and he was. He felt acutely conscious of his size and her slightness just now. Their thighs weren't touching each other, quite, but she was barely an inch away in her pink silk gown. If he shifted just a little… He could smell her perfume – light and floral, just an elusive hint of it under the overpowering scents of summer. He felt achingly aware of his body, and of hers. Of his blood in his veins. He moved restlessly on the stone, then realised this brought him closer to her, and edged back. But if he moved any further away, he'd fall off the end of the bench like a damned idiot. *Jesus.*

'What shall we say to them?' she asked. He wasn't sure if she was talking to him, or musing aloud to herself. If she'd noticed his fidgeting, she was considerate enough not to mention it. He could only hope that she didn't know what it meant. And why should she? He wasn't entirely sure himself.

'It doesn't matter what we say, as long as we don't allow them to force their crazy scheme on us. I've never seen anyone look so terrified as you did when she proposed that we should marry in two days' time. If we show the least sign of agreeing to it, everything will be out of our hands for good.'

She sighed deeply. Possibly it was Marcus's imagination, but it seemed to move her bare arm a little closer. Tantalisingly so. It was a most attractive sound, her soft exhalation of breath in the warm dusk. He would like to hear a different kind of sigh from her...

'I'm sorry,' she whispered. 'It's all my fault.'

'It obviously isn't. You did not plan this... this madness. Nobody could have. You certainly didn't plan to get pushed down the stairs.'

'Very well. I'll say we want to be married at Wyverne on a date of our choosing. Not this Thursday. It's not true, of course, none of it's true, but I have to say something. If it's my choice, my home, it's harder for them to question it. If they continue, I'll... I'll say I feel unwell.'

'You don't, do you?'

'My head is swimming slightly, perhaps. But it's not at all unpleasant.'

'That'll be the wine,' he said resignedly. 'It can do that, you know.'

'I'm not inebriated,' she replied with dignity.

'Not foxed, of course. You're not about to start breaking windows and singing vulgar songs, I don't suppose. Just up in the world a touch.'

'I don't know what your horrid slang means. I'm not an expert in the degrees of inebriation as you plainly are.' She pronounced this sentence with excessive care. 'But I really don't think I'm drunk. It's just, I don't know, Marcus – I'm tired, and I feel a little reckless.'

'Wine can do that too.'

This was very bad. Very, very bad. A reckless Amelia was the last thing he felt able to cope with out here, as warm, scented darkness fell and they were all alone in it.   •

'It makes me want to say and do things. No, that's not true at all. I would normally want to do them. And say them. But I wouldn't actually do them. Or say them. Does that make sense?'

'Yes... No!'

'It makes sense, but you don't want it to,' she puzzled out. 'Oh, I see. You know I want to kiss you again, but you don't want me to.' Her voice was small and sad.

'Of course I want you to – of course I want to!' He hadn't meant to say that at all. But it seemed he couldn't endure that she thought he didn't want to kiss her, because he did. Very, very, very badly.

'Well, then?'

They'd both been looking ahead – staring blindly at the darkening garden and the rising moon, in his case. Trying not to gaze at her, see how lovely she was, because he'd known it would only make things worse. But now she turned to look up at him, her cheeks flushed and her soft lips slightly parted. She was breathing fast, and he could just see the swell of her breasts above the modest neckline of her gown. Her shoulder brushed his arm. Such a slight, accidental contact, to have so powerful an effect. An electric jolt shot through him, from his shoulder to his toes. And other places.

Desperation edged his voice. 'I can't kiss you, because you're not in full command of yourself. You said you wouldn't normally do it. You said that yourself, Amelia. So you must see why I can't.'

'I think I said I would want to, but I wouldn't do it. Normally.'

'Exactly.' *Exactly.*

'So we both want to, and we've both admitted we want to, but we still can't. Even though we did once. And both liked it. Presumably.'

'You were sober then.' How many men, he wondered, would be sitting here in a summer garden in the moonlight trying to persuade this lovely girl – his fiancée – that they mustn't kiss? It wasn't even as though it was a stolen, clandestine moment – they'd been all but forced into each other's arms. It seemed she wanted it as much as he did, or thought she did, which made it so much harder. But he couldn't help it. He couldn't take advantage of her vulnerable state.

But she was triumphant. He had made an error, he realised, and she pounced on it, moving even closer. 'So you'd kiss me now, if you didn't think I was drunk? Which I'm not, by the way.'

'No!'

'So you *don't* want to, after all. Though you said you did a moment ago. It's very confusing. See how I remember what you said before, because I'm not horridly drunk. I'm sure a drunk person wouldn't remember.'

'If I were to kiss you...' This was highly dangerous territory. 'If

I were to kiss you... Amelia, it's not at all a question of wanting to or not wanting to.' This was a bare-faced lie. 'I can't take advantage of you. It would be dishonourable – not the action of a gentleman. You must see that.'

'Well, I'm no gentleman, thank goodness. What if *I* took advantage of *you*? What if I stood up and moved to stand in front of you so I could kiss you? Again?'

And then she did.

28

Marcus had accused her of being drunk, and perhaps she was, but she knew it wasn't the wine. It was him. They were alone here in the warm night at last, and his big, strong body was so close, but not close enough. Occasionally, the soft cloth of his evening coat brushed her skin. She had goosebumps, but not from the cold – from the wanting.

On that memorable occasion, they'd kissed, and it had been wonderful, but since then, she'd been violently assaulted. The last physical contact she'd had with him had been that terrible fall, when he'd saved her, and the brief, precious moments when he'd carried her in his arms afterwards. They'd not been alone since the painfully intense occasion when he'd shared his secrets with her – they had barely seen each other except on those frustrating visits of ceremony he'd paid, when they had not spoken apart from commonplaces about her health, the weather... It had seemed to her that he was avoiding her, and certainly there had been no chance for further closeness between them, or any exchange of confidences. He said he wanted to kiss her, so perhaps he did desire her, lonely and frustrated as he must be, but it seemed he didn't want any more than that. If that was true, she must accept it. Soon, they would part forever.

She was tired of it all. Damn tired of it. Everyone seemed determined to force them together – apart from the people who most emphatically wanted to keep them apart and possibly also wanted her dead. It was more than fatiguing, being so subject to other people's wishes and expectations, whether they meant her well or ill. Marry him immediately – don't marry him at all! Go here, go there, do this, don't do that! It wasn't her immediate family, Rafe and Sophie, Grand-mère and poor Charlie, but it seemed to be almost everyone else.

All she knew, and she knew it with certainty, was that she wanted to kiss Marcus again. Lots of men had wanted to kiss her in the past, had wanted to put their hands on her body. They'd been concerned about their own pleasure, never hers, and perhaps they'd also wanted to compromise her, trap her, steal away her fortune and her freedom. She had not asked for their desire, nor done anything to encourage it. She had fought them off; they'd been repulsive to her. But she wanted to kiss Marcus, and he had said he wanted to kiss her, except that honour prevented him, or some such nonsense. If that was all she could have from him...

'I want to kiss you,' she said now, rising to her feet. 'I don't care what anybody else in the world wants, apart from you. And I know I don't like it when people try to touch me against my will, so in fairness, Major Marcus Thornfalcon, I should ask you, do you object if I kiss you?'

'In fairness? And you won't do it if I say yes, I object?' His voice wasn't steady. But then neither was hers.

'I won't. I am not like those awful people. I will not take advantage of you.'

'God, I wish you would!' he groaned in a sudden moment of piercing honesty.

She was standing between his legs now; it was the only way she could get close enough. Though she was beginning to wonder what *close enough* could possibly be. Closer than this, it seemed. His muscular thighs were parted, and enclosed her. It seemed as though she could feel the warmth of his skin through the fabrics that separated them, though that might not be true. Perhaps the heat was all hers. Silk slid over hot skin, and thin muslin, and over heavier fabric.

'You want me to take advantage of you?'

'You'll have to. Because I won't.'

She put her hands on his broad shoulders to steady herself – no, she put her hands on his shoulders because she wanted to. It wasn't, it turned out, the easiest position in which to kiss him, because his head was too low, his head was... She snuggled in between his thighs and reached out for him, so that she could run her fingers lovingly through his silky hair. He sighed then, and instead of kissing him, she pulled him close. His head lay on her breast; his warm breath tickled her bare skin above the bodice of her gown. She liked that. She could even feel his long eyelashes, tickling. Someone's heart was beating fast, though she wasn't sure if it was his or hers. Both, perhaps. Her senses had never been so heightened. His arms came around her and cradled her; again, silk slid over muslin and skin.

'You're not kissing me,' he said. His voice was a little muffled by her body, and his breath was warm on her flesh. She felt his lips move against her and shivered deliciously. Pressed herself closer, wanting more of this precious contact.

'Well, I can't easily reach. But this is good too, don't you think? Especially if you keep talking.'

'Why...?'

She was almost sure he knew why. He was teasing her. But she was reckless, had she not decided? So she would tell him. 'I like the feel of your mouth against my skin.'

'You do?'

He *was* teasing her. 'Mmm.'

'Well, so do I.' She thought she could feel his lips curving in a smile. 'What else do you like, my lady?'

'Your hair is very soft. I remember noticing that, last time.' She was still running her hands through it, still holding him deliciously close to her.

'Just that?'

'And your legs are... not very soft.'

He'd been gripping her hard between his thighs – perhaps he hadn't realised, because his hold lessened instantly. 'Too tight?' he said.

'*Not* too tight,' she corrected him. 'Tighter, if anything. And I like your hands on me. But they don't move.' They were secure about her waist, which was pleasant, but she had an instinct that there was more they could be doing. A great deal more.

'Believe me,' he said with feeling, 'they could move. I'm having a lot of trouble stopping them from moving.'

'Don't. Don't have the trouble. We have troubles enough.'

He groaned, and his big, warm hands slipped down and cupped her buttocks. They fitted very nicely there, it turned out. Silk slid again, and muslin. Now she could be sure the growing heat wasn't just hers, because his hands were burning through the flimsy fabrics. But she liked it. He squeezed her gently, his thumbs moved on her, and she too moaned a little. Just a tiny sound in the night.

Her nipples were hard, and the thin material that covered her breasts chafed them. They felt heavy, aching, wanting. Could he feel her tight buds against his face, through the bodice of her gown and her chemise? His lips were so close...

He could feel her, she thought, because he pressed his cheek closer, rubbed his face against her, and she whimpered at the contact.

He said raggedly, 'Oh, Amelia, perhaps you should fulfil your promise and kiss me now. It seems like the safest course. Because if you don't...'

'If I don't...?' She stroked his face, the side of it that wasn't pressed against her, exploring the hard planes, enjoying the stubble of evening as it bristled against her palm and fingers. His mouth pressed the soft flesh and she shivered; his tongue licked it, then his teeth nipped the pad of her thumb and made her gasp.

'I fear I'll either turn my head and fall on your breasts like a starving man given food, or pull up your skirts so that I can touch your skin. Your secret places. And surely either thing, Amelia, though wonderful, would be a mistake.'

She heard the wicked pout in her own voice. 'You couldn't do both? It seems to me as you describe it that you could easily do both at once.'

'I could do all sorts of things I shouldn't do. I'm touching you now, and I shouldn't be.'

She said very low, suddenly ashamed and doubtful, 'I know people demand things of you – your sister-in-law, and all those other women. I don't want to be like that, but I fear I am. They don't care what you want, only what they want – it isn't fair. It's no different at all to the way I've been treated. I can see that now. I'm sorry. You don't need to pretend you want me just to make me feel better.'

He shook his head against her breast, and his silky hair caressed her. 'You're not like them, my dear. You couldn't be. And

good God, if you think I am pretending, you are fair and far off. If
we're really talking of my desires...'

'Yes?'

'Amelia, I want more than anything in the world to pull up
your skirts and touch your beautiful bottom with no barrier
between us. I want to pull down your gown and kiss your lovely
breasts. I've said as much, but there is more. I want to slip my
fingers into the curls where your thighs meet and feel your
wetness, and make you wetter – I want you to gasp and moan as I
touch you. I want to make you come, and cry out with the release
of it, and know I did that. I want to lick my fingers to taste you,
and then I want to unbutton myself, here, and slide into you as
you straddle me, and move with you until we both see stars.
That's what *I* want. And yet more. A great deal more.'

She was weak with desire, with the thought of all he'd named,
and felt boneless, liquid almost, in his arms. If he had not held
her so close, she might have fallen. She was wet, as he had said,
and needed his hands and his mouth on her skin, bringing her
the sweet release that felt so tantalisingly close. Needed him
inside her, something she could only imagine, wanted to move
with him, wanted see stars with him.

'God, Marcus...' she breathed.

'But someone will open a door and come to fetch us soon, my
dear,' he said, his voice hoarse with the effort of control. 'You
know they will – their indulgence of a supposedly engaged
couple will only go so far.'

Supposedly – the word, so true and so cruel, hit her like a
bucketful of cold water.

'If they find us like this, doing no more than this, we can
spring apart. It will be obvious, I suppose, that we have been
embracing, but we must imagine they expected something of that
nature. One does not send a man and a woman out into the

summer night together and think that they are discussing the latest fashion in bonnets.' He was still holding her, and his breath still feathered the upper swell of her breast, his thumbs still stroked her bottom. His thighs were still hard about her. 'But if we go any further, there will be no coming back from it. And then you really will have to marry me.'

'You're right,' she told him flatly.

He could hear the sudden alteration in her voice, she knew, because he let her go.

29

Rosanna Wyverne looked at herself critically in the spotted mirror as she used a rag to wipe away the chalk powder and rouge that coloured her face. The light was poor backstage in the shabby little theatre this late in the evening, candles and lamps being expensive, and her dressing room – more of a stuffy cupboard, really – was dark and dingy, but she could see well enough for her purposes. Stronger light wouldn't necessarily have been welcome. *Not bad,* she thought, comforted. *Still not bloody bad.*

The last couple of years had left their mark on her, she had to admit, but that could hardly be surprising. In the spring of 1811, she'd been living in the lap of luxury for more than fifteen years, and had grown accustomed to an army of servants scurrying to obey her every whim. She'd been able to afford the most expensive and outlandish aids to beauty – pineapple water, raw veal, Lotion of the Ladies of Denmark. She could have bathed in fucking asses' milk if she'd wanted to, like a queen. She'd been a marchioness, living in a palace, lying on silk sheets, dripping in jewels – her, Rosie Cooper, from the back slums behind the

Ratcliffe Highway. True, she'd had to do some startling things on those silk sheets, some things she preferred not to dwell on now, in order to get rich and stay rich, as anyone with any wit might expect, the world being what it was. But now her notorious husband was dead and all that was behind her – the good and the bad in her marriage, all gone. She was here, in a dirty little makeshift theatre not so very far, as the crow flew, from where she'd started off. She could smell the familiar old river now – the mud and the shit and all the broken, rotting things. Eau de Limehouse.

How in God's name had she ended up here? Well, that was a tale and a half. She'd gone straight to Bath after Gervais had died and they'd thrown her out of his mansion in the country. That might have been partly her own fault; she could see that now. She'd lost her temper once too often in her panic and shock, had caused memorable scenes. But Bath had been a failure. A humiliation. What was the use of rooms at the best hotel, the finest black silk mourning dresses, and hired carriages with glossy matched horses and smart liveried servants, if nobody apart from the lowest of toadies would so much as talk to her? Her reputation had preceded her; she snorted at her wavering reflection in the glass.

It had preceded her also to louche Brighton, where you'd think standards might have been lower. It had preceded her even to Yorkshire – to Harrogate, to York. She couldn't even get the time of day from anybody in fucking freezing cold Yorkshire, except from hangers-on – parasites who wanted her money and didn't even try very hard to conceal it. Bills had mounted faster than she could have believed: modistes, milliners, jewellers, wine merchants, blood-sucking servants, people who sold mouldy cabbages and stinking candles and most unreasonably expected to be paid for them. Dowager marchionesses of obscure origins who weren't on terms with their late husband's family, it transpired, didn't get much in the way of credit from anybody. But she had to live. She borrowed money from those shady characters who'd agree to lend it to pretty much anybody at extortionate rates, so that the next instalment of her jointure was gone as soon as it arrived, and the next, and still the debts grew and grew somehow. Matters waxed unpleasant with terrifying rapidity. There was talk of prison, and even worse things. Threats of violence, of a pretty face marred.

So it hadn't even been a year after her widowhood when she was forced back to the stage, putting a brave face on it up west. It hadn't been so bad at first, she thought now. Her noble, notorious name had been a draw, written big and bright on the posters, bringing in the guineas.

We are proud to present the lovely Lady Wyverne, the Scandalous Marchioness and talk of the London Ton, in positively her First Appearance on any stage in over fifteen years!

Society people had flocked to see her, even if only to point and stare and snigger, and she hadn't cared – had liked it, in fact, because the Wyvernes, those that were left in possession of all the wealth and estates now her husband was gone, must surely hate it, and that had made her smile. They wouldn't receive her, they wouldn't give her any part of her due, but they couldn't forget her either. Not with her name – and theirs – blazoned everywhere, not when their friends and their enemies both were coming to see her and whispering furiously about it.

But the debts and the duns made it impossible to stay in the fancy theatre. Having your name written a foot high on a poster meant that everyone knew exactly where to find you. There had been more scenes, and the theatre management had not been amused. So now she was here, under another name, but even here they'd tracked her down. The duns were growing even more pressing, their threats more urgent, and the fine silk gowns and fancy horses and all the rest were long gone. She was living hand to mouth again, hating it. All her long, hard journey had brought her back east, from poverty to wealth to poverty again, getting her much-admired bubbies out twice a night for a far less select audience in far less classy pieces. And it was still a form of revenge, in a sick sort of way, though a much less satisfying one. Lots of people, she knew, thought that she was receiving no more nor less than she deserved – sinking back to her natural level in the Thames mud, from which the dissipated lord had so mistakenly raised her. But some less censorious types must think that the Wyverne family had treated her badly – stolen what she was owed as the Marquess's widow. This was an idea she encouraged at every opportunity, though it didn't bring her much consolation any more.

And it wasn't true, of course, not really. Her late husband had been a terrible sinner – the worst kind, the kind that didn't even seem to enjoy it all that much – but there was no denying that he had left her well enough provided for. If his frosty-faced son had wanted to overturn the provisions of his will and leave her penniless, he'd soon found he couldn't. She had that widow's jointure, paid quarterly, and by most people's standards, it was ample. But when you'd been living as a grand lady for so many years – a marquess's mistress and then his wife – it turned out that it was hard to get by on a fixed income that had to cover everything. Impossible, in fact. She hadn't come close to managing it. She'd love to tell herself that if she had the last two years to live again, she'd do it differently – live frugally and sensibly, within her means. Save money for her old age, which loomed closer tonight than it ever had before. But she knew in her heart it wasn't true.

She'd long ago got out of the habit of being sensible, of scraping by.

The quiet theatre and her dark thoughts had lulled her into carelessness. She'd heard no footsteps approaching, but the door creaked open suddenly, dragging her rudely from her bitter musings, and she twisted quickly round to see who it was. It was quite likely to be a most unwelcome visitor, at this time of night, and she was tense, instantly watchful. Men who wanted her and were prepared to pay for their pleasure had been woefully thin on the ground lately – she couldn't fool herself it would be one of them, come to get to know her better after watching her perform. And if by chance it was someone looking for a bit of female company, it'd be no gentleman. Those days were over. If she wasn't careful, she'd soon be back on her knees in the shadow of the rotting dockside warehouses, where she'd started. A bloody great big pointless circle.

It was a cloaked figure – that couldn't be good – but not a man, a woman. Rosanna relaxed a fraction. They surely weren't sending women out to collect on bad debts now. No, she must be some sort of messenger or go-between, some doxy with a note, making a production of it, all wrapped up as if in disguise. Maybe she had aspirations to the stage herself, the foolish jade.

The mysterious visitor put her hood back... No, not a messenger woman, not an abigail, a *lady*. An icy beauty in what she probably thought was a plain gown, though it had still obviously cost a small fortune, youngish but not a green girl, with silvery fair hair that gleamed expensively even here, and unreadable violet-blue eyes.

She looked so out of place in this nasty little room that it was almost laughable, like a visitor from another world. An angel come down from heaven in some piece of stage machinery, just missing her wings. What the devil did such a fine lady want with her? Rosanna would bet Mrs Princum Prancum hadn't come to grant her three wishes, wave a wand and say she could go to the ball and dance with the prince. She'd set to it on a satin sofa with a prince once, but then, given the nature of the prince in question, who hadn't? Not this chilly piece, probably. She seemed like butter wouldn't melt in her mouth, nor anywhere else either, but to Rosanna's experienced eyes, she had a bit of a crazy look about her. Feral. As though all kinds of powerful emotions were being just barely held in check. You might not want to cross her, fine lady or not. She looked like she'd bite.

The strange woman was composed, even in these unfamiliar and lowly surroundings. 'Lady Wyverne,' she said, her voice tinkling like tiny silver bells. She even sounded like money. 'Though we do not know each other yet, I hope you will forgive the informality of my approach, and the lateness of the hour. After all, we have some acquaintances in common – more than acquaintances, I suppose, since they are your family. Your dear stepchildren, to be precise. And perhaps we may discover, if we chat a little, that we have common interests too, you and I, and can help each other. May I sit down? I have a proposition to put to you.'

There was another rickety chair in the tiny room, currently piled high with discarded garments. No lady's maid for Rosanna, not any more. She scooped the soiled clothes up in one economical movement and shoved them all anyhow in the corner. 'Sit down, then, whoever you are. Talk,' she said. 'I'm listening.'

30

When her unexpected visitor had left, Rosanna felt a sudden wave of extreme tiredness sweep over her. It was late now – past time she dragged herself to her aching feet and out of here, back to the cheap and insalubrious lodgings close by that she currently called home. She sighed and rose, pressing the small of her back with her hands and then stretching, but then – would this night never end? – the door creaked open again. And this time, she'd been listening for footsteps, in case the strange lady who'd made her indefinably uneasy might have decided to come back, but she'd heard nothing. Not a whisper.

It was a small, spare man in respectable but not expensive clothing – not quite a stranger from another world, like the woman who had flitted away a few minutes ago, though, because this fellow looked perfectly at home in the broken-down old playhouse, and what was more, she knew him, even though it had been years since she'd last set eyes on him. 'Jesus Christ,' she said blankly. 'What are you doing here, Ezekiel? Come to lock me up at last?'

'Not unless you've done something wrong, Rosie,' Mr

Pennyfeather said genially, seating himself comfortably in the chair that Lavinia Thornfalcon had so lately occupied and looking about him with interest. He missed nothing, she knew. '*Have* you done something wrong, my love?'

'Not lately,' she said shortly. She'd done quite a few things in her time that weren't illegal but still weren't right – but she had no intention of telling him about them. Apart from anything else, they'd be here all night. And he was no innocent, either.

'Well then,' he said, producing a long earthenware bottle and two small, heavy-bottomed tumblers from one of the capacious pockets of his overcoat, 'very happy I am to hear it, both in my official capacity and as an old friend. And that being so, why not take a glass or two of heart's ease with me? You look like you could do with it.'

'Isn't that the truth?' she muttered. She still didn't give the impression of being precisely delighted to see this fresh arrival, but she took the glass of gin and tossed it down all the same, as one accustomed to the action, then held it out for more directly.

'Long day, Rosie?' he asked as he poured. His deep-set eyes were shrewd and bright as he regarded her.

'Long week, long month...'

'Long life!' he finished neatly, toasting her, and draining his glass as quickly as she had.

'It doesn't seem all that likely at the moment.'

'Oh, nonsense, I'm sure, nonsense. You may be in low water just now, but you'll come about. You're still a great lady and a great actress and very lovely woman. A phenomenon. Yes indeed. I don't like to think what Mrs Pennyfeather would say if she saw me with you now, so cosy together. She'd have my guts for garters, so she would.'

'Ezekiel Pennyfeather, you can't gammon me like all the rest, so save your breath to cool your porridge,' she said tartly. 'You always did like to play your little games of pretence, but there's no need to try it on with me. The only Mrs Pennyfeather living is your old besom of a mother, and if she thought you were claiming to be getting cosy with me, she'd laugh herself into a fit. She knows better than that and so do I, and have these last thirty years. You're not in the petticoat line, Zeke, and never were.'

'Well, that could be because you broke my heart in a thousand pieces when I was no more than a green young chub,' he replied, not the least disconcerted. 'Of course I've never looked at another woman since – who would? No one could ever compare to you, my lovely. And didn't your illustrious future career prove my superior taste and judgement?'

She scoffed, and drank, and a little silence, by no means uncomfortable, fell between them.

'More,' he sighed at last, not apparently referring to the gin. 'It's more than thirty years, though, Rosie. We're neither of us getting any younger. And I'm glad to hear from your own lips that you haven't been getting in the suds, and I do devoutly hope that you plan to keep it that way. It'd break my poor old heart all over again to have to take you in charge.'

'You always talked too much, even as a whelp,' she said lazily, stretching and yawning as the gin warmed her. And then when his words sunk in, she straightened and looked at him with fresh suspicion. 'What the devil do you mean?' she shot back.

'The thing is, Rosie, I happen to know the lady who just paid you a visit,' he said calmly.

'My God,' she said, grabbing the bottle and sinking another glass of daffy without blinking, staring back at him fixedly. 'You were following her, Miss Sugar Bubs.'

'That's Lady Sugar Bubs, I'll have you know, and yes, I was,' he admitted with a quick grin that made him look like a mischievous boy again for a moment. 'In the execution of my official duties, of course. And can you imagine how surprised I was when she led me here, pretty much the last place you'd expect a gentry mort of her type to go, all the way from Berkeley Square in a hackney carriage? You could have knocked me down with a feather.'

'We used to say, "You could have knocked me down with a sailor",' she said, suddenly wistful. 'Do you remember?'

'Of course I do. And God knows it was true.'

'Of you and me both, my dear. It's not some trap then, Zeke?'

'Not on my part,' he said gently. 'I had no idea she was coming to see you when we set off on our little adventure, though of course I know now why she did.'

'It's that obvious?'

'She seems to think she's subtle, but she really isn't, Rosie. She's about as subtle as a brick in the face. Did she tell you what she wanted?'

Rosanna shrugged carelessly. 'She means to serve the Wyvernes a bad turn, that's all she said, and thought I might help her. Would pay me handsomely for it. I've no fondness for them, as all the world knows. Neither does she, it seems.'

'And did she tell you why?'

'No, not properly. Some stupid ton catfight, I thought. Why should I care, if she's sporting the blunt?'

'So you don't know that young Lady Amelia Wyverne – your stepdaughter, in case you'd forgotten – has just recently got herself betrothed to Lord Thornfalcon?'

'Who's likely to tell me?' she said with a touch of bitterness. 'I'm not taking tea with the old Queen every Wednesday and chatting about the latest news over little iced cakes. I've never met the chit, and they won't be asking me to the fancy wedding, you can be sure of that.'

'Nor her, if they can help it. She's Lady Thornfalcon, Sugar

Bubs is, and she was married to the present lord's older brother, but he died. She and the current lord were childhood sweethearts first – just like you and me, my love, but a good bit hotter and heavier, is my guess – and she's desperate to take up where they left off. She means to marry him. He's a fine, big figure of a man, my dear, such as any woman might get a yearning for once she's had a taste. Not just a woman, if we're being honest. And then it's a different matter, as you know yourself, to be a wife with an indulgent husband than a poor widow counting out the pennies.'

'Her husband's brother, though? Is that legal?' Despite herself, Rosanna was interested. It was a distraction from her own desperate situation – a glimpse of a world she'd never truly been part of, and which seemed even more distant now.

He held out his hand and rocked it from side to side. 'It's tricksy, like a lot of things – it looks legal if nobody questions it and goes to hell in a handbasket the instant anybody does. But whatever the rights of it, he's not keen on being leg-shackled to her, for which I can't blame him, for in my opinion, she's as mad as a horse, however much of a prime article she is. Now he's engaged himself instead to your young Amelia, and Sugar Bubs is far from pleased, as you'd imagine. And what I'm sure your new friend didn't rush to tell you is that somebody, as yet unidentified, pushed the girl down a set of steps a few days ago in the middle of a ball, and damn near finished her off. Would have, probably, if Thornfalcon hadn't jumped in quick as a flea to save her. Very touching, I hear it was.'

'The chilly bitch did it? That's a bold move. Dangerous. Mind, I did think she looked like she was queer in the attic.'

'Dicked in the nob, for sure, she is. And no, not in person she didn't. Can't have done. But she's up to her pretty neck in it all the same. There's a lot of foolish wenches take her as their heroine, and who knows what they'd do if she asked nicely?'

'And you're investigating.'

He tipped his glass in toast to her, emptied it down his throat, and courteously drained the last drops from the bottle into hers. 'Bow Street's finest, my angel, called in on cases of particular delicacy. Scandals in high life, and so on, such as this.'

'So you're warning me off,' she said slowly. 'For my own protection.'

'Not exactly,' he replied, pulling his chair closer to hers in a confidential manner. 'God forbid I should come between you and a nice little purse of yellow boys, which I know you need just at the moment, being temporarily embarrassed as you are. This is what I have in mind, Rosie...'

31

Amelia and Marcus went back inside the Aubertin mansion of their own free will, not waiting to be fetched, with all the comment that would cause. She couldn't remember later if they'd discussed going back indoors or just done it by silent agreement. If they appeared dishevelled or otherwise distracted after their time alone together on the terrace in the moonlight, nobody was tactless enough to tell them so, and she was grateful for it. She then plucked up her courage and told their hosts that she was very sensible of their many kindnesses, but that she had always since childhood dreamed of being married at Wyverne House, and hoped that they would understand. 'The tenants will all wish to attend, and the household staff, and the grooms and gardeners,' she said winsomely, so sweet, she made herself feel slightly sick, 'and it would be wrong, I think, to deprive them of that pleasure. There was a great celebration when my brother and Lady Wyverne were married, and we could hardly do less, I think.' There was some truth in what she said, she realised as she said it, but as she wasn't actually getting married at all, possibly ever, it didn't signify in the least.

'My dear child,' said Sir Humphrey, much moved, 'though I am sorry, of course, that you cannot find a way to accept our offer, your delicate feelings do you credit. Enormous credit!' And he fished out his handkerchief and blew his nose with some energy. Even Lady Aubertin appeared to find her words unexceptionable and unarguable, which couldn't be a common occurrence, and there was no more talk of Thursday, much to her relief.

Lord Wyverne soon contrived it so that they all began preparing to take their leave, saying firmly that he could see that his sister was tired. They departed, interchanging many expressions of mutual esteem as they parted from their hosts and from the Thornfalcons in the marble atrium.

'Do you, in fact, wish to be married at Wyverne House, Melia?' Rafe said once they were safe in the semi-darkness of the carriage. 'I can appreciate that you would have said almost anything that came into your head this evening to prevent our hosts from quite killing you with kindness, so I don't know if what you told them was true.'

'Perhaps we can leave this discussion until a later date?' Sophie suggested quickly. 'It is important, I agree, but there is no need for such haste, and I think Amelia really is tired, as you said she was. I know I am.'

'Very well,' he responded readily. 'It is exhausting to be the object of such relentless benevolence, it's perfectly true. I am positive they will give you a splendid wedding gift, Amelia – I heard Lady Aubertin muttering something about an epergne. Surely you need nothing more to begin married life with than a truly monstrous silver epergne to set between you and Thornfalcon at the dinner table.'

Amelia made some sound that could have been construed as agreement, and then thought better of it. 'Rafe, please don't question me, because I couldn't bear it now, but the engagement isn't real. It never has been, and I wish now that I had told you long ago. It was all a foolish ploy, to improve my reputation, and matters have become more and more involved, till we find ourselves in this ridiculous situation.' She could feel Sophie stirring, and knew she was about to take responsibility for it all, perhaps risking Rafe's displeasure, and that was the last thing she wanted – more unnecessary conflict to be set at her own door. 'It's my own fault, nobody else's, but I will put an end to it soon enough, I promise you. Can we stop talking about it, I beg you? If you are angry with me for being so reckless and need to tell me so, for which I wouldn't blame you, I am sure it can wait.'

Rafe was silent for a moment. 'I understand you,' he said gently, 'and if Sophie and I should need to have a conversation on this topic, it shall be in private and nothing you should worry about for a second. But it's the cursed legacy of our father, isn't it, making our lives complicated again? Damn him to hell, I wonder if we can ever be free of him? No, I won't say anything more, don't worry. Charlie, I can hear you thinking furiously beside me, and I promise I'll explain, but let's spare Melia, shall we? She's been having a very trying time.'

Amelia, finding herself very close to tears, made a noise that she hoped Rafe would know signified her grateful thanks for his forbearance, and turned her head to gaze sightlessly out of the window at the passing lights, the familiar streets rendered mysterious by the moonlight and the sharp-cut shadows. It was a lovely night still, but she felt thoroughly miserable and on edge, and could not appreciate it. There would be no marriage, and no ridiculous epergne to celebrate it. At least Rafe knew now – that was something to cling to. It was plain that Marcus, though he desired her – he had said as much, in memorable detail that she was bound to believe – would not allow himself to be drawn any further into the coil that she had made for them. The last thing in the world he wanted was to be trapped into marriage with her. *That* was why he had called a halt to their... intimacy. And it seemed to her that desire by itself meant nothing; it was certainly not enough for him to base the rest of his life and all his future happiness on. Probably he, or any man, would desire almost any woman who flung herself at him as shamelessly as she had. The artists ought really to be making prints about *her*, not other, much more blameless females. They merely threw themselves from horses; she forced herself into his arms and... and pressed herself against him. Seized his head and rubbed it... A moan of mortification escaped her.

'What's that, my dear?' Rafe asked.

'Nothing,' she muttered. 'Nothing at all. I merely have a slight headache.'

She went straight up to bed upon reaching home, and fell eventually into a restless sleep, full of confused and fragmentary dreams that sometimes showed Marcus doing all the things he'd said he wanted to do with her, and sometimes showed him pushing her away disdainfully so that she fell down endless flights of steps, from which he showed no inclination at all to save her this time. Lavinia was there too, laughing at her in cold triumph as she tumbled down and down with no end in sight. She was more tired when she woke than she had been the night before, and her feigned headache had become a reality. And all of it was entirely her own fault.

32

Lavinia, Lady Thornfalcon, sat in her blue and silver bedchamber that fine morning, busily writing notes. She had told the household in the strictest of terms that she must not be disturbed, and they were all of them accustomed to obey her without question, with one exception. She could hear that exception, her lovely daughter, shrieking energetically in the distance, but it did not disturb her in the least. The house was full of people, one of whom would no doubt deal with her, probably by bribing her with sweetmeats. Lavinia had more important matters to concern herself with. These matters, after all, concerned Priscilla's future as well as her own.

There was a great deal to organise in a short time, and her Friends must be mobilised in her aid. Most of them had been waiting for such an opportunity, and would ask nothing better than to help their idol to achieve the happiness that they all agreed she so richly deserved. As she now had Rosanna Wyverne's vital co-operation – for a price, naturally – she could set her plan fully in motion. The Wyverne girl would soon be ruined – her notorious stepmother would make quite sure of that.

She would never be received in society again, nor would the rest of her family. Their reputation had been precarious enough already. All it needed to destroy it once and for all was – she tittered to herself genteelly at the thought – a little push. Perfect.

It seemed to Lavinia most unlikely that Marcus would wish to marry the chit when her good name lay in tatters, since it was ridiculous to imagine that he cared for her in the slightest, but it really didn't matter one jot. That was the beauty of it; people were so easy to manipulate for one of her intelligence and insight. She had taken the silly girl's measure in an instant, and was almost positive that she was the sort of idiot who would nobly insist on ending her engagement once she was ruined, rather than dragging the man she loved down into the dirt with her. Lady Amelia would cry off, and since Marcus didn't give a damn about her, he would hardly insist on leading her, unwilling, to the altar. He couldn't – he was a gentleman, and must accept her rejection without argument. Gentlemen were so restricted by their ridiculous honour, which was wonderful as it left a large field open to those who were constrained by no such considerations. To those who were prepared to be utterly ruthless to get what they wanted.

He'd then be free, and Lavinia would redouble her own efforts at seduction, and eventually, she could not doubt that she would be successful. If Marcus found her warm and naked in his bed one night, she thought, with the Wyverne girl lost to him forever, he would not have the strength to resist her. She had not failed to notice that he dared not lay a hand on her now, not so much as a finger, and not, she thought complacently, because he found her repulsive. That was a preposterous idea. The reverse was true: if once he touched her, desire would overwhelm him and he would be hers entirely again.

He *was* hers, and always would be. She would give him a son, as quickly as possible, and there would be no more ridiculous talk about the marriage being voided; Papa was an influential man, and had promised he would make certain of that, no matter how many bribes he might have to pay. She would be *the* Lady Thornfalcon again, with all the status of a wife and not a poor, sad widow, and this time she would remain so. There would be no more need for accidents; she and Marcus would be blissfully happy, as they always should have been, the last eight years forgotten. Ambrose had loved her – worshipped her – as was her right, but he had been so dull, loving the country, never wanting to spend the Season in London. She had warned him that he shouldn't oppose her, because people who opposed her never prospered, but he had ignored her warning and now he was dead. Really, it had been his own fault.

And if she and Marcus *weren't* blissfully happy, after a year or two and a son or two, well... she had rid herself of an inconvenient husband before and got away with it. If necessary, she would do so again. But this time, only once her position was entirely secure. No more mistakes. If his mother and sister stood in her way, they too might find themselves unexpectedly unwell. The girl Helena was irrelevant and could easily be married off to somebody or other, preferably somebody who lived a good long way away in some tumbledown castle in Scotland – she would see to that as soon as possible. And the old lady was quite feeble enough already, which would make it even easier. A slip on the stairs – well, perhaps not that, but she would think of something. She was so clever and resourceful. And nobody in the world had the slightest suspicion of it. She had run rings round that bumbling Bow Street Runner; she ran rings round everyone.

She was writing what was effectively the same note a score of times, pressing hard with her pen to underline significant parts, and would have her maid or one of the other servants deliver them – discreetly, of course. She wasn't so foolish as to put her name to the missive, and was disguising her hand as she wrote. If she should later be charged with responsibility, though she was sure she wouldn't be, she would be able to deny it without blinking. And really, even if she had to admit authorship, there was nothing criminal in what she proposed. There would be a touching family reunion in a very public place – again, she smiled at the thought – and all she was doing was inviting a few friends to witness it.

The notes said:

Supporters of Lavinia! You have spoken fine words in praise of your Persecuted Heroine, but it has not been enough. It is time for her suffering to be put to an end. If you attend the Opera House Masquerade on Saturday, you will be present to witness a shocking event that will change everything for the better. An Unworthy, Base Wretch of a Female will receive her just desserts, and you shall see it happen.

All the Poor Unfortunate Lady you so love could ask of you is that you tell the world of what you have seen. To bear witness will be enough. Victory is near, and you may, if you have the courage, play a part in it that will never be forgotten.

I am confident that She may depend on your enduring affection.

A Friend

33

Amelia's downcast state did not improve over the next few days, which were a dizzying whirl of social engagements – balls, breakfasts, dinners and picnics. When they were at home, a great number of calls were made on her and Sophie, and cards were left for their attention by ladies who had never previously paid them such honour. The doorknocker was never still, and the mantel was thick with invitations for yet more events in the coming weeks.

The attack on her seemed to have brought about a noticeable change in the way she was viewed by the greater part of society. Perhaps even some of the more sensible Friends of Lavinia could see that things had gone too far, and welcomed this opportunity to pull back and to moderate their behaviour before any more harm was done. Mr Pennyfeather had not been seen or heard of in a while, and Sophie had agreed that this must mean that his enquiries had petered out into nothing, as they had always suspected that they might. Probably, it was for the best – she had had enough of scandal.

And so there was no more hissing and whispering when she

danced with Lord Thornfalcon, and though she still attracted glares, there were far fewer of them, and they could be ignored. Though Miss Muswell and Miss Archer still scowled at her, Miss Lancaster actually went so far as to smile feebly at her, and pass a remark about the fine weather.

If there were still any whispers at all about her reputation, she did not hear them, and the men who had previously made her life miserable by their unwelcome attentions no longer bothered her in the least. It was ironic, she thought, that her plan had essentially worked exactly as she had hoped, and yet she was thoroughly miserable in a manner she could not have anticipated.

She saw Marcus, of course, but always in company, and when they danced together or drove together in his phaeton, they were always surrounded by people, and had no sort of private conversation. She could not doubt that he was avoiding her on purpose; his expression was as closed to her as it had been when they had first met. The conviction grew upon her that he was waiting for her to tell him that she must break off their engagement, as she had always planned to do. He might be impatient for such an event, impatient to move on with his life – but naturally, he would never betray as much to her.

She ought to do it. The intimacy between them – the dances, the drives, the fact that she was acknowledged by all the world as his prospective bride – would end then, but it was illusory in any case. It must be, if they never spoke in private nor shared any part of their private thoughts, as once, briefly, it had seemed that they might. A kiss and a... whatever their second moment of physical connection had been, they counted for very little, and she must not dwell on them. She needed to find strength enough to end this once and for all.

But still she hesitated. She might tell herself that it would be better to wait till the Season came to an end – that there'd be less gossip that way, which would be better for both of them and for their families. She might even think that she simply could not bear being the subject of rumour and conjecture so soon, and that she could surely be permitted a little respite from it. But neither of these reasons for staying silent were genuine. The sad fact was, once she told him it was over, and once all the world knew it too, she would no longer see him. Not really. He might be glimpsed in the distance, like any stranger, or acknowledged with a slight, awkward smile at some social event. But they would not speak, or dance, or ever be together again even in the unsatisfactory ways they were now. And sometimes, it seemed to her that she couldn't bear it. All the colour would go out of her world, she thought, if he was no longer a part of it. She realised how foolish that was – she barely knew him, and their betrothal had never been real. But it was what she felt, even as she despised herself for the weakness of it.

It was in this mood of despondency that Amelia received a note early one afternoon. It was a mysterious missive, left by some errand boy who had, she was told, impressed upon the maid who received it that it must be passed to its recipient only when she was alone. Presumably, money had changed hands to ensure that this would be so, but once she opened it, all such rational thoughts were driven from her head.

My lady, you must attend the Opera House Masquerade tonight! Come alone, tell no one, burn this.

Lord Thornfalcon is in the greatest peril – his life as well as his reputation – and only you can save him. Wear a dark-red domino and arrive at ten o'clock. I will be watching out for you. Do not fail.

A well-wisher

Amelia stared at the extraordinary words until they swam in front of her eyes. At first glance, they appeared preposterous – what peril could he possibly be in that she could save him from by attending a dubious masquerade in a place respectable young ladies certainly never went alone? It might as well have had *THIS IS A TRAP* inscribed upon it in red ink capitals. But she thought she knew who had sent the letter – she thought it must be Lavinia Thornfalcon. And that changed everything. It might easily still be a trap, meant to damage her, but perhaps that didn't matter.

There were not many people who knew the disreputable secret – supposing it was true – that Lavinia and Marcus shared. The secret of the child's birth. It wasn't important whether it was true or not, after all. If Lavinia was truly desperate, she might reveal it, and that would be terrible. It was like a loaded gun pointed at his head, and none of the gossip any of them had ever suffered would be as much as a drop in the ocean compared to that. If it were ever revealed that he had lain with his brother's wife – she had not been his wife at the time, but nobody would care for that – his reputation would be utterly ruined. He was *not* a rake, and did not deserve to be seen as one by the world. Lavinia's good name would be destroyed too, and so would her daughter's, but perhaps she did not care for that if she was desperate.

But if Amelia made it plain that she had no intention of marrying him, if she swore to break off the engagement directly and kept her promise, perhaps Lavinia would grow calmer. Amelia did not know if Marcus would ever marry Lavinia, assuming he were free to do so; she thought not, since he appeared rather to dislike and distrust her than to love her. But that was not within her control; all she could do was end this farce and set him free. Which meant that she would go to the

Opera House, no matter the risk to herself, and tell Lavinia so to her face.

34

It was all surprisingly straightforward. If Sophie had been present, Amelia might have told her where she was going, as a form of insurance against any mishap, but she was not – she and Rafe had taken little Louis out of London for a night or two, to visit Rafe's mother's family in Essex. The Marquess had had very little contact with any of his maternal relatives in the past, but one of his cousins had recently reached out to him to mend fences, and, as Lord Wyverne had said drily, they had few enough presentable connections to be glad of it, and to accept the unexpected invitation. Amelia and Charlie had no blood ties to these people, and as a result had not been included. They dined alone, chatting over indifferent topics, and soon after dinner, she pleaded the headache and went up to bed; nothing could be easier. Charlie, bless the boy, was the least suspicious person in nature.

* * *

The hands of the silver clock in her bedchamber moved agonisingly slowly as she paced the room, but at last it was time to make her way very carefully and quietly down the back stairs. Her maid had been bribed again, this time by her, and was waiting for her by the entrance to the area, holding the dark-red domino. Amelia had worn this once before, to a ball a few weeks ago, and could only assume that Lavinia – it must be Lavinia – had been paying attention. Perhaps she even knew through her spying of Sophie's absence, which was an uncomfortable thought.

The abigail had called up a hackney carriage, as they had arranged, and assured her mistress that it was waiting a little way down the street. The girl didn't appear to be nervous – she seemed quite astonishingly practised at clandestine behaviour, which she had certainly not learned in Amelia's employ. *I could have been meeting secretly with Marcus all this time*, she thought dully. *We could have been spending time together. But probably, he would not have wanted to – he showed no signs of it. And it is too late now.*

Amelia made her way up the steps and along the pavement to the vehicle, and climbed swiftly in, feeling enormously conspicuous. But nobody spoke to her or tried to stop her, and soon they were rattling away over the cobbles towards Covent Garden. She had no idea how she'd get home from such a highly unsafe area for a woman alone, even in daylight, but she could not allow that to deter her. She had a mask clutched tightly in her hand – a plain black loo mask – and she put it on, fumbling with the strings. How was it possible to feel horribly nervous and perfectly ridiculous at the same time?

She had some money in her purse. She realised now that she didn't know if one was supposed to obtain tickets for the masquerade in advance – how could she know this sort of detail, when she had never been? But surely, if someone urgently wanted her there, they would have thought of that, and perhaps paid for her to enter. And it seemed they had, for when she reached the impressive building, just on the appointed hour, she was admitted by a burly attendant, who shot her a penetrating glance and waved her in without question.

There was no point scanning the throng for slim women of medium height who were also masked and wearing dominoes; that description would cover a large proportion of the people present, any one of whom could be Lavinia Thornfalcon in disguise. The note had said that her correspondent would find her – *very well, let her do so.* Amelia stood to one side in the entrance hall and waited. What else could she do?

It was a busy, lively crowd. Those who did not sport dominoes were elaborately costumed in all manner of inventive and colourful ways, and people were laughing and calling to each other in a manner that would be considered not at all the thing at a gathering of the haut ton, where aristocratic indifference generally prevailed. Perhaps such open enjoyment was vulgar – Amelia could very easily imagine what her Aunt Keswick would have to say about it all, and her face while she said it – but it also looked to be enormous fun, at least at this early stage of the evening. No doubt, like an event at Vauxhall Gardens, it would be unsafe and rowdy later, and one would need protection from unwelcome advances. Amelia had thought of this while dressing, and had worn her sturdy shoes and once more concealed pins about her person, including the long, wickedly sharp ones in her hair. It had been a long time since she'd felt the need to equip herself thus, and she'd wondered if, after all her scheming, she would be obliged to do so again, forever, once she was no longer betrothed. But that was a pointless reflection, and she had done her best to banish it. It would be a sad thing indeed if these weeks as

Marcus's false fiancée had served only to make her less brave than she had been before she met him.

A voice said in her ear, making her start, 'I am glad to see you took the note you received seriously, Lady Amelia.'

She turned swiftly, a sudden lurch in her stomach assailing her. She knew, even before she saw the tall, statuesque woman who stood beside her, smiling down at her with painted lips, that that rich, melodious voice did not belong to Lavinia Thornfalcon. It was a complete stranger who had accosted her and who somehow knew her identity.

They regarded each other in tense silence for a moment. The woman had a black domino thrown back a little over her shoulders to display a fiery red, shockingly low-cut gown and a barely covered, magnificent bosom. Her hood was up, but still gave a glimpse of rich blonde curls at her brow. She was beautiful – the mask did not conceal this – and not young, perhaps in her forties or fifties, her face skilfully painted. Amelia was sure she had never laid eyes on her before, and yet...

'I would offer to unmask,' the stranger said, 'but there would be little point, because I've realised you don't know me from Eve. And that's a shocking thing, isn't it, my dear, when you consider that I'm your own stepmama?'

'Lady Wyverne!' Amelia gasped. And then she asked in puzzlement, 'Was it you who wrote to me, then? I had thought it was another.'

'Oh, it was,' Rosanna said, still smiling rather maliciously. 'I have a nickname for her, which perhaps I won't share with you, but you know her as Lady Thornfalcon. Lavinia. And I must tell you that she brought you here tonight on purpose to ruin you.'

'I thought she might have done,' said Amelia steadily, since this was not news to her, but merely confirmation of her suspicions. 'But I don't know what you're doing here, and why you seem to know all about her plan – unless you're her accomplice? Do you intend to participate in my ruin?' A few weeks ago, this fresh disaster would have horrified her; now she was just vaguely interested.

'She thinks I am to be the instrument of it,' Rosanna Wyverne replied, her fine eyes sparkling behind the mask. 'She came to me because she understood that I might well want revenge on your family for the way I have been treated.'

'Have you been treated badly? I am sorry if this is so. I know I have never harmed you, though perhaps I have spoken carelessly of you in private – not in public – when I should not have done, since I don't know you. I've fast been learning how pernicious gossip is – all gossip. But as far as Rafe is concerned, I think he showed you a fair amount of forbearance, and you might acknowledge it. After all, you spread a shocking story about him that was untrue, and that damaged him greatly. To be thought the lover of his stepmother when he was little more than a boy was dreadful for him.'

'Has he told you of it, his innocent little sister? I am somewhat surprised, but I can't deny I was first responsible for the rumour, though others spread it with great abandon afterwards.' Was that regret in the woman's voice? It seemed unlikely. 'But we should not stay here in idle chat, where anyone can see us. Let us go apart and talk, but make it quick. If we remain in such a public place, that woman who loathes you so much will be able to carry out her plan and it will be too late to stop her.'

'I don't understand. Don't you mean to help her?'

'I did intend to, I won't lie. And she has certainly paid me handsomely – in advance, as I insisted – and even bought me this fine gown so I might present a suitable figure here. But no, I don't, as it happens. I have been persuaded by an old friend to think better of it. Now come away, girl, before she sees us!'

Rosanna took her arm in a strong grip and hurried her out of the vestibule into one of the long corridors that led to the boxes. People were passing, laughing and chattering as they made their way to their places, but nobody paid them any attention; Lady Wyverne angled their position so that her own back, clad in sober black, was to the passing crowd, and Amelia's bright domino was somewhat concealed behind her body.

'There isn't much time,' the older lady said energetically. It seemed to Amelia that she was enjoying the drama of the occasion, though for her part, she was not. 'Her plan is for me to confront you, in the most public setting possible, in such a way to make it clear that we are on intimate terms, as a green girl like you should not be with a woman of my reputation. She made no bones about that – the fact that I'm poison to respectable people – though of course I knew it already. She's arranged for some of her Friends to be here – though there won't be as many as she thinks – to witness the scandalous meeting and spread it abroad so far and so fast so that your good name would never recover from it.'

'Thank you, then,' Amelia said instantly. 'I don't know why you've changed your mind and decided to warn me, but thank you for it.'

'I'm not quite sure why I did either,' Rosanna said frankly. 'I suppose it's true enough that you've never harmed me – how could you? You were no more than a child. And as for your brother, the older one, I mean, not the young gudgeon, I did him wrong and no pitch hot. He was just a greenhorn when I first met him and deserved much better from his stepmama. I could blame your father for everything I did in those days, but... Well, talking pays no toll. An old friend of mine came to see me unexpectedly a few days ago, and I suppose he reminded me that I was a young girl myself once. I've never been what you'd call a good 'un, but I don't need to go round spreading misery either when there's enough in the world already. And that Lavinia, for all she looks so prim and proper, she's a terrible bad lot – a proper hellcat.'

Amelia didn't understand everything that her stepmother said – she used such queer words sometimes – but she certainly got the gist of it. 'I know she is. But I came here to tell her that I had no intention of marrying Lord Thornfalcon, so she might as well leave me be. I can't hand him over to her – that's up to him, he's not a parcel – but I won't be in her way any more.'

'I'm not sure she'll ever leave you be, whatever you do or don't do. She's got her nasty cold eye fixed on you. It's my opinion, and my friend's too, that she's not quite right in the head. She's a woman obsessed, as you might say, and that makes her more dangerous than you know. And that's what I need to tell you – my friend has arranged matters so that she springs her own trap. He seems to have taken a powerful dislike to her, and he's not a man you'd want to get on the wrong side of, as she's about to learn.'

'Who is he?' Amelia couldn't imagine who could possibly be interested enough in her affairs to be intervening on her behalf and yet also be a friend of her stepmother.

'It's only me, Lady Amelia – Ezekiel Pennyfeather.'

Amelia had been so absorbed in her intense conversation that she had not heard or seen anyone approach; perhaps too the Bow Street Runner had learned to be particularly stealthy in his movements. For he was here now, close by, standing behind Rosanna and smiling at them both, small and crumpled and unimpressive as ever, but with a light in his eyes that bespoke his utter self-confidence and mastery of the scene.

'Good God, Zeke, must you creep about like an area sneak at midnight and make a woman jump clean out of her skin?' said his friend in exasperation, but Amelia didn't think she was really angry, only wound up. 'Is it all set up?'

'It is, my dear, and it is time for us to go and throw the dice. Rosie, you have your part, and I am sure you will make it all come off perfectly. But Lady Amelia, I have a black domino for you – that red one is far too conspicuous, and Sugar—Lady Thornfalcon will be looking out for you impatiently by now. I think it is much better if she does not see you at all, so she has no chance to abuse you and draw unnecessary attention to your presence.'

Amelia obediently took off her cloak and put on the other that he handed to her, pulling up the hood to cover her hair so that she was, she hoped, quite unrecognisable. She could see the sense in what he said, though she had not the least idea what was about to happen. He bundled her own domino away under his arm and led them back down the corridor, into the huge auditorium, which had been transformed for the evening into a sort of grand assembly room.

The boxes were almost full by now and the stage was covered in whirling couples; it was a colourful scene, with candlelight reflecting off the gilded decoration and catching sparks from the gold and silver lace and sequins that adorned many of the more exotic costumes. The orchestra was playing a country dance with vigour, those who were not dancing were making a great deal of merry noise of their own, and Amelia could not imagine how any scene, however dramatic, could unroll here that would attract a single person's attention away from their own exuberant pursuit of pleasure.

'There she is,' said Mr Pennyfeather, touching their shoulders and nodding in the direction of the entranceway. 'I've had my eye on her since she arrived, and I have a couple of reliable men watching her too. She thinks she's missed you in the crowd, look, and she's getting agitated now.'

There was no doubt that he was right. The woman was disguised in a black domino much like their own, but the tension that radiated from her slight figure was unmistakeable, and her head was in constant motion, scanning the groups of people that passed to and fro with desperate focus. There were three or four persons present in red dominoes, but none, as it happened, who could have been Amelia herself – they were either too tall, too short, or too obviously male. And so the anxious eyes flitted backwards and forwards in constant restless motion, seeking her victim.

Lavinia wasn't alone. Several cloaked figures had gathered around her in a sort of anxious huddle, though she paid no attention to them at all. Watching them, Amelia thought it was obvious that they were very young ladies, and also that most of them were exceedingly nervous now that they found themselves actually here, having presumably deceived their parents or guardians so that they might attend an event that was by no means proper, since it was open to the public with no means of control upon who attended as long as they could afford it. They clustered together as if for protection, and shrank away if any stranger seemed to pass too close. They had come at Lavinia's call, but they were no means happy about it.

The dance came to an end, and there was a brief lull as the musicians prepared for the next set; the stage cleared a little as some of the dancers decided to seek rest or refreshment or new partners. 'Let's have some fun, Rosie,' Mr Pennyfeather said unexpectedly, shaking out the red domino and wrapping it adroitly around himself. Amelia realised that she and he were much of a height, and at a glance, they would be indistinguishable. He slipped easily through the crowd, and she saw the precise moment that Lavinia spotted him – her whole posture changed, becoming triumphant, the attitude of a predator who had sighted her defenceless prey. A ripple of excitement seemed to run through the little group around her; they saw it too, especially since they had presumably been prepared and waiting for such a sign.

'My turn to go on stage,' said Rosanna, grinning at her. 'My God, there's no better feeling!' And she headed after her friend, the domino flung back still to show her red gown. The crowd parted before her impressive figure, which drew admiring looks from many men and quite other sorts of stares from the women who accompanied them.

'You – you in the red domino!' she said in rich, carrying tones that must have served her well upon the stage. 'Stop!'

35

Mr Pennyfeather's pace faltered when he was so loudly and abruptly addressed, he stood stock still for a long second or two, and then he turned to face his accuser. A space opened up around him as people unconsciously pulled away. No doubt they were eager to witness this unscheduled piece of entertainment, but equally keen not to be too closely involved in it. He was the very picture in stance and gesture of a frightened young woman, shrinking from public attention. Rosanna was quite close to him now, but she did not lower her voice. 'Take off your hood and mask and reveal yourself,' she said in ringing accents, 'or I will do it for you, and I promise you that you shall not like it!'

Amelia was watching Lavinia intently as the red-robed figure raised shaking hands and let down the hood, then ripped off the mask with incredible quickness. The woman's triumph changed to puzzlement and then to horror; it was plain that she recognised the Runner, and equally clear that her quick brain realised that more was wrong here than a simple mistake. Rosanna was smiling broadly, and nobody could think that she had made an error in identification.

'I am an officer in the employ of the Bow Street Magistrates, here about my lawful business,' said Mr Pennyfeather loudly, his whole bearing and mien changed in an instant in a remarkable fashion. A fascinated murmur ran through the crowd. Now that the attention was off her and fully on her former quarry, Rosanna began making her way slowly and carefully back through the crowd to Amelia's side. Nobody paid the least attention to her now; the Runner held them all in the palm of his hand as he spoke.

'I am come to make an arrest for blackmail, attempted murder – and, most heinous of crimes, murder itself! I arrest you, Lavinia Thornfalcon, and I suggest you come quietly, or it will be the worse for you.'

There was a great outcry from the assembled people, and the orchestra, which had just started up again, broke off in a discordant scraping of fiddles as they became aware of the disturbance. Everyone in the body of the theatre was staring and pointing, and those in boxes leaned forward shamelessly for a better view, as did the fascinated musicians. Mr Pennyfeather made a sort of quick dart through the crowd and seized Lavinia by the arm, and a pair of stout individuals who could only have been fellow Runners materialised out of the throng at either side of him and converged relentlessly on his prey. One of them pulled back her hood, and her lovely, silver-gilt hair was revealed. The more impressionable members of the audience gasped to see her, so beautiful as she was and so obviously a lady of high rank. 'That mask needs to come off too,' Pennyfeather said sternly. 'I have to be certain sure I've got the right woman in such a serious matter.' Rough hands tugged at the strings for a second and she was exposed to public view, her enormous eyes wild and her face set in lines of anger and disbelief.

'This is nonsense!' she cried angrily. She didn't seem to be afraid, only furious. 'Complete nonsense, and I will make sure you pay for it! You will wish you had never set eyes on me before you are done. *You* will be the one rotting in prison, you insolent nobody – my father is a powerful man and will make sure of it. I am quite innocent of everything you accuse me of! I do not know why you are persecuting me so, but you will be sorry for it soon enough!'

'I don't think I will, my lady. I have a witness whom I shall not name who will swear that you blackmailed her into pushing an innocent young woman down a flight of steps, which could easily have killed her,' said Mr Pennyfeather inexorably, not in the least cowed by her defiance. He seemed quite glad, Amelia thought, to have this opportunity to share Lavinia's crimes with all the world. No doubt it was more usual to hurry arrested persons away without such a public recitation of their misdeeds, but she had chosen to take the Runner on and it seemed she must take her medicine now. 'Scared for her own life, she was, poor silly creature, when you threatened her, as you were so wild and menacing that she did not know which way to turn. And as for murder...'

The group of former Friends who had surrounded their idol had shrunk as far away as they could well go, pulling back even their garments as though contact with her would sully them. Amelia thought that if any one of them should be charged with knowing Lavinia, still less with having come here to support her and help her engineer another woman's humiliation, they would play St Peter's part and deny her with great emphasis, as many times as proved necessary.

'It is preposterous to accuse me of murder!' Lady Thornfalcon said, putting out her hands wide in a highly theatrical gesture and looking about her for confirmation, as if to say, *I am beautiful, so very beautiful, and therefore, I must be innocent! How could a woman with such a face commit any sort of crime?*

'There's no denying you got away with it for a good long while,' said the Runner complacently, 'but I have been down in Somerset doing a bit of investigating, and I believe I can make a case for the deliberate and premeditated killing by poison... of your own husband.'

The sound that ran around the huge auditorium was an extraordinary one: a sort of sibilant whisper of shock and disgust. Amelia too was astonished, and looked at her stepmother in sharp enquiry. Rosanna shrugged expansively and whispered, 'I don't know any of this part of it. Zeke plays his cards very close to his chest, and always has. But no wonder he didn't want me getting mixed up with her. Murder, he says! I'm as shocked as you are.'

'Now, I'm an officer of the law and not a canting parson,' Pennyfeather went on loudly, clearly relishing his large, captive audience, 'but when a moral lesson smacks you round the face, as you might say, it seems to me that others would do well to heed it. I dare say every married body here has had their moments of irritability with their life's partner. I'm sure Mrs P, woman in a million as she is, has had many such with me, not to speak of my own sentiments. Little daily habits can grate on your nerves, as we all know. Snoring and the like. Jiggling of the legs, loud slurping of beverages. But as for murdering your loved one by putting something nasty in their tea, well, however much they slurp it, that's a step too far, and is bound to get found out in the end. Because once a person starts off a-murdering, they most often find they can't stop. If you'd called a halt at just one victim, my dear, it's likely you'd have got away with it, because you're a clever piece, as I'd be the first to acknowledge.' He gave his prisoner a friendly sort of a shake. 'But you couldn't stop, could you? They never can, ladies and gents! They never can.' And on that unanswerable remark, he and his colleagues led her away, with no more than a conspiratorial grin in the direction of Amelia and Rosanna. This was no time or place for explanations.

'Good God,' Amelia said blankly as the door closed behind them and the room erupted into excited comment. 'Can it be true?'

'If Zeke says it is, I dare say it is. Not that she'll hang for it like an ordinary woman would. If I'd bumped your father off, for all his wickedness, I'd have been up swinging on the nubbing cheat for all to see within a bare fortnight. What a scandal that would have been for the Wyvernes! But this fancy bit won't be paying that price, I'll go bail. You wait and see if I'm right.'

'I don't know exactly what the nubbing cheat is, but I expect that doesn't matter,' Amelia said. 'You didn't murder my father, did you? I feel as though I ought to ask. He did die very suddenly, or so I understand.'

Rosanna laughed mirthlessly. 'That I didn't! He had a paralytic seizure, just like they told you. Whatever he was, and he was a proper bad lot, you know, a rakehell and a satyr and worse, I'd hardly kill the goose that laid the golden egg, now, would I? I was dependent on him, remember, for all that came with being a marchioness. All those fine things I thought I couldn't live without. Jewels and silks and servants and such. Yes,' she added impatiently, seeing what her stepdaughter was about to say, 'I get a jointure now he's dead. It's very generous. But I couldn't manage to live on it, and I've got into debt so deep, it's hard to see how I can ever get out.'

'We should help you,' Amelia said impulsively. 'You've helped me, and you didn't need to.'

'I'd bleed you dry and you'd soon regret it,' was the cheerful answer. 'You're talking to me now, but you know you can't afford to be seen with me in public. But I'm well blunted, just at the moment, because of what the murdering wench paid me, and I've a mind to go abroad and leave all my debts and my creditors behind. I've had enough of England, and it seems like England has had enough of me. You Wyvernes won't be sorry to see the back of me either. Perhaps your precious reputations will recover in the end if I make myself scarce.'

'I'm not sure it matters, really. Anything that can be destroyed so easily by baseless gossip can't be worth much in the first place, it seems to me. But where will you go? We're at war with practically everybody, and I should think that would make things rather difficult for you.'

'It's a shame and no mistake,' Rosanna acknowledged wistfully, 'because I quite fancy Paris. I've never been – your father had an unaccountable dislike of risking getting his head chopped off, even before the bloody wars started. Perhaps I should be bold and head for America instead.'

'We're at war with them too,' Amelia said, suppressing an impulse to laugh.

Her stepmother waved this inconvenient fact away as a mere detail. 'I'm sure there are ships slipping through the blockade every day of the week. There's always smuggling to be done and profit to be had, and if I don't have any connections down on the docks, I'll wager Zeke does. He knows everybody. And I'm positive I could make a big splash in New York or Boston. I expect they have theatres – they must have. "The notorious Lady Wyverne appearing for the first time on an American stage!" Can't you see it?'

'I can,' Amelia admitted. 'I should wish you good fortune, then. Not that I think you need it. It seems to me that you can very well look after yourself.'

The older woman grinned at her wryly. 'Well, I've needed to often enough in my life; I should be an old hand at it by now. Talking of which, how's that sister-in-law of yours? She's a cunning baggage and no mistake. I hired her as your old grand-mother's companion, when I was in my pomp, and before I could so much as blink, she was cosying up to your brother with designs on him plain for all to see. I bet she never told you about all that.' There was just a faint trace of malice still in her voice, and though Amelia couldn't help liking her, she wasn't sure she was entirely to be trusted, and certainly not where Sophie – the new Lady Wyverne, her replacement – was concerned.

'It's none of my business how they met.' It was also true that Amelia didn't feel her own conscience was clear enough these days to want to sit in judgement on anyone else. 'They're very happy, and they have a baby son they both dote on. I can't imagine anyone else who would suit Rafe half so well. He's a different man since he met her – as though the weight of the world has been lifted off his shoulders. He was always worried and anxious before, and seemed much older than his years.'

'If that's to my account, there's no need to rub it in. I've said I wronged him, haven't I? I'm no hand at apologising – I don't have a lot of practice at it – but will you tell him for me that I'm sorry? I doubt he'll credit it, but I really am. Some of the things I did when I was married to your father don't sit easy in my mind, and the way I treated him is one of them.'

'I will tell him, ma'am, I promise.'

It seemed there was nothing more to be said, but then Rosanna added abruptly, as if against her will, 'I can't ever be a mother to you, or to anybody, God knows, the idea is ridiculous, and I dare say you've wished me at Jericho often enough since you've been old enough to know who and what I am. I know my existence by itself makes things harder for you. But when people tell you of all the scandalous things I've done, which I'm sure they will once you're married and more fit to hear them...' She stopped, and then said, 'The gossip's probably all true in my case;

the most malicious old cat alive would struggle to invent things when what I've really done is bad enough. I can't dodge the tittle-tattle – I expect it'll follow me even to America and I'll end up selling myself again, one way or another. But you don't have to – not in the ways I have, and not in the ways so many society ladies do. One man or a dozen – you'd be surprised how little difference it makes if that one man's cruel, and so many of them are. Don't do anything because a man tries to make you, girl. Don't do anything that hurts you just so you can keep him. It isn't worth it. No man's worth it, and a bad man's worth less than nothing, no matter if he has a fancy title and riches and a bloody big house.' And with these words of wisdom, she turned and melted away into the crowd, and in a moment, Amelia couldn't see her any more.

She shook her head to clear it. The music had started up again, and many more couples had taken to the stage, keen to continue enjoying their evening. Others were gossiping hard, shocked faces outnumbered by gleeful ones. Had it ever happened before that a woman – a lady of quality – had been dragged by the Bow Street Runners from the middle of a masquerade at the Opera House? And the charge was murder. It would be a subject of scandal for days or even weeks, and these fortunate individuals could say that they had been here to see it, every thrilling moment of it. That was worth the price of admission by itself.

But nobody was paying Amelia herself the least attention, and she thought she should profit from it by leaving. She had to make her way across London – she hoped she would be able to hail a hackney, and that the driver of it would not take it into his head to murder her, or kidnap her for purposes she'd prefer not to contemplate. Having got her here – for she now knew that although Lavinia had thought she had been pulling the strings, the real author of the evening's proceedings had been Mr Pennyfeather – she thought the Runner might have arranged that she should get home safely too. After all, it hadn't been strictly necessary to bring her here to witness Lavinia's downfall, except as some demonstration of the operation of justice. But it seemed that even a being as omniscient as he appeared to be couldn't think of absolutely everything.

Amelia turned and began pushing her way through the crowd towards the exit. It was ridiculously difficult to get by the knots of avidly chattering people, and it seemed her way was blocked at last by a particularly solid body – a man, a very tall one, who showed no disposition to let her pass. *Not now, please God,* she thought, *I'm really not in the humour to be accosted now. I just want to go home!* She looked up, scowling, ready to stamp on a foot or drive a pin deep into someone's groping hand.

But it was Marcus.

36

Marcus had had a thoroughly disagreeable few days, ever since the nightmare evening of Sir Humphrey's dinner. He'd gone home from that event in a kind of daze and lain awake all night, prey to all manner of roiling thoughts. It wasn't even the intense, almost painful sexual frustration he was experiencing that tormented him so. Nor even, really, the shame of the shockingly frank things he'd said to Amelia, though they brought a fiery colour to his cheeks as he lay in the darkness and remembered them in excruciating detail. He'd told her he wanted to... And God knows he had wanted to, and did still want to. All that he'd said and much, much more. But that wasn't by any means the worst of it.

It was the knowledge that he loved her that had hit him like a thunderbolt. He thought himself an idiot for not realising it sooner when all the signs had been there. But when they'd been speaking of their speedy marriage, he had been almost overcome by a fierce desire to agree, to add his voice to those of Sir Humphrey and his wife, and demand that Amelia should become his without further delay. This week. Tomorrow! And it wasn't, he'd realised a moment later, just because he wanted her in his bed. Though he did. It was because he needed the engagement to be genuine. He loved her, and he could think of nothing better than to marry her as soon as possible. What had started as a fiction had become a fact for him. For him, though not, he knew, for her.

She was everything he had ever wanted in a woman, though he'd spent no time at all before this moment puzzling out what that might be. He could easily have said, *She is lively and clever, kind and caring and funny; she teases me out of my ill humour so that I cannot even remember why I was downcast. She is brave and beautiful and makes me want to be a better person for her. I want to make love to her so badly not just because I desire her, but because I want a deeper connection with her than I have ever had with another person. I want to know her utterly, and for her to know me. I want to grow old with her.* This was all true. But it didn't matter, none of the detail of it, beyond the plain fact that he loved her.

And she didn't want him to. He could see that. He was attuned to her now, even for knowledge that would hurt him, and he knew that over the last few days, the words, *I think we should break off this foolish engagement!* had been trembling constantly on her lips. If they'd been alone at any point, she'd undoubtedly have said it, which was why he had made sure that they never were. He could see it in her lovely, stormy eyes: the false betrothal was making her deeply unhappy, and she wanted to put an end to it and take back her own life, free from the chaotic entanglement with his.

It was no consolation, or very little, to know that she desired him too. She'd made that plain enough in those few precious moments when they'd held each other. They had a physical bond, they shared that much, and it was all too easy to imagine what might have happened if their time together had been prolonged, and if one of them – he could not remember who it was now, but he thought it had probably been him – had not called a halt to their dangerous moment of intimacy. He did imagine it, over and over again, imagined reaching ecstasy with her. But he must be glad that it had not happened, because the last thing in the world he wanted was for her to be obliged to marry him because he had compromised her honour. Well... that wasn't true. The last thing he wanted was to lose her, or – hellish thought – for her to marry someone else, some oaf who didn't deserve her. But he couldn't bear to have her forced into his arms. She was too open, too honest, to be able to conceal her regret, and he thought that it would slowly kill him. Imagine if they'd even conceived a child, and that had tied her to him forever when she wanted to be free.

He should, he supposed, himself raise the subject of parting, as a matter of honour. Give her the opportunity to reject him that he knew she wanted. But he couldn't quite bring himself to do it, because he knew that when their engagement was over, they would meet in the future as no more than awkward semi-strangers. What a hideous thought that was; he found it close to unbearable.

And it was his own fault. He'd shared all the disreputable details of his involvement with Lavinia with her, and revealed to her all the shoddy, painful secrets of his past. He'd had to do it, in common decency, so that she knew exactly what she was involved with, but it was impossible to blame her for wanting rid of it all, and of him. She must think him a heartless rake, a man without morals, like her father. That stung, but he could see that it could be so. Maybe she hadn't even believed him when he'd told her he'd only lain with Lavinia once. She knew that Priscilla could be his child, so why should she believe him when he tried to minimise his transgression? She must think he was desperate to play down his involvement with Lavinia so that he looked less ramshackle in her eyes. Men lied to women, and women knew they did. Her father's daughter of all people had every reason to be aware of this.

And it was impossible to forget that the disorder of his private life had nearly killed her. She had not asked for nor anticipated that added complication, he would have cut off his right arm to spare her it, and every moment she was still publicly tied to him, she was still in danger. For that reason, if for no other, he should set her free immediately.

It did no good to imagine what might have happened if he'd had as much chance to woo her and win her love as any other man; his foolish, reckless actions at the age of eighteen had made sure he could not come to her with a clean conscience now. Lavinia was like a ghost from his past, haunting his present, tainting his future. And after all Amelia had suffered because of her father and his dirty reputation, did she not deserve a man who had no such sordid ties? He knew the answer well enough. No wonder he was miserable.

His mother was resting in her room that evening after a shopping trip earlier in the day had over-tired her, and his sister Helena was attending some damn dreary, pointless ball or other with the chaperonage of a friend's grandmother. Marcus had been intending to go with her, but his interest in dancing and making conversation on this occasion had plummeted dramatically when he had discovered that the Wyvernes did not mean to be there. Neither Helena nor Lady Thornfalcon had been so inconsiderate as to laugh at him or otherwise mock him when he said that, as it happened, he really didn't feel like going, though he didn't suppose that they had missed the significance of his volte-face. They might have mentioned that his engagement was not, in fact, genuine, and teasingly said that it was therefore odd that he should so burn to meet his faux fiancée and be despondent at her absence; he could only be grateful that they had not.

He was sitting in his library with Jeremy Gastrell then, a not particularly welcome visitor who did not seem inclined to take a hint and go away. Thorn was aware that he was very poor company indeed tonight, gazing gloomily into the depths of a brandy glass as though he might find some solution to his predicament there, when a note was brought in to him on a silver tray. He didn't suppose it could be from Amelia, but still, he tore it open with pathetic haste, ignoring his friend's ironically lifted brow. Marcus then sat staring at the paper in a manner that had the footman who had borne it in to him shifting uneasily in his buckled shoes, probably wondering if his master had run mad, and what if anything he might be expected to do about it.

The missive read, in an antique, wavering hand with many blots:

Lord Thornfalcon

I write in great urgency, and have no time to explain how it comes about that I know all of your ridiculous doings – be satisfied to know that Sophie told me. I have just discovered that Amelia has gone, alone, to the Opera House Masquerade this evening. She claimed to be unwell after dinner, and I sent my maid up to her room to see if she could make her a tisane, but helas, she was gone. My woman found a note discarded there – anonymous, but plainly from your sister-in-law – telling Amelia that you were in terrible danger if she did not attend. It must be a trap, and I expect my poor granddaughter knew as much. But she has put herself in danger in this reckless manner because she loves you. Perhaps you do not care for her in the same way, since in my experience, most men are fools, and I am sure that you cannot deserve her, but even if *you do not love her, please find her and make sure she is safe. La méchante folle surely means to hurt her. Do not delay, or you will have me to answer to, and when I die, I will come back and haunt you in the most disagreeable manner possible, I promise.*

Delphine Wyverne

Marcus dragged himself out of his reverie and jumped to his feet, startling the waiting footman further, and Mr Gastrell too. 'Come, Jeremy!' he barked. 'I may need you.' There was no time to get a mask or domino – she could be in terrible danger, in pain, even now. He must go. As the footman stood staring, Lord Thornfalcon ran out of the room in the direction of the stables, following by his vainly expostulating friend. A door banged, and they were gone.

37

It was not usual for a peer of the realm to drive to London's Opera House late in the evening in a curricle drawn by a pair of fine bays, still less to do so at reckless, breakneck speed. Nor was it at all the done thing to leave such a two-wheeler waiting right outside the august institution – minded by a reluctant and most self-conscious gentleman who was trying very hard to be expressionless as he waited and not entirely succeeding – while one dashed inside, hatless, pushing through the crowd willy-nilly and shoving a handful of guineas into the hand of the protesting attendant. That puzzled individual, who had barely recovered from the recent excitements of Runners, accusation and arrest, eyed the Major's tall, muscular frame and agitated mien, and decided that discretion was the better part of valour. He stepped promptly aside to let him pass, but pocketed several of the excess guineas for himself, as no more than his due.

Marcus stood just inside the entranceway, panting, brushing his dishevelled, auburn locks out of his eyes and using his superior height to survey the scene around him, first swiftly and then more slowly. She wasn't here, or not that he could see. But then she'd surely be disguised, probably in a plain domino, just one among many. She could be anywhere in the huge building. Or worse, she could already have been exposed to some terrible insult, or tricked somehow into leaving. He must find her and make sure she was safe. There was no time to dwell on what else Lady Wyverne had told him, to wonder if it could possibly be true. He had to find her directly.

Some tiny part of his watchful soldier's mind told him that the people around him were surveying him with great interest, and whispering about him, and no wonder, as he was dressed in ordinary day clothes and boots, not sporting any sort of fancy costume nor even a concealing domino, and clearly in a state of great emotional turmoil. He could not know that they had already been greatly entertained, and were hopeful for more enjoyable scenes that they could gossip over afterwards.

She wasn't here; he was almost certain of it. He had to go deeper into the building and look for her, and pray he was not too late. But which way should he turn in this enormous theatre? It would be all too easy to miss her. She surely wouldn't be dancing, not of her own free will, not after receiving such an alarming missive, but she could be in any of the many boxes on different levels, or in one of the corridors that led away on either side, or in the supper room, supposing there was such a place. Marcus cursed, for the first and probably the last time in his life, his complete and lifelong lack of interest in opera. He'd never been here before, had strenuously avoided coming here, and yet if he'd know the place, he might be more confident of finding her. But he must choose a side to start searching...

He went left, since he had to go somewhere, moving through the staring crowd with muttered apologies, but he had not gone five yards before a hurrying young woman in a black domino collided with his chest. He looked down, impatient with this fresh delay, and then froze. Incredibly, it was her.

'Amelia!' he cried. 'My God, I have found you! Are you well?'

She looked up at him in astonishment. 'I... I am. I was just leaving. But what in heaven's name are you doing here, Marcus... my lord, I mean.'

He reached out, almost unconscious that he was doing it, and held her by the shoulders, as if to assure himself that she was real. Having once made certain of that, he did not let her go – perhaps he could not. 'Your grandmother sent me a note in desperate haste. She said that you had been tricked here by Lavinia, that she was sure she meant to do you harm once more, and that I must come to rescue you. Of course I rushed here immediately, almost out of my mind with worry. But was it untrue – some devilish ruse?'

'No,' she said shakily, 'no, it was all true, though I have not the least idea how my grandmother of all people came to know of it. Lavinia had set a trap for me – she had arranged that my step-mother, Rosanna, the actress, should be here, and meant to use her presence to destroy my reputation forever in a huge public scene that nobody could fail to notice. Some of the Friends were here with Lavinia to watch, so they could spread the gossip all the better. But Rosanna had instead made another plan with Mr Pennyfeather – I am sorry if I am not explaining it clearly; it is all so fantastical – and Lavinia herself was exposed, and then – yes, I see you stare – arrested! And I have something even worse to tell you...'

He was astonished, and could hardly take in the full import of her words. 'What has Pennyfeather to do with it, and how could he have enough evidence to take her in charge? I can't make head or tail of this, my dear.' He was still holding her, he might never let go, and the crowd perforce had to part around them, with many a curious glance. Marcus and Amelia were oblivious to them, and to their muttered comments. They could have been quite alone in some quiet, private place, not surrounded by dozens of curious and noisy onlookers.

'I'm not surprised you're puzzled; I was too. I still am. He has been investigating her all this time, he said, and discovered at last who pushed me, and that she had been blackmailed and threatened into it by Lavinia, out of fear for her own safety. But Marcus, there's more...'

'I hope there is, my dearest!' Now that he knew she was unharmed, now that she was warm and real under his hands, the rest of it, including Lavinia, didn't matter – and he could turn to the revelation that had broken on him like a glorious dawn. 'The Dowager Marchioness told me you had been lured here because you thought I was in terrible danger, and you needed to save me. Is that true?'

Amelia blushed adorably and looked down. 'That was what the note said, to make me come here. It was a trick, of course, and I knew as much as soon as I saw it. I'm not a complete idiot.'

'You're wonderful in every respect. I shall plant a facer on anyone who dares to call you an idiot. You knew it must be a trick then, and yet you still came.'

She had no answer for that. Something was clearly troubling her, and he had a vague notion that she was trying to tell him some fact or other, and that it was probably important. He would gladly hear it later, but just now, one thing alone had possessed his mind to the exclusion of all else. 'My darling, my angel, the note I received said you came here because you loved me.'

She was instantly scarlet. 'My grandmother said that? Sophie must have... I'll kill her!'

'I don't care whether you do or whether you don't just at this moment. But with all my heart and soul I need to know if it is true. I've never asked anyone a more important question in my whole life, nor been so desperate to hear an answer, and at the same time terrified, in case that answer is not what I hope and long for. Do you love me, Amelia?'

'Do you want me to?' Her lovely face was a mixture of confused emotions, and her eyes were full of tears, but he thought a smile was breaking through despite all that.

'No, my love, it's much worse than that – I need you to. Because I love you desperately, and I had thought there was no hope... I have been so miserable, knowing you planned to break with me at any moment and thinking that for your own sake, you probably should. Damn it, woman, answer me in plain words before I lose my senses entirely: do you love me?'

She *was* smiling; he was almost sure. A teasing little smile that made his heart leap and the blood pound in his veins. 'What will you do if I say yes, Marcus?'

'Next week I'll marry you, as soon as a licence can be got, but just now, I'm going to kiss you very thoroughly, here in the vestibule of the Opera House with all these people watching.'

'Very well then, my lord, it's true. Yes! I do love you. I love you terribly, and I've been miserable too. I realised it long ago. And I'm still going to kill—'

But she never finished her murderous sentence, because Marcus seized her in his arms and claimed her mouth hungrily, and she responded with equal enthusiasm, her arms sliding up around his neck. He lifted her quite off her feet and held her tight, and a small cheer went up from the surrounding crowd. Some of them broke into applause, though the embracing couple were quite oblivious to it, entirely absorbed in each other.

One of the most enthusiastic watchers said breathlessly to her friend, 'Is it always like this here, Alice? Because it's so much better than the play, and it's not even eleven yet. What do they do for an encore, and when can we come again?'

38

Eventually they came back to their senses, and slowly, reluctantly, Marcus let Amelia slip out of his arms, and set her back on her feet. 'I don't want to stop kissing you, ever, my love,' he said, still holding her hands, 'but I know you were trying to tell me something. I could say I'm sorry I interrupted you, but I'm afraid it wouldn't be true.'

'Yes, Marcus! But we cannot discuss it here. Come away in the corridor for a moment and I will tell you.'

She pulled him, unresisting, through the crowd, and in a few moments, they had some measure of privacy, though their conversation seemed to necessitate standing very close all the same. 'I told you about Lavinia threatening the young woman, though I'm not sure you were listening.'

He grinned at her unrepentantly. 'I was listening, up to a point. I'm sorry, my dearest love. But I did have more important matters on my mind.'

'Well, yes, I expect so, but listen now. I cannot tell you if you look at me like that! Mr Pennyfeather didn't mention the young woman's name in front of everybody, though we must suppose she has agreed to bear witness, or matters could hardly go further. But that's not the worst of it. Marcus, I'm so sorry, but he said that Lavinia murdered your brother. He seemed quite sure of it. If I understand him correctly – I was astonished – he spoke of poison. I'm assuming you know nothing of this?'

The laughter faded from his countenance, to be replaced by shocked incomprehension. 'My God, Amelia, I most certainly did not!'

'I know it sounds grotesque, but I assure you that's what he said. It's not the sort of thing I would be likely to mishear. And he arrested her for murder of her husband. Dozens and dozens of people must have witnessed it.'

Lord Thornfalcon stood stock still, an expression of horror creeping onto his face. 'Can it be true? No, no, it can't be. My brother died in a riding accident – fell from his horse. Or so I was always told. I was abroad...'

'I thought Mr Pennyfeather might have warned you in advance, when I had absorbed the shock and my brain began to work again. But I can see that he has not. I'm so sorry, Marcus.'

'I don't... It's not that I struggle to believe it, my dearest. I feel no impulse to throw up my hands and say it is impossible that Lavinia should ever do such a thing. Is that terrible? But there has never been the least suspicion of it, as far as I am aware. Not a whisper. I suppose he must mean that she drugged him and caused his fall? I cannot make any other sort of sense of it. It's such a dreadful thought. And it's poor Ambrose I can't help thinking of... He loved her, Amelia. That was always some consolation to me, when I was still enthralled by her – that he loved her and treated her like a queen.' He was silent for a little while, and then said, 'My God, Priscilla! That poor child. What an atrocious thing.'

She sought to comfort him, though in truth, there was little

she could offer in consolation and what she said to him made her
uneasy even if it turned out to be the truth. 'My stepmother said,
and I imagine she is right, that a woman in Lavinia's position will
never pay the full penalty for such a crime, even if she is found
guilty, which she might not be. It might never come to trial even,
do you think? Lavinia herself said as much regarding her arrest,
before the full extent of what she was accused of was revealed –
that her father is a rich and powerful man who will use his influence on her behalf.'

'Perhaps so. Perhaps Lady Wyverne is right. But he cannot
hush this up, however hard he tries – there will be an enormous
scandal; Pennyfeather has made sure of that by acting so publicly.
I am not saying it should be kept quiet, if she has truly killed my
poor brother. He deserves justice, if there is such a thing in the
world. But Priscilla, to discover when she is a little older that her
mother is a murderess... Oh, Christ, Amelia, and poor bloody
Jeremy, too. He's waiting outside in my curricle – he was with me
when the note arrived, and I was so overset, I could not think to
do anything but bring him. He drove me here, in fact, as he said I
was not fit to do it myself. How will I tell him? I fear it will destroy
him.'

'Tell him what, Marcus?' She did not understand how his
friend could be supposed to care so much.

'He loves Lavinia – has done so for years, ever since we were
children together. He told me so a few weeks ago. Then, he was
hopeful that they might one day have a life together, with
Priscilla. But whatever happens, surely that is impossible now.
And I must tell him without loss of time, before he hears it from
another source.'

'I suppose you must.'

'But first, I must take you home. It will be a sad squeeze, love,
in the curricle, but I see no alternative. I can't send Jeremy off

alone, I need to tell him after we have you home safe, and I did not delay long enough to fetch out a closed carriage.'

'Or your hat.'

He gave her a ghost of a smile at this. 'Or my hat, or a coat or cloak. I was so desperately worried about you. But we must go.'

Amelia's head was whirling after the events of the last hour, wonderful things so mixed with what looked like, and surely was, disaster. It must be a horrible shock for all Marcus's family to discover that Ambrose had been murdered and they had never suspected it at all, but had condoled with his murderess on her bereavement and kept her as a close member of their family in the years since. And the concern for her child's future – his niece, assuming that was all she was – must be a constant worry, whatever happened to Lavinia.

'Yes, you must tell him, but then also speak urgently with your mama and sister, before they too hear this elsewhere.'

'I know it,' he said grimly. 'I fear this will be a terrible blow to my poor mother, whose health is not good and who has suffered so much already. Let us go, my love.'

Mr Gastrell's face betrayed his relief when he saw Marcus emerging from the theatre, though it lessened somewhat when he realised that the three of them must squash in together to convey Amelia back home. He offered to step down and fetch a hackney for his own use, and was plainly puzzled when Marcus refused this generous offer. The carriage journey was most uncomfortable but thankfully short, and the three conversed little during the time, beyond a stilted exchange of commonplaces.

Once in Brook Street, Marcus jumped down and helped Amelia to descend. She had had him stop the horses a little way from the house, and he walked with her along the silent street and saw her safely inside, via the area steps rather than the main entrance.

'Goodnight,' she said, smiling up at him and pressing his hand. 'It's so dreadful… it's hard to know what to say to you. But we will cope with it all, Marcus, now we have each other. You know you can rely on me for support, I hope.'

'I never doubted it,' he said. 'I take great comfort from knowing that we will see this through together. My love, I hate to be parted from you, but I will see you tomorrow, and let you know… everything. Goodnight!'

She turned to look when she had reached the bottom of the stone steps, and waved, and he raised a hand in response, watching until she had closed the door behind her and disappeared.

39

A little while later, after a most painful conversation with his friend, Marcus was tapping on his sister's door. She had not long returned from the ball she had attended, the footman had told him, and so he found her still dressed, with her maid at her side helping her to take off her jewellery and let down her hair. One look at his face had her dismissing the girl with a mechanical smile of thanks.

As the door closed behind the abigail, Helena said, 'In heaven's name, Marcus, what's the matter? Has something happened to Amelia? I have been told that you left the house in a terrible pelter a short while ago – I hope there has not been another attack or any sort of accident!'

'No,' he said heavily. 'No, she is perfectly well, I am very glad to say. But she was at the Opera House masquerade – it will take too long to explain why now, more trickery of Lavinia's that has fortunately misfired – and she witnessed Pennyfeather arresting Lavinia. Arresting her for arranging the attack on Amelia, Nell, but also... but also for Ambrose's murder. I cannot... Amelia understood him to say that Ambrose was poisoned. It is not the sort of matter about which anyone would be likely to make a mistake, but...'

He had sunk into a chair while he was speaking, suddenly aware of how drained he was after the emotional turmoil of the evening. Helena sat silent, but he could see the shock on her face, and almost hear her quick brain whirling as she struggled to comprehend it all.

'Marcus, Ambrose died in a riding accident. You know that much, though you were not in the country at the time. I am sure I must have told you the horrible details. I know I did. He took Baphomet out late one afternoon when it was getting dark, and the horse must have put his hoof into a rabbit hole that was obscured by the dusk, and done so while moving quite quickly, because Ambrose was thrown and hit his head. Lavinia became worried about him when it grew fully dark and he did not return but the horse came back without him, and she organised the servants into a party to look for him. They found him at the edge of the Home Wood, with a wound on his temple caused by a rocky outcrop. He was cold; it's always distressed me to think of him so cold and alone. Nobody was near to him, there was no possibility of poison, just a stupid accident that could have happened to anyone out riding in such conditions. Perhaps it was rather reckless of him to go out so late, though it pains me to say so. No, no, it can't be true; it must be some mistake.'

'Were you in the house when it happened, Nell? Was Mother?'

'No, I was at school in Bath still. Mama was ill that winter, you know how the cold affects her, but she insisted I left her all the same after Christmas.' She paused, as if struck by something, and then went on reluctantly, 'Ambrose and Lavinia were not on the best of terms; they were arguing – or she was, you know he never raised his voice – and Mother thought it best if they had a little space. She kept to her chambers, I was away, they were alone except for Priscilla and the servants. But it cannot signify in the least. Ambrose cannot have been poisoned! It was just a foolish, petty argument about whether they should go up to London for the Season. One does not poison one's husband because one wants to attend a few parties and he will not...' Her words trailed off into silence.

'Most people would not do so, certainly,' he said expressionlessly. 'I dare say no more than one person in ten thousand would, but can you say that Lavinia is not that one person? I loved her once, and I cannot swear it. Not after the extreme way she has behaved towards me this Season, and her attack on Amelia. Nell, I think we need to speak to Mother about this now. Was she awake when you came in?'

'Yes, I went to kiss her goodnight and see how she did, and she was reading comfortably, and seemed most caught up in her new book, which was making her laugh. I do not suppose she will be asleep yet; she said something about just one more chapter, and you know how she is when she is absorbed in a story. Let us go and see.'

A short while later, brother and sister were sitting at the end of their mama's comfortable bed, and she had set down her volume with only a slight expression of regret and a wistful glance at it. Marcus set out on his explanation, which he was aware was not as coherent as it might have been, but much to his surprise, his mother stopped him before he had told her very much at all. He didn't think she could possibly have understood him so quickly, but he was mistaken.

'He found the proof then,' she murmured rather blankly. 'I truly did not think he would be able to.'

They both stared at her in astonishment for a moment, then

Helena said in a bewildered tone, 'Mama, you knew about this, and you did not tell us?'

'You set Pennyfeather on to investigate, if I understand you correctly?' Marcus put in. 'I thought you would be appalled to hear all this, but you *already knew*?'

She sighed and pulled her shawl more tightly about her thin shoulders. 'I had a suspicion, nothing more than that. I did not tell you, my dears, because I thought that even if it were true, it could never be proved, and you, Marcus, had quite enough to worry over without that. If I had thought you meant to marry Lavinia, I must have told you, but I was sure you would never do such a thing. And I knew she would not make an attempt on your life while she still hoped you might be hers. Afterwards, if you have been foolish enough to commit yourself to her and you had thwarted her wishes in any way, well... I would have been most anxious.'

'"Most anxious"? Mama, please explain!' her son said with commendable patience.

'I told Mr Pennyfeather everything a while ago, when he came to see me and by chance you were both out. He had called on me on purpose to warn us to be cautious around Lavinia – he said she worried him, and he thought her capable of anything, like many murderers he had met. He considered her entirely wrapped up in herself, in a way he had previously seen in very dangerous people. So I shared my fears with him, of how they were arguing that winter and how odd Ambrose's manner was on the day he died – how he was not himself, and seemed confused and distressed, though he denied it. I knew that the fall had killed him, but I thought there was something more – perhaps that if he was unwell, he might not have been able to control his difficult horse as he normally would. Of course, he always went out riding on that dreadfully wild stallion at any hour if he was upset, and Lavinia knew that as well as anyone. I thought it was just possible that she had given him something and then deliberately provoked an argument. Told him... something shocking, perhaps. Lied to him. And Mr Pennyfeather very kindly said that he would look into it, and went down to Somerset directly to do so. Someone there must have known something all along and kept it hidden – one of the servants, maybe. At any rate, he must feel he has sufficient proof.'

'I understand why you did not tell us, Mama, when it was just a vague suspicion in your mind and no good could come of airing it. But why did Pennyfeather not alert us to the fact that he meant to do so public and irrevocable a thing, once he had his precious proof? I cannot understand why he would not write us a note of warning, at the very least, if he could not find time to call on us in so important a matter.'

She said, taking his hand, 'I think you may lay that at my door too, my dear. And I am not sorry for it. I told him that one of the reasons I had not shared my fears with you was that if you believed them to be true, you would feel obliged to confront Lavinia, because that is the sort of man you are: direct and honest. And if she truly is a wicked murderess, that would be the last thing in the world I wanted. If she thought you of all people had turned on her, I dare not imagine what she might do. This whole fantasy of a perfect love that she has created is dependent on you, and her fixed belief that she will win you over in the end. If you knew or even suspected that she had killed your brother, all that would be over and she would be furious – uncontrollable. That, I suppose, is why he made it so public. Even if she is released, she cannot think to blame you for this. Or me, for that matter, or Helena. Nor, surely, can she take revenge on us, not after being so exposed once already. And Mr Pennyfeather, he assures me, can look after himself. I promise you, I am most grateful to him, though I see you stare. I think he is a wonder.'

'You're a wonder too, Mama. And I understand why you feel this makes us safer. But at what cost – what of Priscilla?' he said wearily.

She looked a little uneasy now. 'My conscience is not clear there, but I ask you, is it safer for a child to grow up without a mother, or in the care of a mother whose solution to any opposition is to murder the person who stands in her way? I don't know if I will be here to see what Priscilla is like when she reaches that awkward age, but I recall quite well enough Helena's temper tantrums at fourteen or fifteen, and I cannot picture Lavinia enduring a fraction of them with complaisance.'

'Mama! Are you saying you might have murdered me a mere four years ago because I was occasionally a little irritating?' spluttered Helena.

'I'm saying I never would have done such a thing, because I love you and because I am a woman with a normal woman's reserve of patience, which is to say a great deal – after all, I put up with your father for twenty years without felling him with a candlestick, and he was an infuriatingly stubborn, foolish man and drove me to distraction several times a day. But I have no confidence in Lavinia's patience, nor in her normality. I think she is unbalanced, and might do anything if opposed. So Priscilla must be better off without her, difficult as it must be for the poor child. I only hope that you do not find yourself saddled with her at the very start of your married life with dear Amelia. That would be a trial indeed, and must be prevented if at all possible.'

'Mama, have you forgotten that the engagement is not genuine?' Helena asked a little tartly, still apparently smarting from the criticism of her younger self.

'Isn't it?' Judith said comfortably, looking at her son with a twinkle in her eye.

Marcus felt a smile break out upon his face, despite everything. 'In fact, it is real, my dears. It has become real, and I am so happy to be able to tell you. We have decided only this evening that we shall suit very well, and must be married as soon as possible. I think in my delirium, I may have mentioned a special licence, and next week as a date, and I believe she agreed. So you must prepare yourselves. It will be a great deal to cope with – planning a wedding, even the simplest of ones, and marrying, while all this trouble with Lavinia is breaking about our ears.'

'That doesn't matter,' said Lady Thornfalcon robustly. 'What matters is that you will be very happy together, and I am excessively glad.'

'And so am I!' said Helena. 'I like her enormously, and have from the very beginning. I mean to take credit for bringing you together, I must tell you!'

There was a flurry of embraces and kisses, and Judith and Helena were both crying a little. Marcus would not have sworn that there was not a tear or two in his own eyes as he left them. No doubt the next day would bring its difficulties, but he would face them. He had Amelia, and could face anything – even the difficult visit to Bow Street he must now make.

40

Amelia had not expected that her grandmother would still be up when she returned home, and indeed had hoped that she would not be, but when she slipped into her own bedchamber at last, having entered the house with the help of her disturbingly devious abigail, she found the Dowager Marchioness's own maid, Marchand, waiting for her. The Frenchwoman was sitting silently in a chair, hands folded in her lap, and the sight was so eerie and so unexpected that she gasped and started, almost dropping her candle.

'Madame La Marquise is awake, and awaiting you impatiently in her chamber,' Marchand said composedly, as if such nocturnal conversations were entirely commonplace. 'I beg of you, milady, remember her great age and do not tire her more than is absolutely necessary.'

'I'd rather not tire her at all!' Amelia said frankly. 'I'd rather go to bed directly. But if she is waiting for me, I suppose I must come.'

A short while later, she was curled up at her ancestor's side, holding her small, wrinkled hand. Delphine was fully alert, her wise old eyes glittering in the candlelight. She didn't appear to be tired in the least, but full of life and sparkling irresistible curiosity, and she listened intently and without the least appearance of shock when her granddaughter described Lavinia's arrest, and the dreadful crime of which she had been accused Possibly she had known so many women who murdered their husbands in her long life that she took it as a mere commonplace.

'I had not the least idea you knew anything at all about my ridiculous situation,' Amelia said resignedly at last. 'But I should not be surprised. I suppose Sophie told you?'

'Once she had told Rafe, she thought she might as well. And she was a little worried about you when she was obliged to go away at such a delicate moment, and thought quite rightly that a person of sense should have an eye on what you were about. Marchand has been watching you, saw you leave the house with such a parade of secrecy, and found that preposterous note, which she instantly brought to me. I, of course, seized the opportunity to write to your young man to make sure he was present at your sinister rendezvous. If you and he between you could not make good use of such a moment, bah! I would wash my hands of you. But I see from your whole manner that you did. Young Sophie will be forced to agree that she could not have managed matters better herself. I trust that all is now resolved between you, so that your engagement has become genuine at last?'

Amelia leaned over and kissed her grandmother's soft cheek. 'Yes! He said you had told him that I loved him, and insisted I admit if it was true. But I think – it's all a little confused in my mind now – that I made him tell me first. And then he picked me up and kissed me in front of everyone and said we should be married next week. I believe many of them cheered, though I wasn't really paying attention.'

'Good!' Delphine said with profound satisfaction. 'I would

have cheered too, if I had been there. I wish I could have been, you understand. That you have both come to your senses is all that really matters. The rest is mere detail.'

'The fact that Lavinia Thornfalcon murdered Marcus's brother is not a mere detail! It will be terrible for the family.'

The old lady shrugged and said ruthlessly, 'They will survive it. One does, I have found. It is surprising, what one can survive.'

'I know you have earned the right to say that, Grand-mère, in bitter experience, but there's no denying the fact that there will be a great scandal that will be most unpleasant for Marcus's family, and for hers.'

Delphine shrugged. 'As for hers, bah! But you don't care about scandal, and nor does Rafe. There is something to be said for being a Wyverne, after all. We will stand proudly by the Thornfalcons as another family might not. There will be no nonsense from us about blaming them for unknowingly having had a killer in their midst, which after all is an unlucky thing that might happen to anyone, nor about breaking off your engagement because of it.'

'Of course not!' Amelia said hotly. 'I would marry him in my shift, and woe betide anyone who tries to stop me!'

The Dowager smiled and said, 'I am almost certain that that won't be necessary, *ma petite*. Perhaps now the two families are equal in terms of reputation – it is undeniable that at least your father never murdered anyone, or at least not that we know of. I do not wish to shadow your joy when it is shadowed enough already by circumstances, but I hope you do not end up having to look after that child. I have heard a great deal about her, none of it good. She clearly cannot be left with her mother, whatever happens or does not happen to that woman in the way of justice.'

'Marcus was most worried about her. We cannot turn her away, and her grandparents brought Lavinia up to be what she is, so I am not sure they are fit guardians for Priscilla. We will have to discuss it.'

'First fix the date of your wedding,' Delphine advised. 'There may not be time to go down to Wyverne Hall for it, if it is really to be next week. That will be most convenient for me, of course. I hope your Aunt Keswick will approve of your haste – is it not what she wanted all along?'

'Oh God, Grand-mère, I had forgotten Aunt Keswick. She won't approve at all of Marcus having a murderer in his family! Can you imagine her reaction? I am certain she will take it as a personal affront.'

'Let her!' said the old lady with a martial glint in her eye. 'I am quite ready to put her firmly in her place, child, I assure you!'

41

When he arrived at Bow Street around midnight, the first person Marcus saw in the panelled vestibule was Sir Lionel Hall, and it was plain at a glance that he was a broken, bewildered man. Marcus, who had always disliked the pompous old fool, took him by the hand and said, 'I'm so sorry, sir. I learned what had happened a short while ago, and came here as soon as I had told my mother. Is there anything I can do to help?'

The baronet, who seemed to have aged ten years in a couple of hours, said, 'It's very good of you, Thornfalcon. Your brother... I have never been so shocked in my life. This bumptious Runner fellow says he has all sorts of evidence, which he has laid before the magistrates, and they authorised him to arrest my poor daughter. Arrest her, like a common criminal, and bring her here!'

'Will they release her on your recognisance, do you think?'

'My lawyer fellow believes they will. A lady – a widow of a peer, and a mother of a young child, they surely cannot drag her off to some filthy gaol populated by the scum of the earth. He's in there arranging matters now, and then I will be able to take her

home where she belongs. My poor wife, and the innocent child –
we must keep it from the dear little thing at all costs. But how?
That's what I ask myself, Thornfalcon: how? It will be all anyone
can talk of! It will be spread across the newspapers, every gutter
rag, and we shall be disgraced!'

Marcus could not fail to notice that Sir Lionel had made no
great protestations of his daughter's innocence; he seemed more
horrified that someone of Lavinia's rank should be arrested at all,
rather than anxious to stress the fact that she couldn't possibly
have done any of the things she'd been accused of. Perhaps it was
just shock and it was wrong to refine too much upon it... The
man could hardly know what he was saying.

Sir Lionel's eyes brightened suddenly and he said, reaching
out and clutching Marcus's arm in a fevered grip, 'If you sit down
with them and reason with them, it may help! You must tell them
directly that you are positive your brother cannot have been
murdered in this preposterous fashion they speak of, or if he was,
they should look first at his servants and other such low persons
rather than Lavinia! His own wife! Go in there, man, and tell
them!'

'I have no knowledge of what happened, sir, and they would
doubtless tell me so directly,' Marcus said a little stiffly, greatly
disliking this assumption, however desperate the man was. 'I
was not even in the country at the time. I cannot believe they
will pay any mind to a bare assertion of disbelief from me, if
they do feel they have proof. And as you say, they must have
evidence of some kind, or the magistrates would not have authorised Pennyfeather to arrest her. I am very sorry for it, but I
cannot see that my intervention could do any good at all. I
certainly shall not be slandering my own staff without a shred of
evidence.'

'Damn your staff! But you know the encroaching fellow

responsible for this disaster?' Sir Lionel cried, suspicion darkening his features.

'Only because he was set on at Sir Humphrey Aubertin's insistence to investigate the attack on my fiancée. He came to interview us about the matter, and I met him then. I have no further
knowledge of the officer.'

That wasn't quite true, of course, but Marcus had no intention
at all of allowing this weak man's ire to fall on his invalid mother.
It would be unconscionable if Sir Lionel thought to pressure her
to set aside any hope of justice for her son's killer for the sake of –
what? The avoidance of scandal? So that that killer could live an
easier life, and escape the consequences of her actions? It was not
to be thought of, and he was sure his mother would agree. She
would tell the baronet no, but the scene would be painful for her,
especially if Sir Lionel in his rage and grief began abusing her,
and he must prevent it if he could.

'I must go, I think, sir, if there is nothing else that can be
done,' he added. 'I am glad for you, if you will soon be able to
take her home where she will be comfortable.' It seemed he
couldn't say her name, not here. 'I am certain she would not like
to encounter me in such circumstances and in such a place, and it
would be best then if I am gone before she comes out, to spare
her that embarrassment.'

Sir Lionel was perhaps about to agree, or to demur – Marcus
would never know. An inner door opened as he spoke, and
Lavinia emerged on the arm of a spare, greying man who must be
the baronet's lawyer, and behind her, one of the magistrates, by
his dress, and Pennyfeather, and trailing after them all, another
younger officer, a burly man in a frieze coat.

The senior Runner seemed to wince when he saw Lord
Thornfalcon, a sentiment which Marcus could only share, but if
had meant to speak, even just a word of greeting, he had no

chance. Lavinia hurried into speech the moment she set eyes on her former lover. 'Oh, Thornfalcon, you have come to save me, and to tell these foolish men that it is all a mistake!' she said brightly. 'I am so glad that you had the goodness to come on my behalf, and I thank you for it.' The words were rational, extremely so, but there was something disturbing in her tone – it was not that she was agitated, which would have been understandable, but that she was not. She might have been speaking about some mildly annoying error with an order in a shop – the wrong sort of muslin, perhaps, had been delivered, or a piece of china, not a very expensive one, had been discovered to be broken and must be replaced. It was not the tone of a woman who fully understood that she had been accused of deliberate murder, still less the murder of the brother of the man she was smiling so graciously on. Marcus had seen her icily furious in the recent past because a footman had spilled a drop or two of wine on her silken gown. And yet now she smiled.

Her father must have had the same reaction, for he said in a flustered voice, 'Don't worry, my dear, Lord Thornfalcon is here to see if he can help, as you say, but there is no need for him to trouble himself. I shall take you home directly now. It is late and I am sure you must be very tired.'

'Not really, Papa,' she replied with a smirk that seemed to imply that her father was making rather a fuss over nothing. 'I was at a masquerade – but of course you can all see that by my domino; how silly of me – but I had no opportunity to dance tonight, I can't recall why, and I do so love dancing. Do you remember how we used to dance together, Marcus? People used to say that we were the handsomest couple in the West Country, and I'm sure that was true.'

'Yes,' he said in as level a tone as he could manage. 'I do remember.'

'Come, Lavinia, dear,' her father insisted, taking her arm and tugging at it. 'This is no time to stand talking. The carriage is waiting outside. The horses will take cold, and your mama will worry if we are late home.'

'Very well,' she said with a touch of impatience, her eyes still on Marcus. 'I will come, but only if you agree to visit me tomorrow, Thornfalcon. Priscilla is longing to see her... her uncle. I was about to say father, but of course you are not that. But you could be, if you wished to. Yes, Papa, I do not know why you must be in such a rush, but I am coming.' They passed outside without further discussion, and the burly young Runner followed them, as he must have been instructed to do.

'You know my views on this travesty,' the lawyer said in exasperated tones to the magistrate once they had gone, ignoring everyone else who was present. 'You can't put that woman in the dock. She's not in her right mind. She doesn't fully understand what's happening to her. It makes my hair stand on end to hear her talking as though she were at a damn tea party and they've run out of her favourite cake.'

'Doesn't want to understand, perhaps,' the other man said shortly. 'She was sufficiently agitated, as I understand it, when her crime was first put to her. Made all sorts of threats that showed she knew exactly how serious it was. But that's enough for tonight. Go home. All of you—' he waved vaguely '—go home! Even you, Pennyfeather. I don't know if you've done a good day's work or a bad one, but it's plenty for now. Try not to arrest anyone of high rank for a few hours, if you can manage it. Stay away from White's and Brooks's and Carlton House, I'm begging you.'

Marcus and the Runner made their way slowly outside, neither of them wanting to encounter Lavinia and her father again. A light drizzle was beginning to fall and the streets were gleaming where lamplight struck them.

Pennyfeather shivered and said, 'The lawyer's right in a way; she is crazy. She thinks the whole world's organised for her convenience, as if she were Marie Antoinette. But then a lot of aristocrats seem to think that, don't they? Are they all mad, my lord?'

'Maybe. But they're not all killers, or I hope they aren't. I wasn't meant to be a lord, you know – that was my brother, and he was a good man, not some spoiled, conceited fop. I'm just a soldier, or I was.'

'Yes, I expect you've seen a thing or two in Spain and Portugal. But I'll wager you never saw anything like tonight.'

Marcus laughed mirthlessly. 'No. And I don't ever want to see it again.'

'You don't think she ought to be tried? A poor man, or a poor woman for that matter, could be crazy as a coot and would still hang for crimes much less serious than hers.'

'I don't know. It's not my decision, and I'm glad it isn't. I believe my mother would want me to thank you, Pennyfeather. If my brother really was killed, I suppose I too must be glad you got to the bottom of it. I should not dwell on our long ignorance of the truth. He didn't deserve such an end; that's one thing I am certain of.'

'I'm sure he didn't. She drugged him with belladonna that she supposedly uses to make her eyes bright. They are always very bright, aren't they? So perhaps she does. There was a little bottle in her chamber that was full, the chambermaid saw it there when she was cleaning, and then next day after your brother's accident, it was almost empty. She can't have used it all herself in so short a time – it's powerful stuff, one of the strongest poisons in nature. The maid's a sharp girl and suspected some manner of foul play, but was too canny to let her mistress know. She very wisely kept her counsel, showed no sign of awareness, then gave up her job for some invented personal reason and moved away as soon as she was able. Out of her reach. Your servants down in Somerset all have strong opinions about Her Ladyship, and no desire to cross her. I talked to them, and after a bit of back and forth, I was given the maid's direction, and she was persuaded to tell me what she saw. She'll make a good witness; she's obviously telling the truth, or so it seems to me. Whether it's proof enough for a judge and jury – well, we'll see.'

'I'll have to tell my mother – she will want to know exactly what happened.'

The Runner shook his head. 'I know it will be hard for her – for you all. It's not what you need, when you're about to be married. But dangerous people like Lady Lavinia need to be stopped.'

'That's what my mother said. She thinks very highly of you.'

'It's mutual, I assure you, my lord.'

Marcus smiled, somewhat against his will. He couldn't help liking this eccentric man. 'You won't be dragging her to the guillotine, then?'

'Not just yet. They keep me busy enough catching criminals, and there's always more of those.'

They parted, and Marcus made his weary way home, though he did not expect to sleep, his brain so torn between happiness and distress. It had been a quite extraordinary day, and he could not imagine what tomorrow might bring.

42

Marcus slept badly, falling into a restless sleep around dawn, and woke late, clearing his head with a brisk ride in the park before breakfast. He would very much have liked to go straight to see Amelia, to take her in his arms and kiss her again and reassure himself that their engagement and their new-found love really were genuine, not figments of his disordered imagination, but it was still too early, he thought. He couldn't wait till normal visiting hours, which decreed that 'morning visits' should be paid in the mid-afternoon, but he could let his love sleep a little longer. She must be tired too, after all the dramatic events of the previous evening.

There were the morning newspapers lying on the breakfast table, like so many unexploded bombs, but he resolutely refused to look at them. He had never had occasion before to wonder exactly when the day's early editions were printed, and whether they were able to include news that had happened late the night before, and he did not choose to enlighten himself now. If there was nothing there, as he thought there would not be, it would only be a temporary reprieve. The storm of scandal would break soon enough.

The natural and direct way from Half-Moon Street to Brook Street would have taken Marcus through the pleasant environs of Berkeley Square, but he felt an odd reluctance to pass Sir Lionel's mansion today, and so set out on a circuitous route that led him down to Piccadilly, in the wrong direction, and then eastward along it and up New Bond Street. He was fortunate enough not to meet anyone he knew on his way, and arrived at the Wyverne home unaware of whether his brother's murder and his sister-in-law's very public arrest for it were yet the subject of common gossip.

He was shown into Lady Wyverne's jewel-bright sitting room and found it occupied by his beloved's aged grandmother, whom he wished at Jericho though she had every right to be there; Amelia, smiling at him in a way that made his heart leap; and a most unwelcome visitor: the terrifying Lady Keswick.

'I hope, Lord Thornfalcon,' she said, barely giving him a chance to greet the old lady and his betrothed, 'that you have come to discuss very speedy arrangements for your marriage. My niece has implied that this is so, in fact.'

'You're right as ever, Lady Keswick,' he responded promptly. 'The blame for the delay is mine, but I am determined to set matters right, and we are to be married as soon as it may be arranged.'

Lady Keswick was no doubt about to tell him that it was about time, and read him a lecture on his previous unsatisfactory behaviour, when Mr Gastrell burst into the room unannounced, dishevelled and panting. He was unable to speak for a little while, and they all stared at him with varying degrees of surprise, concern and, on Lady Keswick's part, strong disapprobation. 'Forgive me!' he managed when he had recovered a little of his breath. 'Dashed bad ton, crashing in on you like this. Ma'am, Lady Amelia, Lady K, I do apologise, and your butler is most put out and will take a week to recover, but I thought you should know directly. Most extraordinary thing. They've gone – vanished from Berkeley Square! The whole lot of them!'

Lady Keswick swelled up like a pigeon, about to put this unmannerly intruder firmly in his place, but Delphine somehow stilled her with a sharp, imperious gesture very reminiscent of old Versailles. 'Sir Lionel and his family?' she asked sharply. 'You are saying they have fled? How do you know?'

'Yes,' he panted. 'That's it exactly, ma'am. In the middle of the night, I suppose. Saw for myself what had happened. The whole house is in an uproar – none of the servants had the least idea what was afoot, apart from the one or two they took with them. Went to call to see if I could help in their trouble – couldn't seem to stop myself from going along, despite everything I learned last night, for which I hope you'll pardon me, Thorn, old man. Found the butler drunk and unconscious on the front step and the housekeeper and all the maids having hysterics in the drawing room, while knocking back Lady Hall's ratafia by the half-pint and lamenting their back wages, which I'll go bail they'll never see now. Hideous scenes, I assure you. Neighbours can't be ignorant of something dashed fishy going on. Bound to leak out, probably already has.'

'Young man,' said Lady Keswick in a dangerous tone, 'I perceive that there are things you know – that all of you know – that you have not thought fit to share with me. I must insist that someone does so immediately, or I shall go off into strong hysterics myself.'

This was hardly Jeremy Gastrell's tale to tell, nor should he be forced to relate it and do violence to his tender feelings. Marcus explained, in as few words as possible, that Lavinia had been

arrested in public late last night for the murder of her husband –
yes, his own brother – blackmail of someone whom he couldn't
name because he didn't know, and attempted murder – yes, of
Amelia. He thought it best not to mention Amelia's presence at
the masquerade, and Rosanna Wyverne's involvement was also
tactfully omitted. Though his love added nothing to his tale, she
sent him a very speaking look of gratitude.

His terse recital of the facts left Lady Keswick speechless,
opening and shutting her mouth like a stranded fish. It couldn't
last, but while it did, Jeremy prepared to take his leave, drawing
Lord Thornfalcon aside for a moment's private speech. 'Thought
you should know first,' he said. 'Went to your house from
Berkeley Square; they told me you were here. Ran all the way like
a bedlamite, devil of a thing, sweating like a horse. Not sure if
they've had time to get overseas – probably not by normal means,
not with the dashed war on, unless they simply bribed their way
onto the next ship going who-knows-where out of the Port of
London with the morning tide. In which case, they're long gone
and there'll be no stopping them, not by the Runners nor
anybody else. But wherever they are, they won't be travelling
under their own names. Matter for Bow Street, in any case, and
rather them than me. Dashed quick work, didn't know the old
man had it in him.'

'They had a Runner watching them,' Marcus said suddenly.
'Maybe more than one, but one for sure. I saw him leave Bow
Street with them last night. Just a precaution, I suppose, but not
enough of one, it seems.'

'Well, he's not there now. Bribed, or knocked over the head,
or...?'

'Let's hope they bribed him a vast amount. I hate to think of
the alternative. My God, whoever would have suspected such a

sudden flight? I wonder now if Sir Lionel was as shaken as I thought he was. Maybe everyone underestimated the old fellow.'

'It's possible. He was certainly keeping secrets of his own. From what the housekeeper said in her lament, they've not been paying bills or wages for a good long while. Everything mortgaged to the hilt, I shouldn't wonder. So perhaps this flight was planned, and it was just brought forward when the Runners came calling.'

'You're taking it all quite well,' Marcus said, eyeing his friend consideringly. 'I was worried about you when I left you yesterday.'

Mr Gastrell shrugged with a fair show of unconcern, and said with nonchalant understatement that no doubt cost him some effort, 'It was a blow. Can't deny it. But perhaps I'm not the marrying kind. Can't trust my own judgement – thought she was an angel for ten years or more.'

'She looks like one, but she isn't,' Marcus said. 'I think that was a big part of the problem. No one alive is as perfect as she set herself up to be. And perhaps we all share the blame for that.'

As Jeremy left, Amelia slipped her hand into Marcus's arm and said, 'Let's leave Aunt Keswick with my grandmother. She spoke with great enthusiasm of giving my aunt a set-down last night. I don't think you need to hear any more of Aunt's recriminations over something that scarcely concerns her at all, and *we* deserve some time alone, it seems to me.'

'It seems so to me too, my love!'

43

Amelia shut the door of the small sitting room behind her, turned the key in the lock and looked expectantly at Marcus, who had not moved very far into the room away from her. He must, she thought, be deeply shaken by this fresh revelation and its implications, but if so, he didn't show it. He seemed surprisingly cheerful, as though he had finally resolved to put the past behind him and focus on the future.

'Have I ever asked you to marry me properly, my love?' he said, smiling. 'Did I ask you last night, in front of all those people?'

'I can't remember,' she replied, though of course she did, and thought he did too. 'In any case, if you did, there is no harm in doing so again. I shall tell you when I become tired of it, if I ever do. I thought you were about to say something of the kind in my aunt's presence, which I must tell you, Marcus, is not at all what I should wish for. I can't imagine anyone would. But now we are alone.'

'I had observed,' he said, taking her up in his arms and

holding her tightly against his heart. '*You* have asked me to marry you, though, let us not forget. On the occasion of our first meeting, indeed, which is a shocking thing.'

'But that wasn't real.'

'This is, though, my love.' To demonstrate this, he claimed her lips with a hungry urgency that she matched, and they were silent for a long moment, locked together, until at last he said unsteadily against her cheek, 'Nothing in my life has ever been as real as this. As you in my arms, and your lips on mine. I feel we owe each other a debt of kisses that we must instantly set about repaying.'

She chuckled, and snuggled even closer in his arms. 'What do you mean?'

'Well, you kissed me first, did you not? And then you offered to kiss me again, in Sir Humphrey's garden – I do recall that I almost begged you to – but you did not do it. Do not think that I have forgotten. Now you owe me what you promised, and I mean to claim it, with interest.'

She remembered holding him in the scented night, his head between her breasts, his lips on her skin, his hands hard on her body, and she shivered. 'We have kissed each other since,' she teased him.

'Last night? But that was in public.'

'And now the door is locked. I locked it. Marcus, do you mean to do all the things you told me you wanted to do, when we were together in the moonlight?'

'I mean to do all of them and more. I've lain in my bed at night and tortured myself with all I said to you, when I thought there was almost no chance that any of it would ever happen, however desperately I wanted it. I hope you want it too.'

She smiled up at him in loving mischief, her answer in her

expression. 'I too,' she said. 'God knows, I too. And more, as you say. Do you know how it affected me, when you described your nakedness – your bruises?'

'No, I don't, my love! How could I? It sounds most promising – I wish you'd tell me.'

'I'll show you, that'll be better.' Her eager fingers were at his cravat, tugging at the knot. 'I don't think you can have considered, sir, the sad case we women find ourselves in. Our dress, especially evening dress, is so flimsy and revealing...'

'I had noticed,' he said with feeling, as she unwound the snowy muslin from about his throat, then tossed it aside.

'You have seen my arms bare almost to the shoulder, my lord, and a good portion of my chest...'

'Not enough, I swear. Never enough.'

'Yet all I have seen of your skin,' she continued, dealing ruthlessly with the buttons of his shirt, 'till now, is your hands and face. They're excellent in their way, naturally. But it's not enough. It's not fair.'

The strong column of his throat was exposed now, and the deep vee where his shirt opened, and she made a little sound of appreciation and reached up to stroke his warm skin, tracing her way down and down. She could feel the blood thrumming in his veins, and his breath coming fast where her hand caressed the muscles of his chest. She pressed her lips to his flesh, closing her eyes for a moment as she drank in the beloved scent of him.

'Is that better?' he asked a little raggedly.

'Well, it's definitely somewhat better,' she whispered, her breath tickling him and making them both quiver. Her hands were still running over the hard planes of his chest under his shirt, tangling in the hair she found there. There was a deep scar that puckered his right shoulder, and her fingers traced it gently, wanting to know and love every inch of him. 'But you told me you boxed shirtless. You can't expect to say that sort of thing and not have it lodge in a woman's mind. You said you had bruises in surprising places, and my immediate thought was that I wanted to kiss them all better.'

He groaned deep in his throat, and reached to pull the shirt over his head with astonishing swiftness; she helped him, and it was gone in a second, thrown aside to land they knew not where. 'I think there are still a few traces of them on my back,' he said very low. 'I'm sure they would benefit from being kissed better by you. How could they not?'

It was true. Not really bruises, but the shadows of bruises, yellow and brown, still lingered upon his broad shoulders and across his back. The biggest of them was still distinct in shape, as he had said, and vanished tantalisingly beneath the waistband of his breeches. She ran her fingers lightly over them all, from top to bottom, and then brushed the highest one with her lips as she stood close behind him. She kissed each bruise, and when she came across a lesser scar here and there, each one a relic of his dangerous life and an unmistakeable sign of how excessively lucky she had been that he had lived to find her, she kissed that too.

The room was very quiet, save for his soft gasps, and hers. Her hands explored him as her lips did, and her fingers traced along the line in front where soft buckskin met flesh, and where the fall of his breeches was closed with buttons. She caressed the round buttons too, slowly, one by one, tracing each circle, and his big hands captured hers, and held them there. 'Oh,' she said, 'yes, put my hand on you, Marcus. I did not quite dare, though I wanted to.'

He did not seem able to speak, but he guided her right hand

so that it lay over his length, his highly aroused member pressing through the buckskin leather into her palm. She stroked him through the covering, and his hand still lay over hers; she was crushed tight against his back now, her lips at his neck, her breasts and belly moving against his naked flesh though the thin fabrics that abraded her heated skin, her other hand on his hard thigh, holding him close. His hand moved on her hand, and they panted together; she was nipping at his neck now with her teeth, tugging on the tendrils of hair that curled there, his urgency spurring her on, her breasts swollen and heavy and liquid fire pooling between her thighs. In a moment he let out a great groan of release, and pressed himself into her hand. 'My love, my dearest love,' he gasped out.

They were still for a moment, breathless, then he turned and seized her ruthlessly in his strong arms, lifting her up and carrying her to the sofa. He set her down among the cushions, throwing up her skirts and kneeling beside her. She was entirely exposed to him, as she had never been to anyone before in all her life, but she did not feel shy. They had passed far beyond that, into a place where there was only love, and trust, and always desire. 'Now it is my turn to put my hand on you,' he murmured. 'Will you guide me, too?'

She took his hand without hesitation and pressed it straight to her core, whimpering at the first contact of his fingers with her hot, aroused flesh, writhing under his touch. She was wet for him, and the slightly roughened pads of his fingers slid across and around her engorged pearl of Venus in a confident manner that suggested that he hardly needed her direction. But she was enjoying the intimacy of their hands being joined still, and so she did not pull hers away, but moved with him, her whole body – and his – focused on the sensations of pure pleasure that built and crested and broke, carrying her away.

When she came back to herself, she found that Marcus was still on his knees at her side. 'I think we have thoroughly compromised each other, my darling,' he said tenderly. 'I hate to think what your Aunt Keswick would say. Let's not tell her. Will you really marry me next week, by special licence? How does Tuesday sound?'

44

They had somehow found themselves sitting together on the sofa, and Marcus said, as she snuggled close to him, 'Is it too soon? I don't want to pressurise you, and perhaps now everything is resolved, you may wish to have a little time really to be engaged, rather than the pretence we made of it before. Maybe you would even prefer to be married at Wyverne, as you once said. I don't want you to feel that I am rushing you if you would rather wait.'

She shook her head. How complicated it all was. 'I want to be alone with you, that's the plain truth of it. We always seem to be surrounded by so many people, and while we remain betrothed, that will not change. I love Sophie and my brothers, I am sure I will quickly grow to love your mother and sister, and I am even fond of Aunt Keswick, who has always been very good to me despite her gruff exterior. But they are always here, or about to burst in at any moment – it is a wonder we have had these few precious moments alone.'

'We could go down to Thornfalcon for our honeymoon,' he told her, caressing her cheek and making her sigh and press her face to his hand. 'It's a good deal more than a day's carriage ride from London, and some of the roads are bad, so we'd have to break our journey somewhere on the way. But once we got there, we could be private together.'

'Does it hold many memories for you, Marcus?' She knew that Thornfalcon in Somerset was where Marcus had grown up, which meant that it was also where he had fallen in love with Lavinia, his neighbour, and lost her. And they now knew that his brother had died there at her hands. It must be full of all sorts of recollections, both good and bad. Was it really wise to go there straight after their wedding?

She was relieved that he did not fail to understand her. 'You are worried that at home, I will see Lavinia in every room and on every walk and ride – you fear she will haunt us? And if she does not, my poor brother's fate will?'

It was something that had never occurred to her before this conversation, but when he put it to her in that stark manner, she could not deny it. 'I know we will be obliged to go there eventually, even if we do not do so straight away. It is your principal seat, is it not? And so I can understand that you want to live there, or even that you might decide you *must* live there even if you don't want to. I have no idea what you feel about the place – whether that might be love, hatred, or indifference, or something altogether more complex. We haven't discussed it at all, have we?'

'You are right, we should,' he said, leaning back. 'We should talk about our expectations and our hopes and fears, should we not? Where and how we shall live. It has never crossed my mind before – how unjust it is that a woman marries a man and is merely expected to live where he says they shall live, with no discussion. Nobody would question my right to tell you grandly, "We shall live at Thornfalcon", which is a place you've never even seen and know little about.'

'It's a conundrum. It's foolish to imagine that I might think of saying to you that I don't wish to live there, supposing I should visit and dislike it, and that you might simply agree. Because in practical terms, if you own an estate, it would be negligent of you not to spend a substantial portion of your time there. Even if you don't care for it at all, or you wife doesn't, you are committed to the place and its people. I know this from my brother, who hated being at Wyverne when my father was alive, and yet had a duty not to abandon it completely.'

'My feelings are mixed,' he told her, and she could see that he was trying to puzzle it out for himself. 'Perhaps less mixed than your brother's, for there is no question of anything as extreme as hatred. It was a wonderful place to grow up, and it's beautiful, I think – not in a dramatic but a quiet way. It's not a great mansion with Palladian columns and a lake.' He grinned at her – plainly, he had heard what Wyverne was like. 'It's a big, old, rambling house built around a courtyard, with parts of it very ancient indeed, and lots of unexpected steps here and there, and secret corners such as children love. Yet it was never meant to be mine. I could not tell you when I realised that Ambrose would inherit it, not me – I seem always to have known it, and I swear I never resented it. It wouldn't be true to say that I never allowed myself to become deeply attached, because it was my home, and I was happy there. But I always expected to leave it and make my way in the world, in a way that my brother did not. I found it odd, when I came home after I was wounded, to walk about the place and think it mine for the first time. I still haven't grown accustomed to that. And I can't claim to any deep knowledge of how to run an estate – my father never thought to teach me, since there was no need. I dare say Helena knows more of such things than I do; my mother certainly does, and she has been a great help to me. So you see, it's all new to me still, my love. And you're right, I cannot neglect it. I don't want to, and it's not just a matter of obligation and duty; I want to do right by it. I would never have come to London at all this spring if Helena had not been making her come-out.'

She couldn't help but notice that he hadn't mentioned the powerful connection the place must hold with Lavinia, and her uncertainty must have been written on her face, because he said, 'I didn't find Thornfalcon haunted by Lavinia when I went back, rather to my surprise. My mother had the tact to make sure that I did not occupy Ambrose's chamber, and... does it make sense to say that my youthful feelings for her seem very distant from me now? Perhaps because I was away so long – almost eight years! – and I came back as a different person. A man, not a boy, and more importantly, a soldier. I may have little faith in my current knowledge of the running of the estate, but I am sure that I can learn, and my military career has given me great confidence in my ability to manage people, which is more than half the battle. If I had ever seen Lavinia there as Ambrose's wife, or mistress of the house, it might have been different, but I never did. And if you are worried about taking her place, my love, you should be aware that the servants never cared for her – I had not realised quite how much until Pennyfeather told me. But the last thing in the world I want is to make you uncomfortable, least of all on our honeymoon. There must be dozens of other places we could go. Wyverne, even – it's your home, and it's much closer and easier to get to. I am sure there might be a corner found for us in such a palace.'

Amelia smiled, but said, 'It's not really my home, you know, Marcus. I was born there, but I don't have any memory of living there as a child. My mother died when I was small, and my Aunt Jemima came and took Charlie and me away to live with her and her own children, outside St Albans in Hertfordshire. My Aunt

Keswick's home is nearby, so we were a great group of cousins all quite close in age, and spent most of our time together, including our lessons. We lived there happily till Aunt Jemima died and my uncle quickly remarried. His new wife made it quite clear that she did not want a houseful of great overgrown children, some of whom who were not even his. Then we went to live with Rafe, because by then he was old enough to take care of us, but at his own small home, not at Wyverne, where my father was. I'd barely been there at all until two years ago, and it holds no special significance for me. We used to sneak in like a pack of thieves sometimes when my father and Rosanna were away, to visit my grandmother in secret – can you imagine how ridiculous?'

He was looking at her with sympathy and understanding. 'You haven't really had one settled home in your life, then?'

'No, although for the last few years, my home, and Charlie's, has been wherever Rafe was. I don't think my experience has been all that unusual. So many people I know have parents who remarry, or have grown up as orphans, passed between relatives. But if you had been thinking that I grew up in the grandeur of Wyverne and expected to be in charge of such a palace when I married, that's not the case at all. I've almost always lived in much smaller places. And yes, I would like a home of my own at last. My portion is all invested in the Funds, and does not include any property.'

'That I can give you. A home that is yours. Do you think, then, that you would be content to go to Thornfalcon? Or would you like to think about it for a while, and consider other alternatives?'

She shook her head. 'If we are to be married on Tuesday, I had better not think about it for very long!'

Marcus laughed. 'You are a constant delight to me. My dear, you are right in all you say – we shall be obliged to spend a good part of our year at Thornfalcon. It would be idle to pretend that we shall not. Now that I have resigned my commission, as in all honesty I should have done a good while ago when Ambrose died, the care of the place is my job. I cannot be sitting idle when there is work to be done and nobody else to do it. But that doesn't mean we need to go there now.'

'I would like to, I think,' she said slowly. 'I want to be with you, and I want it to feel... permanent. However happy we might be in some other place, it can only be an interlude, and not our real life. I would like our real life to begin, far away from all this gossip and scandal and deception.'

'So would I,' he said. 'My darling, so would I.'

EPILOGUE

The wedding was small and private in the end – a rather subdued but valiant best man in the shape of Mr Gastrell, both families, and Lady Keswick and her adult children. They held a wedding breakfast in Brook Street, so that the Dowager Lady Wyverne was able to attend and still retire when she grew weary. But she was on exceptional form that day. 'Oh, if I had met you eighty years ago,' she told Marcus with a completely straight face, 'I would have cut the child out and won you for myself, I promise you!'

'I take that as a great compliment, Madame La Marquise,' was his grave reply.

'So you should!'

The couple spent their first night together in Half-Moon Street, rather than in an inn upon the road, which must be less comfortable as a beginning to their married life. Amelia remembered little of her first hours in her new home afterwards; she could not take her eyes from Marcus. She had drunk a glass or two of wine in celebration, but he was her intoxication, not the champagne. At last they could be entirely private, naked in a bed without fear of interruption. It was of course not the first time they had touched each other, not the first time they had given each other pleasure, but it was the first time Amelia had welcomed Marcus into her body in the ultimate intimacy. She was glad, afterwards, drowsing in his embrace, that any discomfort or awkwardness they may have felt was momentary, because of the knowledge they were already gaining of each other. And much more important was the fact that at last they could fall asleep in each other's arms, and wake together, and reach out again in mutual desire and need.

They left early the next morning, though not perhaps quite as early as they had originally intended, stopping that night at the Castle and Ball in Marlborough, taking up where they had left off. Another early start, and now in the late afternoon, their chaise had turned off the post road to Taunton along the lane that led towards the house. The heavier, slower vehicle with Amelia's maid, Marcus's valet and all the luggage had kept pace with them to Marlborough, but today, they had outdistanced it.

They'd been passing along a tall, well-maintained sandstone wall on their right for several minutes, and Marcus had told Amelia that this was the southern boundary of the Thornfalcon park, though many of the farms belonging to the estate lay on the other side of the road. At last, the wall fell back to create a wide, gravelled space, which led up to a pair of Jacobean gatehouses and a set of elaborate, wrought-iron gates. Amelia swallowed and smoothed down the skirts of her smartest amaranth pelisse, feeling ridiculously nervous suddenly, and Marcus squeezed her hand in silent sympathy.

There was no need for the coachman to blow his yard of tin officiously, or get down and seek admission; they'd clearly been looked out for, and the gates were swinging open as they drew up to them. A man, a woman and a group of rosy-cheeked children had spilled out of the right-hand gatehouse, and Marcus leaned out to greet them all by name and introduce Amelia to them. But it was a brief pause; soon they were moving along a winding, tree-lined drive cast into dappled shadow by the boughs that arched and met above the carriage.

'I'm so glad to be coming home with you,' he said, still holding her hand tightly, his voice a little rough with emotion.

The chaise crested a low hill, and the trees gave way to open parkland that rolled gently down into a shallow valley and then rose again to where the house stood, backed by more woodland. It was, as Marcus had said, low and rambling, its roofline an irregular jumble of chimneys. The central portion was Jacobean, like the lodge houses, and the wings on either side more modern in appearance, though she knew that much of that was mere façade, and some parts of the building behind it were medieval. Sections of the stone walls were covered in climbing vines which had been clipped into shape around the mullioned windows, and great swags of yellow and white roses in full bloom. It was much less grand than Wyverne, and because of it, much more immediately welcoming and homely. The many panes of old glass in the irregular-sized windows caught the sinking sun and threw back flame.

'Home,' Marcus said, a wealth of emotion in his voice.

The carriage passed under an elaborate central archway and into a stone-flagged courtyard heady with the scent of more roses. 'We don't normally make such a grand performance of merely driving home,' he told her. 'There is a more convenient modern entrance to the coach house and stables at the back, which is in general use. This is all done in your honour, my love.'

Amelia saw that what she presumed to be the whole household staff had come out to greet her. Marcus handed her down from the carriage and once more, she heard a flurry of names and saw the faces that went with them. But he had thought to prepare her last night, trading kisses for remembered names and titles, and with that excellent incentive, she had managed to memorise most of them and knew them still so that she could greet them individually. She did not dare meet her husband's eye as she shook hands with everyone from the butler and housekeeper to the shyest scullery maid and most blushing stable boy; she knew he would be grinning wickedly at her, remembering just as clearly as she did how he had rewarded her when she had in triumph produced all the names of the kitchen maids without hesitation. She did not know what recompense would be hers later for remembering them all correctly now, but greatly looked forward to finding out.

When all the greetings and congratulations had been exchanged, Marcus lifted his bride in his arms and carried her effortlessly over the threshold, which provoked an outburst of cheers among the assembled staff. This turned to laughter – some of it scandalised but most of it raucously approving – when he did not set her down in the wood-panelled entrance hall, nor pause to remove even his hat, but continued on across the chequered marble floor and up the grand Jacobean staircase. Rows of gold-framed Thornfalcon ancestors looked on with varying degrees of approval as he took her down a long passage into an apartment that contained a large four-poster bed, and no doubt a quantity of other furniture that Amelia did not concern herself with just now. It was a bright chamber filled with golden light, which presumably offered fine views over the parkland at the front of the house, but this too was of not the least interest to her at present.

Marcus set her down on the bed with just the right balance of haste and care, and stripped off his overcoat, hat and waistcoat, flinging them aside with no thought at all for their final destination. Amelia was busy with her gloves, smart bonnet and pelisse in much the same fashion, and hurled her half-boots aside with equal abandon, hearing them thump to the floor in some unseen corner.

'I have been wondering,' she said breathlessly, 'how you would decide to reward me for my most impressive feat of memory downstairs, my lord.'

'So have I,' he said, his voice muffled for a moment as he dragged his shirt over his head. Freed from it, he stood looking down at her for a moment, bare-chested, and then he seized her ruthlessly by the ankles and pulled her towards him across the coverlet. This had the interesting additional effect of rucking up her gown and petticoats about her waist, leaving her long legs and bright-red garters uncovered to his hungry gaze. She had not the least thought of attempting to cover herself, but smiled up at him, her face flushed and expectant. 'And this is what I settled on, my deliciously wicked Wyverne bride.'

He threw himself down on the bed between her thighs and lifted up her legs so that they wrapped across his broad shoulders and down his back, then began pulling at the knots of her garters with his teeth, first one and then the other. When they came free, he flung them aside impatiently too, and pushed down her stockings, kissing the tender skin of her inner thighs where the ties had marked them. She closed her eyes and forgot the room, the house and all the people in it, losing herself in the sensations his lips, his mouth and his clever fingers were teasing from her. He slipped his big hands under her buttocks to hold her tightly, and kissed his way up towards the dark curls where her thighs met. Once there, and armed with the knowledge of exactly what pleased her most that he'd gained last night and the night before, not to mention in a couple of highly enjoyable snatched encounters in the week before their wedding, he began licking and kissing her most sensitive places with a fierce focus that soon had her gasping and clutching at the sheets, digging her heels into his back, raising her body eagerly to meet him. She felt gloriously wanton as he lay between her legs and devoured her with the savage, passionate attention she was coming to crave. This was her new addiction and she could not imagine tiring of it. She hadn't known a few days ago that men and women did this sort of thrillingly wicked thing to each other; now, she wondered why they ever used their time to do anything else. He freed his right hand from beneath her body and slid a finger inside her and then out again, and her electric jolt of pleasure and the incoherent cry that accompanied it had him smiling against her – she could feel his cheeks curve – but did not make him stop. She would have been most annoyed if it had; he'd scarcely begun. A second finger joined the first, and found the particular place that made her arch her back and open herself to him wider still, the edges of her vision darkening as the urgent desire for release built within her. And still his mouth worshipped at her altar of Venus, but now suddenly she wanted more, more of him, a deeper union; she was moaning his name in a confused plea she hoped he could understand.

He moved away from her and she whimpered at the sudden absence, cold on her exposed skin, but he was unbuttoning himself, leaping free, pulling her closer, slipping his hardness inside her where it belonged, finding a rhythm, and that was even better, that was what she needed now. 'It's when you do that,' she gasped as he thrust into her and slowly, tantalisingly withdrew a little before thrusting once more to fill her again. It was so good it was almost unbearable.

'I know, my love,' he said. 'I know.' He was standing tall and powerful at the foot of the bed and holding her hips just as tightly as she liked, and she locked her legs about him and moved with him, passing beyond rational thought into a place where there was only sensation, and that sensation was the most intense pleasure she had ever known. She climaxed before he did, her release prolonged beyond what she would have thought possible by his continuing, powerful thrusts and by his cries as he came and gasped out her name, and fell into her waiting arms.

A short while later, they lay naked together, idly caressing and kissing, talking or being silent and, most of all, revelling in the time alone that was so new and so precious to them both.

Amelia said lazily at last, 'So your sister-in-law and her entire family are gone from England...?' She didn't want to say her name, not here and now, but there had been no time before the wedding to ask, and afterwards, she had not found the right moment till now.

'They are,' he told her easily enough. 'Pennyfeather tracked them without difficulty to a disreputable ship that left on the early-morning tide, supposedly bound for Ireland but, he thinks, bent on running the naval blockade and heading for Boston. At any rate, they are beyond his reach, and I cannot say that I am sorry.'

Was it still, despite everything, delicate ground over which she must be careful? Would it always be? 'You do not wish to see your brother's killer brought to justice, Marcus?'

He took her hand and kissed it, then held it against his cheek. 'It will not bring him back, will it? I can see that you hesitate to say her name, my darling, but let us have no secrets between us, no places where we fear to tread. I think the outcome of justice is always uncertain in this world, and even though I do not love Lavinia, and ceased to love her long before I met you, no person of any sensibility could wish to know that someone he once cared for was to be put to death. To have a child learn one day that that was her mother's fate, for killing her father. A trial would have mired us in the sad past again, and I am more than content to put that past and all its pain behind us where it belongs and look to our brighter future together. Not least because – and perhaps this is selfish and discreditable, but I hope you will be understanding if it is – I would feel obliged to go and watch if Lavinia were to climb the gallows steps at Newgate, and I would wish to spare myself that. Those images in my head.'

She shuddered, and held him more tightly. 'You'd feel you owed her that? I suppose it is natural, but it would be terrible to see. I am sure you have thought of the crowd too, clamouring for the best view. I don't think it's selfish to wish to avoid such a dreadful experience.'

'I do not know if I'd owe it to her – she is a murderer and cares nothing for others – but I would have that debt to my brother and my mother. To see an end made, however hard it would be. To say, "Yes, it is done," rather than rely on the reports of others.'

'To bear witness.'

'Exactly. But I shall be spared that because it will not happen, and if it is weak to be glad, then so be it. Lavinia, dead or alive, here or abroad, is no threat to our happiness – I hope you know that. But before we leave this dark topic, I must make you smile. Pennyfeather knew details of the ship and its ultimate destination already, I strongly suspect, because he had previously arranged for another to take clandestine passage on it. He hinted as much, though he did not say so in plain words. I wonder if America is ready?'

Amelia gasped and choked with laughter, sitting up to stare at her husband. 'My stepmother!' she cried. 'Rosanna did say that she was toying with the idea of going to New York or Boston and taking the stage by storm, which I'm quite sure she would. But she has betrayed Lavinia and taken her money for nothing, Lavinia knows it, and they will meet on board ship, with no escape possible for either of them!'

Marcus grinned. 'You have met and talked with the lady, and I have only seen her perform, so you will know best, but personally I cannot doubt that she will be more than a match for Lavinia. Probably she already has been, since over a week has passed since the *Spruce Wench* left port. They will have had their confrontation, though we may never know the outcome, but are forced to imagine it.'

'That is a much more enjoyable picture to have in your head,' she said, leaning forward to kiss him. 'Lavinia icily furious, Rosanna defiant and amused, and Sir Lionel and Lady Hall obliged to acknowledge Rosanna as Lady Wyverne, their social superior. Perhaps she will try to ensnare Sir Lionel out of pure mischief.'

'All this with an audience of highly interested sailors,' Marcus added. 'It was not a large ship, Pennyfeather said, nor a well-appointed one. And they will be obliged to dodge the navy, and be ready at any moment to flee, which sounds most chancy and uncomfortable. I hope they are all good sailors, including poor Priscilla. I am not, and have vivid and unpleasant memories of my own sea voyages. I do not envy them in the slightest.'

'I should hope you do not, sir!' she said, laughing as he pulled her down to kiss her.

They had been far too intent on each other to think of closing the curtains. The moon, almost full, sailed across the star-studded dark velvet sky and painted a silver pathway across the floor, still strewn with discarded clothing, and up to the big bed, where Marcus and Amelia fell asleep at last, dreaming of a vessel tossed in the vast, unfriendly Atlantic and bound for an uncertain destination, while they lay safe and warm in each other's arms.

* * *

MORE FROM EMMA ORCHARD

Another book from Emma Orchard, *A Gentleman's Offer*, is available to order now here:

https://mybook.to/AGentlemansOfferBackAd

ACKNOWLEDGEMENTS

I wrote my first novel in my kitchen in lockdown, five years ago now. I'd never have developed the confidence to do it without the encouragement of all the complete strangers who commented so positively on my Heyer fanfic on A03 (and still do). But the real inspiration came from my good friends in the Georgette Heyer Readalong on Twitter. I'm particularly grateful to Bea Dutton, who spent many hours of her precious time setting up and running the readalongs. I can't possibly name everyone – there are too many of us – but thank you all, amazing Dowagers, for your continuing support with this novel and far beyond it. Your friendship is very important to me. We've supported each other through some tough times, and had a lot of fun too. And one of you was kind enough to note down the name of a village you were driving past, Thornfalcon, and pass it on to me as a perfect surname for a hero. Thank you, Judith!

Thank you to all of the reading community on Twitter/X (it was great while it lasted), and now on Instagram. For this book, I'd particularly like to thank @a_french_augurey for her continuing support, and for the invaluable help with Delphine's naughty French – though any mistakes, of course, remain my own.

I've been obsessed with Georgette Heyer's novels since I first read them when I was eleven. They have their faults, as we all know, but they've provided solace and escape for millions of people in tough times, and still do, so thank you, Georgette, even though you would have hated a lot of what I write, and probably would have thought I deserve to be locked up. I'm always (I mean always) available for Heyer chat on social media...

Thanks also to my family – Luigi, Jamie and Anna – for putting up with me while I wrote one novel and then another in quick succession. And then another six. Thanks for understanding when I just have to write another 127 words before lunch so I can stop on a nice round number.

My lovely work colleagues Amanda Preston, Louise Lamont, Hannah Schofield and Daisy Messent, have also been extremely supportive: thanks, Team LBA!

I am very lucky to have a superb agent in Diana Beaumont of DHH. She has believed in my writing from the first time she read it, and will always be my champion. Her editorial suggestions are brilliant, and she's just an all-round star. Thanks too to everyone else on the teams at Marjacq and DHH. I know better than most people how important the whole team at an agency is.

Many thanks to everyone at Boldwood, including Emily Reader for the fantastic copyediting, and to Team Boldwood as a whole for your amazing professionalism and unflagging enthusiasm – all of you, in every department, all the time. And of course most of all grateful thanks to my wonderful editor Rachel Faulkner-Willcocks, whose superb edits have, as ever, made this a much better book. Rachel Lawston has given me four fantastic, eye-catching covers already, and I can't wait to see the next one. And thanks always to Gary Jukes for making 'doing proofs' a highly enjoyable experience.

One of the many special things about Boldwood is the wonderful spirit of mutual support that the authors share, so I'd like to thank you all, particularly the fabulous Jane Dunn and Sarah Bennett, for your generosity, wisdom and friendship.

Finally, if you're reading this because you've bought the book, or a previous one: THANK YOU!

ABOUT THE AUTHOR

Emma Orchard is the author of several well-reviewed regency romance novels. In her other life she is a literary agent, helping others realise their dreams of being published.

Sign up to Emma Orchard's newsletter to read her exclusive short story "The Lost Jewel of Mayfair"!

Follow Emma on social media here:

 x.com/EmmaOrchardB

 instagram.com/emmaorchardbooks

 pinterest.com/EmmaOrchardRegency

ALSO BY EMMA ORCHARD

A Duke of One's Own

What the Lady Wants

For the Viscount's Eyes Only

A Gentleman's Offer

To Catch a Lord

You're cordially invited to

The home of swoon-worthy historical romance from the Regency to the Victorian era!

Warning: may contain spice

Sign up to the newsletter

https://bit.ly/thescandalsheet

Boldw◎◎d

Boldwood Books is an award-winning fiction publishing company seeking out the best stories from around the world.

Find out more at www.boldwoodbooks.com

Join our reader community for brilliant books, competitions and offers!

Follow us
@BoldwoodBooks
@TheBoldBookClub

Sign up to our weekly
deals newsletter

https://bit.ly/BoldwoodBNewsletter

Printed in Dunstable, United Kingdom